DATE DUE	NOV 0 3		
DO NOT			
SEP 24 04			
10-5-06			
DEC 3 0 200			
K			
GAYLORD			PRINTED IN U.S.A.

When the Slipper Fits

Also by Lynn Collum
in Large Print:

The Spy's Bride

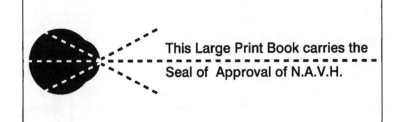

This Large Print Book carries the
Seal of Approval of N.A.V.H.

When the Slipper Fits

Lynn Collum

Thorndike Press • Waterville, Maine

Published in 2003 by arrangement with Kensington Books, an imprint of Kensington Publishing Corp.

Thorndike Press® Large Print Romance.

The tree indicium is a trademark of Thorndike Press.

The text of this Large Print edition is unabridged.
Other aspects of the book may vary from the original edition.

Set in 16 pt. Plantin by Minnie B. Raven.

Printed in the United States on permanent paper.

Library of Congress Cataloging-in-Publication Data

Collum, Lynn.
    When the slipper fits / Lynn Collum.
      p. cm.
    ISBN 0-7862-5846-2 (lg. print : hc : alk. paper)
    1. Balls (Parties) — Fiction.   2. Poor women — Fiction.
   3. Nobility — Fiction.   4. Large type books.   I. Title.
PS3603.O555W47 2003
813′.54—dc22   2003055469

To Irene Estep,
a wonderful writer and good friend

As the Founder/CEO of NAVH, the only national health agency solely devoted to those who, although not totally blind, have an eye disease which could lead to serious visual impairment, I am pleased to recognize Thorndike Press★ as one of the leading publishers in the large print field.

Founded in 1954 in San Francisco to prepare large print textbooks for partially seeing children, NAVH became the pioneer and standard setting agency in the preparation of large type.

Today, those publishers who meet our standards carry the prestigious "Seal of Approval" indicating high quality large print. We are delighted that Thorndike Press is one of the publishers whose titles meet these standards. We are also pleased to recognize the significant contribution Thorndike Press is making in this important and growing field.

Lorraine H. Marchi, L.H.D.
Founder/CEO
NAVH

★ Thorndike Press encompasses the following imprints: Thorndike, Wheeler, Walker and Large Pr int Press.

One

Rain pelted the roof of the hired post chaise as it hurtled along the main road from Guildford. Miss Luella Sanderson, Ella to her friends, could think of nothing but her arrival at Aunt Newton's house in Surrey and hope they made it in one piece as the hired vehicle lurched from side to side. Water leaked round the ill-fitting doors, which only made matters worse. The straw on the floor was soaked and her black slippers quite damp. She peered out the front window, but even the post boy's back appeared as a dark blurry shadow in the torrent. She felt sorry for the lad despite the quantity of spirits he'd imbibed at the last coaching inn while the horses were exchanged. He was surely quite miserable.

Beside her slept one of her aunt's maids, Cilla Potter, a friendly girl who'd told Ella much about Newton Park before she fell into exhausted slumber. Ella wished she, too, could rest, but butterflies inhabited her stomach at the thought of her new situation. She pulled the watch that had be-

7

longed to her late father from her purse and clicked it open, noting the time. Had it only been half a day since she'd parted from her dearest friends?

Sarah Whiting and Lady Rosamund Dennison had been Ella's bosom companions at school, as well as the closest thing to family the orphaned young woman had known for the past four years. But that life ended with the closing of Miss Parson's Academy for Young Ladies of Quality. They were set upon their own courses — only hers was filled with uncertainty. Before departing, the three friends had made one final gesture of friendship: a pact. If one were to marry advantageously, she would invite the others to share her good fortune by bringing her friends to live with her.

Ella sighed as she clicked the watch shut and returned it to her tatted reticule. She experienced a mild pang of envy for Sara and Lady Rose, since they were returning to their immediate families where they would live normal lives, be part of their local Society, and perhaps meet someone to love. Ella's destiny was that of poor relation in her aunt's household. She owned no illusion about what her life would be like, but she refused to dwell on such dark thoughts.

Careful not to wake the young maid, Ella wiped the moisture from the front window with her gloved hand. It did little to help visibility. The wall of rain obscured the landscape and she did not know how close she was to the end of her journey. It had been years since she and her father had visited Newton Park. She'd scarcely been ten when Viscount Sanders had swallowed his pride to go hat in hand to beg funds from his wealthy brother-in-law. Even now, over nine years after the event, Ella remembered how Harwell Newton had enjoyed refusing her father, no matter that he was Uncle Harwell's only brother-in-law.

Father and daughter had managed to survive without Mr. Newton's help, but not well. Lord Sanders fell ill that Christmas of 1806 and within five years passed to the hereafter, leaving behind a noble title but little else to a distant cousin, a grief-stricken daughter, and a will that left guardianship of the young girl to Mr. and Mrs. Newton. The viscount hoped that her life would be better than what he had provided.

Unfortunately, Ella had quickly learned that her Aunt Leona was much like her husband in temperament. She'd arrived at the small rooms where Ella had remained for a week after her father's funeral and announced to the young girl that she would be sent to school at Miss Parson's. There Ella had been ever since. Each year she'd received a single letter from her aunt on her birthday with admonishments that she behave, study hard, and be devout.

By the end of her first year at Miss Parson's, Ella had come to suspect that she would endure a lifetime at school. Determined to make the best of the situation, she had taken an interest in expanding her knowledge of cookery and how the kitchens at Parson's worked. Eventually she hoped to find a post as housekeeper, for a penniless girl, even a viscount's daughter, would be expected to earn her keep, and teaching held no lure for her. Over the years she learned much; even Cook declared her a wonder. But Miss Parson's retirement that May changed everything. The academy would be shut down for good. So, Aunt Newton had summoned Ella to Surrey.

A bolt of lightning flashed at the same moment thunder boomed, and the chaise veered suddenly to the right, tumbling to its side. Ella and the maid flew out of their seats, their legs and arms entangled. At last the carriage settled on its side and water began to rush in. The young servant shrieked at the top of her lungs. After scrambling to right herself, Ella ascertained that neither one of them were seriously injured and worked to calm the frightened girl.

Cilla's wails soon dwindled to mere sniffles. After what seemed a half hour but was only a matter of minutes, the carriage door was wrenched open by the post boy, who stood atop the toppled chaise. "Are ye hurt, ladies?"

"No thanks to you . . . coachman of Satan!" Cilla tried to glare at him, but the raindrops ruined the scowl.

Ella shielded her eyes from the rain as she looked up at him. His hat lay wilted about his head as rivulets of water poured from his chin. "We're uninjured, but we must climb out of here for muddy water is coming in dreadfully." The carriage rested in a water-filled ditch and the murky runoff from the storm continued to edge upward in the interior.

"It ain't no drier out here, miss."

As the water round them rose, so did Cilla's panic. "Stop jawin', you drunken fool! Get us out of here!" She struggled to her feet, the weight of her saturated gown encumbering her movements as she stood in the open doorway. The post boy lifted her out and set her on the roadway. Ella heard an angry shriek before Mrs. Newton's maid began to lambast their rescuer about his rough handling.

He ignored the girl's histrionics and reached back to lift Ella out of the wrecked chaise. He was a tall, wiry lad, but he pulled her straight through the door and deposited her on the ground beside the vehicle. Unfortunately, after several hours of rain, the road was a quagmire of black mud. To her dismay, she sank up to her ankles. The hem of her sodden traveling dress sagged into the mud, leaving her nearly unable to move.

The post boy jumped down to join them. At his landing, a splash of mud and water shot over both women. He received a new peppering of hot fury from Cilla.

He paid little attention to the irate servant. Instead he addressed himself to the young lady. "There be a barn near a mile back, or Newton Park two miles ahead, whichever ye want to try to reach afore dark. Ye'll have to walk, for I can't leave the horses, miss."

The rain whipped round Ella, and she knew she didn't want to spend the night wet and cold in a barn. She eyed Cilla, at last grown silent and looking equally uncomfortable with her wilted bonnet and clinging wool dress. "Shall we make for the Park?"

The little maid didn't look happy, but she bobbed a curtsey. "Whatever you think, miss."

Ella struggled to pull her limbs from the mud. It was as if the earth knew what awaited her at Newton Park and refused to release her on her way. With one final tug, she stumbled forward, but only her feet came free. Her slippers remained lodged under the mud. The rain fell so hard that within seconds the holes where her shoes remained completely disappeared. She stood in her stocking feet on the roadway and looked up at the post boy with pleading eyes.

"Oh, very well." Begrudgingly, he stooped and began to dig around in the mud, but to no avail. The shoes had vanished somewhere beneath the mire. "No luck, miss. Shall I bring your bag out for you to don another pair?"

Ella shook her head. "I don't have another pair."

Somehow the wreck of the chaise and the loss of her slippers seemed a portent of things to come. With a resigned sigh, she realized she had no other options since the rain showed no signs of abating. "Shall we go, Cilla?"

The little maid set off with shoulders hunched against the rain, and Ella trudged behind her down the road to Newton Park. Perhaps it was just as well that the rain was falling in torrents, for the resultant mud buffered her tender feet from the sharp rocks.

Darkness edged upward in the eastern sky as the two women passed through the gates onto the Park grounds. Through the curtain of rain, Ella noted that the old Tudor manor looked much as it had all those years ago. Yet the white-timbered facade was a welcome sight despite the life that awaited within.

Their walk had taken over two hours, and both shivered from the cold and wet. Ella rapped the knocker sharply. Within minutes a starch-faced butler opened the door and looked down his nose at them.

"May I help you?" His tone was so frosty Ella suddenly wanted to turn round and walk all the way back to school.

"It's us, Mr. Bleeker." The little maid was not the least intimidated by the man, but Ella thought his name suited him.

His gray brows drew together, and he

looked beyond them for a carriage. "Where have you been, Cilla? And where is the post chaise? Madam has been most concerned." He stepped back and the little servant hurried inside, then turned and waited as Ella limped into the great hall.

"We was overturned in a ditch, Mr. Bleeker. Had to walk miles home."

Before the butler could comment, the door to one of the drawing rooms opened and Leona Newton exited the room. She stopped just beyond the threshold when she noted the two bedraggled females. To Ella's mind her aunt had changed little in the years since she had seen her.

Not a single brown curl was evident from beneath Mrs. Newton's frilly white cap. At forty, her plain face remained unlined, but a pinched quality about her countenance made her appear older. Slender, she stood scarcely five feet tall, yet from experience Ella was aware that what the lady lacked in stature she possessed in sheer stubborn determination to have things her way.

"Oh, good heavens, Bleeker. They are dripping all over the floor. Take them to the kitchens, and when Miss Sanderson has changed, bring her to the Blue Salon." Without giving her niece the least welcome, she returned to the drawing room.

The butler led the way downstairs, then turned the girls over to the housekeeper, Mrs. Falk, a plump woman with a great deal of white hair and cold dark eyes. Within ten minutes Ella was dressed in a coarse, well-washed shift from the upstairs maid and the tweeny's gray muslin Sunday gown. Her wet auburn hair curled loosely down her back. A problem had arisen with her feet, however. They were so small that not a single servant in the house could provide her with shoes.

After some discussion between the butler and Mrs. Falk, they determined there was nothing that could be done. The mistress would have to purchase shoes for her niece. So Ella padded upstairs in bare feet. After a quick knock, Bleeker ushered her into a room with blue silk wallpaper, blue damask chairs, and blue curtains.

A small fire burned in the oversized fireplace to take the chill from the large room. Seated round the blaze were three females. At the sound of the door, Aunt Leona looked up, and a frown appeared on her brow.

"Come closer, girl. Let me take a look at you."

Ella moved across the blue and yellow

oriental rug to stand in front of her aunt and her cousins, who clearly kept country hours for they were already dressed to dine. She got her first look at the two young ladies she'd not seen since they were scarcely eight and nine years old. Both girls possessed dusky brown curls and piecing brown eyes. Iris, the eldest, was the closest to what one might call pretty. Her hair was cut short in the latest of fashions and curled about her long face. A simple yellow ribbon, which matched her gown, was threaded through the arrangement. Yet her looks were ruined by the petulant set of her mouth as she gazed up at her newly arrived cousin.

Daisy Newton looked exactly like her mother had at that age. She wore her hair long, and it had been pulled away from her face with a series of pink bows nestled among the crimped curls. Unlike her sister's simple silk gown, Daisy's ornate pink dress held three ruffles at the hem, Brussels lace at the neck, and embroidered roses on the tiny puffed sleeves. No matter how many frills and furbelows Mrs. Newton placed on the girl, plain best described the young lady.

Iris swept her cousin with a disdainful glance, stopping at her cousin's rapidly drying hair. "Red hair is never the rage in London. My sister and I were fortunate not to have inherited the Newton hair." She patted her curls and exchanged a smug look with her sister.

Daisy's gaze swept her cousin as well. She giggled. "She's barefoot, Mama."

Mrs. Newton frowned. "Where are your shoes, Luella?"

"Lost in the mud near the carriage accident, Aunt Leona."

"How careless. Well, I am certain one of the girls has an old pair you might use." After that the lady rose, drew her hands behind her, and stared at her niece. "You can have little doubt that your circumstances have changed a great deal since the death of your father, Luella. A viscount's daughter you may be, but you will be expected to earn your keep here at the Park."

Ella sensed that her aunt was enjoying this speech a great deal. Her father had once told her that Harwell Newton, a squire's younger son, was convinced that his wealth would procure Iris and Daisy titled husbands. He hadn't lived to see his plans come to pass, dying from the ague two years earlier, but he'd gone to his grave aware that his wife would do what she must to see his dream come true.

"I understand, Aunt." Ella stared at a painting on the opposite wall, not wanting to give in to the despair she felt.

"I am not a cruel woman. I would not subject you to waiting on your cousins as your current station would demand. Besides, I have housemaids aplenty." Mrs. Newton turned and looked about the lavish room as if to reaffirm her affluence in her own mind. "Still, I intend to do my duty to you, which you in turn must reciprocate. I have decided you will be most useful helping my brother, Mr. Addison Banks, who recently came to live at Newland Cottage. He has only his aged valet with him and could use a bit of help. You will reside here at night, but each morning you must walk to the cottage and assist Harper with the household duties. When you are here in the evenings, you might be asked to help out on occasion, when the girls have a party to attend or should I host an affair."

Ella was too tired to think about how much work lay ahead of her on a daily basis. Instead she merely said, "I understand."

Mrs. Newton folded her hands. "One of the footmen will show you the way to Newland tomorrow. Do you have any questions?"

There were a thousand questions swirling in Ella's brain, but she knew that most of them would only upset her aunt. "None, Aunt Leona." Still, she couldn't deny being relieved that she would not have to be at the beck and call of her cousins. They didn't strike her as the least bit kind as they smirked at her while she heard her fate.

Leona Newton returned to her seat. She looked up at her niece with a jaundiced eye. "Do not think that you can take advantage of my goodness, Luella. If Addison reports that you are not satisfactory, I shan't hesitate to send you packing."

A chill raced up Ella's spine. She didn't doubt her aunt for a moment. The prospect of being alone and penniless in the world frightened her as nothing else did. She didn't even have the funds that would take her to Sarah or Lady Rose. "I shall work hard, Aunt Leona."

Mrs. Newton cast one last glance at the girl, then picked up her needlework. "I shall have Cook send up a tray, for no doubt you are tired and hungry after your long journey. Don't expect such extravagant treatment to be a daily occurrence. When you are at the Park you will be expected to take your meals with the servants or in your own room as you choose. Iris, show Luella her room and see if you have an old pair of shoes to give your cousin."

Miss Newton rose, and in the sweetest voice called, "Come with me, cousin."

Ella followed Iris upstairs to an elaborately decorated room with pink and white roses as the main theme. Her cousin tripped across the carpet, opened the wardrobe, and pulled out a pair of well-worn satin slippers that were a hideous green. A wicked grin settled on her face. "These will do for you, cousin."

"Have you no half boots? I shall have little need for satin slippers." Ella eyed the hideous shoes which her cousin had thrust into her hands.

"Mama warned us that you would likely think yourself superior. Well, you cannot have your way here, Miss Hoity-Toity. I have only the half boots I wear to walk in the gardens, which you cannot have. These will have to do. Come with me." Iris closed the wardrobe door and breezed past a stunned Ella.

They went up one more flight, and Ella discovered that her room was to be a small corner chamber in the attic which possessed one small bed, a chair, a washstand, and a narrow wardrobe. The room was larger than what she'd known at school and she would indeed enjoy the privacy.

Iris looked about the room as if she were seeing it for the first time. At last she seemed to decide the space adequately spartan for her cousin. "Crazy old Uncle Addison rises early, so the footman shall come for you at six. Don't be tardy." Without another word, the young lady exited the room.

Ella sank tiredly to the bed. So much for sentimental homecomings. She had clearly been shown her place, and that was to be with the servants. She dropped the slippers to the floor and tried them on. As she suspected, they were too large. She had nearly an inch of space in the toes. She would have to stuff a handkerchief in them to make them fit so that she would have something to wear in the morning or walk barefoot to Newland Cottage — a prospect that made her sore feet curl.

She lay back on the counterpane. Would this Mr. Banks be anything like her Aunt Leona? They were, after all, brother and sister. Why had her cousin called him crazy? Was she to become caretaker for an insane man? Clearly she had one more ordeal to endure before she knew the true extent of her new life. How would she ever survive? She could only hope and pray that Sarah or Lady Rose married well and soon. Ella wasn't sure how long she would survive her aunt's brand of "kindness."

"Lord Daniel wishes to see you at your earliest convenience, my lord." Timbers held the elegantly cut morning coat as the athletic young gentleman shrugged into the Bishop's blue garment. The clock on the mantelpiece showed half past eleven, but the earl had been up for hours, as was his usual habit. He had joined his friends for their morning exercise before retiring to White's to break their fast and was only just returned home.

"Well, if it's money my brother wants, the paperskull can plead his case with Mother. She's the only one who holds any sway over Father when it comes to Danny's excesses. I've already loaned him enough brass to furnish a small house this quarter. Enough is enough." Gabriel Crowe, Earl of Shalford and heir to the Marquess of Latimer, wasn't a harsh young man, but he well knew his brother's ability to wheedle money from anyone.

Gabriel stepped to the mirror and inspected the slight black swelling under his left eye. A lucky jab at Gentleman Jackson's had found him during his early morning sparring with his friend, Sir John Aubrey. The news of such an event had rapidly spread throughout the boxing parlor, since Lord Shalford's skill with his fives was legend and he rarely took a blow.

The valet stepped up behind his lordship and began to brush any offending flecks from the gentleman's coat. "Blunt ain't his problem at the moment, my lord."

"What now? Has he wagered and lost his horse? Father will ring a peal over him if he has." Gabe owned a great affection for his younger brother, but he'd lost patience with Daniel's fondness for games of chance and birds of paradise. At two and twenty it was high time the lad settled down and began to look about for some gentlemanly occupation, in Gabe's opinion. Or at the very least to exercise some modicum of restraint in his activities, but Danny had always been a neck-or-nothing kind of individual.

At that moment a rapid scratching started at the door. With only a moment's delay, the portal opened and the young man under discussion entered the earl's bedchamber. Lord Daniel Crowe was physically a near mirror image of his elder brother, albeit he dressed in a far more flamboyant manner. A bright green morning coat, yellow waistcoat with shiny gold buttons, and ecru breeches graced his tall frame. He was athletic in build but leaner than Gabriel. Daniel possessed the same thick brown hair with a tendency to curl, a baby face which would eventually lean into the same angular planes of his brother, and piercing blue eyes along with a wide, well-sculpted mouth, which at present was set in a grim line.

Daniel's brows shot up at the sight of his brother's black eye, and despite his mood he grinned. "Who planted you a facer, Gabe? Would that I were there to have seen that. Must have taken you by surprise."

Gabriel shrugged. "A mere sparring accident at Jackson's. What has you awake and pestering me before noon? In Dun Territory again?"

The smile fell from the younger man's face. "I'm in a devil of a coil." He looked at Timbers, and the valet bowed, then exited the room when Gabriel gave a slight nod of his head. Once the door was closed, Daniel moved to the ornately carved bed and sat down. "I've fallen into a bit of a scrape. A bout of fisticuffs in public."

Surveying his brother's face, Gabriel

folded his arms across his chest as he leaned against the mantelpiece. "You seem none the worse for wear. Must have kept your hands up like I showed you. Surely you didn't forget yourself enough to trade blows in the presence of ladies?"

Daniel shook his head, then after a moment, "Drew Lord Chilton's cork at Madame Dupre's last night."

A moment of stunned silence filled the room and Gabriel straightened, disbelief etching his face. "You struck the Duke of Cumberland's godson in a brothel? Confound it, Danny, why not just accuse the Home Secretary of treason while you are about it to completely end Father's political hopes for you."

The young man had the decency to hang his head in shame while his cheeks flushed crimson. "Oh, botheration, Gabe, you know I have no such ambitions. Ain't bookish enough to keep up with all that paperwork, and I don't know the difference between the Corn Laws and a hole in the ground."

There Gabriel would have to agree. It wasn't that Daniel lacked intelligence. He merely was too impatient to sit still long enough to forge through more than a few pages of a book at a time. But fathers often have ambitions that far exceed their progeny's abilities, and the marquess was no different. "Well, you will have a very good notion of a hole in the ground soon, for Father will bury you in Surrey when he hears of this."

"Franklin says he already knows." Daniel often got much of his family information from the butler because his late hours rarely coincided with the rest of the Crowes. "That old gabble grinder, Sir Nate Walker, was here before breakfast wagging his tongue. Word from below stairs is that father is livid."

"What possessed you to trade blows with Chilton of all people? If he takes his grievances to the duke, Father is likely to receive the cut direct from Prinny himself."

Daniel's cheeks flamed with indignation. "The man called Freddie a jaded flirt."

Gabriel put his hand over his eyes for a moment. Somehow it only needed having his sister involved to make matters worse. Lady Alfreda Crowe was in London to experience her first Season. Like many young females, she little understood the power her beauty wielded and had been a bit free in her conduct. He dropped his hand. "Freddie is a flirt."

The young man looked nonplussed for a

moment. Then he straightened. "You may say that and I may say that, but by heavens that toad-eating, fish-faced Chilton cannot."

There seemed to be no way to show Daniel the error of his ways. Then another thought occurred to Gabriel. "What were you doing in a brothel? Has the little opera dancer in your keeping moved on to larger game?"

Daniel's chin rose. "Babbette loves me."

Gabe said nothing to that foolish statement. His brother was young and had much to learn about the mercenary nature of the muslin company. "So why the brothel?"

"I went looking for Charles Welles. He owes me fifty pounds and I needed the blunt."

Gabriel grew silent. A frown settled on his face, and at last he said, "Why are you telling me this? If Father wants to send you down to Surrey for awhile, why complain? The Season is nearly over, and with summer coming everyone will be departing Town soon. I was thinking of joining friends in York for the Gold Cup races, myself."

"Have you forgotten what Father said in March after my carriage wheel ripped down the gatepost at The Green Goose when I was racing Siddy Gilmore to Richmond?"

Gabriel shook his head. He could only remember there had been a great deal of yelling from the library, his mother's icy silence, and Freddie's weeping. "I fear there have been so many misadventures that I cannot sort them all out."

Daniel slid from the bed and came to his brother. "He swore he would send me to the East Indies to manage his business interests there if I fell into another mess."

The earl eyed his brother thoughtfully. For a moment he contemplated such a plan might not be a bad thing. His young brother had been cutting an unruly dash through Society. Scandal always hovered in the shadows of Danny's life. Then Gabriel remembered Lord Yorkton's son who'd gone to the Indies only to return a year later sick and feverish. The young man never fully recovered, and soon developed an inflammation of the lungs the winter after his return and died. One of Gabriel's friends had told him the mortality rate for clerks of the East India Company ran at nearly thirty percent. Too many younger sons were sacrificed in the name of making a man of them in the tropical environments, and Daniel, while not sickly, had always been more vulnerable to disease, he being the one to catch all the colds, measles, and other minor ailments that Freddie and Gabriel had escaped.

"Shall I go to Father and argue your case? He might be understanding since Freddie's name was being bandied about."

"Understanding? Father? It would be a waste of time. He knows the whole tale. Old Walker didn't leave out any details. Father ordered my man to begin packing my stuff."

Gabriel frowned. The marquess wasn't a doting parent. He rarely gave much thought to the punishment of his children, which usually involved a reduction of allowance. Clearly his patience had run out where Daniel was concerned. There would have to be something drastic to stop the momentum of things.

A knock sounded on the door and Gabriel called the visitor to enter. Lady Alfreda Crowe, all blond curls and ivory complexion, entered the room in a swirl of blue muslin. Always the darling of her eldest brother, she sought him out in times of trouble. "Oh, Gabe, you must stop Father. He says he is sending Danny away."

She threw herself into her elder brother's

arms and fell to weeping.

"Don't cry, little one. Your eyes will grow quite puffy and I believe you are to drive with Lord Marlin in the park today." The family had been expecting an offer from the young viscount at any moment.

"I don't care about my eyes," she declared, but she straightened and dabbed at them. "You must do something or Danny won't be here by the end of the week." She turned to her younger brother. "Oh, why can you not behave yourself for more than five minutes at a time?"

"Me?" Daniel's cheeks flushed quite red. "If you hadn't seen fit to dash off into the garden at Lady Willingham's soiree —"

"Daniel! Freddie! This does no good. We must put our heads together and come up with a plan." Gabriel needed something to distract the pair.

Freddie settled in a leather chair beside her eldest brother. "I suppose locking Danny in his room for the next five years is out of the question." She glared at Daniel. Close in age, the two youngest Crowes often bickered like children still, but were the first to defend the other in times of trouble.

Daniel rolled his eyes and turned his back to his sister. "It would seem my only

31

hope would be to slip off the ship Father puts me on and hide in the countryside."

The young lady snorted rudely. "And do you think Father's friends won't hear of your exploits and tell him at once? For I wager you a monkey that you cannot keep out of trouble for a week."

Gabriel chuckled. "Mother will have your tongue, little one, if she hears her gently bred daughter making such a vulgar wager."

Daniel turned and made a face at his sister. "They won't if I pretend to be Gabe. Everyone says we look so much alike."

In the act of buttoning his jacket, Gabriel halted. "Danny, when did this altercation happen?"

The young man shrugged. "Sometime after midnight last night. Why?"

"Can I safely assume that most everyone was deep in their cups at the time?" Gabriel's gaze surveyed his brother's face intently.

Daniel's eyes narrowed warily. "You aren't becoming one of those cursed temperance types, Gabe? Of course everyone had been enjoying themselves. Who doesn't drink when out for the evening?"

Gabriel nodded, then a smile lit his face. "Stay here. I think I may be able to put a stop to this East Indies business."

The earl left his startled siblings in his room and hurried down the stairs to the library where he found his father. Gabriel knew he risked inflaming his father's wrath, for they were all strictly forbidden to intrude during his work.

"Good morning, Father."

The Marquess of Latimer, still a fine figure of a man at fifty-nine, lowered a letter he was reading from his steward, his brows flatting at the interruption, as well as the sight of his son's injured face. "Whatever happened to you?"

Gabriel casually walked up to the desk. "I've come to beg your forgiveness, Father. I may have put you in a difficult situation."

The marquess sat back in surprise. Like his wife, he was rather a disinterested parent. Lord and Lady Latimer were much involved in London Society and politics, which had left their three children to be brought up mostly by servants. Each of the Crowe offspring had reacted to the neglect in different ways. Gabriel had excelled in most venues — shooting, boxing, driving, or any pursuit that kept him from the London drawing rooms which he blamed for his parents' indifference. Yet he'd always hoped for his parents' praise when he had performed well at any event. Daniel had chosen another route. He tumbled from one scrape to another, seeking even the negative attention. As for the youngest, Lady Alfreda was a hardened flirt. She sought her notice from others.

Scarcely aware of his children on any given day, Lord Latimer little understood the depth's of their interests or wishes. What *he* expected from them was foremost in his mind.

"What have you done, Shalford?" The marquess began to shuffle papers on his desk as if what his son had to say was less important than his affairs.

Not wanting to go into a detailed deception, Gabriel merely touched his eye and said, "Lord Chilton."

The marquess halted as the name penetrated his distraction. Disbelief filled his eyes as he stood. "Sir Nate said it was Daniel. How can this be?"

Gabriel shrugged. "As you can imagine, everyone was foxed. No doubt they all merely assumed it was Daniel, what with his reputation. But I cannot allow him to take the blame for me." The earl schooled his face to look contrite. In truth, he owned a bit of trepidation. His father's temperament had grown more irascible with age. Even for minor infractions, the old gentleman had taken to dispensing harsh punishment and always knew where to strike one's soft points.

Latimer sank down in his chair with shock and glared at his eldest as if he'd just grown horns. "This is far worse than I imagined." His face grew flushed and he gripped the arms of his chair. "You must give me some time to think. Chilton could ruin me at Whitehall, and all because you bested him."

Gabriel stood quietly. He knew little of what his father was involved in. It wasn't that he wasn't interested, but that his father brushed off such questions by changing the subject. Yet, Gabriel knew the marquess was often in the company of the Home Secretary, Lord Addington, which indicated that the documents presently scattered about the gentleman's desk were of some importance.

As the silence lengthened, a myriad of emotions played on the old gentleman's face, disbelief and anger among them. The marquess wanted the tale not to be true, but his gaze kept returning to Gabriel's black eye. At last Lord Latimer rose and went to the window, his back to his son.

"When you decide to stumble, you certainly pick the scandal which could do the most harm to me." He looked back at his son. "You may think I shall go lightly, but I won't. You are far too old to be up to such mischief and I shall punish you accordingly. Firstly, you must make your apologies to Lord Chilton. Blame it on whatever you wish, but I want there to be no bad blood between you. Secondly, I know who to blame for this."

Gabriel's brow arched. He hoped that Freddie wouldn't be in for a trimming, as well. True, she was a flirt, but it was all innocent and she would soon be married.

"Daniel!" the marquess pronounced with scorn. "His continuing bad conduct has led you astray."

"Father, it was no one's fault except Chilton for daring to speak my sister's name in such a place as Madame Dupre's." On that Gabriel was honest. Like Daniel, it offended his sense of honor that the man had dared to mention a gently bred female's name in a house of ill repute.

The old gentleman grew silent. He couldn't take his son to task on that issue. His daughter's future depended on her keeping her reputation intact. But by the same token, he couldn't ignore his son's conduct. To have struck a royal duke's godson, and in a bawdy house, would create all kinds of scandalous gossip and possibly even exclusion from the royal circles.

He folded his hands behind him. "I have been far too lax in my supervision of you and your brother. Still, I have little time or inclination to spend overseeing your social conduct. You *and* Daniel will retire to Weycross at week's end. Your mother must turn Freddie over to her sister and accompany you."

A sense of relief settled over Gabriel. Danny's exile to the East Indies seemed to have been averted. A summer at Weycross Abbey was no punishment, in truth.

Yet there was no reason to disrupt Freddie's Season. "Mother needn't come."

But his father wasn't finished. "Of course she must, for you haven't heard your final punishment. It's my decree that you have exactly one month to find and marry one of the ladies from a proper Surrey family. I shall trust your mother to make certain that you choose a young lady with both wealth and position to strengthen our position in Society."

"Marry! But, Father, I have no wish to marry at present, nor any fondness for a particular female." In his worst imagining,

Gabriel would never have envisioned marriage as his punishment. A punishment he didn't even deserve. It wasn't that he didn't wish to marry eventually, but he'd seen what had happened to too many of his friends after marriage. Their life no longer seemed to be their own, either by choice or coercion.

But he had made his bed, so to speak, in an effort to save Daniel from a life in exile, and he couldn't betray his brother even if it meant enduring such a punishment.

Lord Latimer continued. "Marriage settles a man down. It's high time you thought about setting up your nursery, especially at six and twenty. Say your good-byes to your friends. You depart on Friday morning." The old gentleman quirked one graying brow at his son. "And do not think you can defy me, Gabriel. You and your brother are dependent on me for your income. I should not hesitate to cut your allowance to fifty pounds a year if you disregard my wishes."

Fury ignited a fire in Gabriel. Fifty pounds a year wouldn't even take care of his cattle in Town, much less his other expenses. While both brothers were fully dependent on their father as were most fashionable young men of the *ton*, Gabriel was not without funds. His quarterly allowance was more than adequate for his needs, and he often walked away from wagers a winner. He was of a mind to tell his father he would not be coerced into a marriage of convenience, but his limited funds wouldn't last long.

He stayed his outrage and angry words when he realized it wasn't just him who would face the punishment, but Daniel as well. Gabriel knew in an instant where his brother would turn for money — the gaming tables or the moneylenders. The boy would be in Dun Territory by the first month's end.

His lordship took his son's silence as acceptance of the terms of the punishment. He returned to his desk, picked up his letter, and returned to what he had been doing. For Gabriel it was a clear sign that the interview was at an end. A part of him wanted to stay and argue, but things might only get worse. His father might decide that he would *choose* Gabriel's bride. He turned and exited into the hallway.

Daniel stepped from behind a large potted palm. "What happened? Am I still being sent away?"

Gabriel shook his head. "Not to the East Indies. I told him it was me at Madame's."

"You did?" Surprise etched the younger Crowe's face. "And did he believe you?"

Again Gabriel shook his head, being too distracted to speak.

Daniel clapped his brother on the shoulder. "You're a great gun, Gabe. I suppose he found some lesser punishment than the Indies for you?"

"I'm not sure that lesser would describe my punishment." Gabriel's blue eyes locked with his brother's.

Daniel frowned. "But you never cause trouble. Surely he would take that into account. What has he ordered?"

"That I marry within the month."

"I didn't know that you were in love."

Gabriel gave a grim chuckle. "I'm not. This union shall be a marriage of convenience, albeit not for me."

Horror settled on Daniel's face. He shook his head. "I cannot let you do this." He turned and started toward the library door, but Gabriel grabbed his arm.

"This was my choice. Promise me you will say nothing to Father. It is far better than you being exposed to God knows what dangers and illnesses in the tropics."

"But —"

Gabriel held up his finger for silence. "Promise."

"Oh, very well."

He forced a smile he was far from feeling. "You and I are for Surrey on Friday."

Daniel didn't say a word. As he followed his brother upstairs, he made a vow to himself to repay Gabriel for this sacrifice. Just how, he wasn't sure at present, but he would know the moment when it arrived.

Two

The knock on Ella's door came promptly at six sharp the following morning. The young footman gave her a saucy grin when she opened the door. "I be Nate, miss. I'm to take ye to Newland Cottage. Are ye ready?"

Ella had been up for nearly an hour. Her small portmanteau had been delivered near midnight and she'd risen early to put away her meager wardrobe. Afterwards, she dressed in her gray school gown, that being as close to servant's clothes as she owned. She'd stuffed a small handkerchief in the toe of each of the green slippers to keep them on her feet.

Without hesitation, she stepped into the hallway and closed her door, then paused. "Shall I need a shawl?"

"It's a bit chilled, but the walk will warm ye up, miss." He handed her a napkin with another wink. She opened it to discover a chunk of cheese and a slice of bread. "Cook thought ye might want a bite afore ye start yer new position."

Tears welled in Ella's eyes. The servant's

kindness touched her deeply. "You must thank her for me, Nate."

"That I will, miss." He tugged on his cap, then set off downstairs at a jaunty pace. Ella almost had to run to keep up, the cursed shoes hindering her every step.

The kitchen smelled of baked bread and bacon, but all the maids dropped their gazes as the viscount's daughter followed the footman through the huge room. Cook winked at Ella. The housekeeper stood near her desk in prim silence, her hands folded in front of her. Ella couldn't help but wonder if the stern Mrs. Falk weren't there, would the staff have been more welcoming? No doubt the housekeeper took her cues from her mistress. There seemed to be little question that Ella would be accepted neither by her aunt and cousins nor by the servants.

A gray dawn sky greeted Ella as she slipped out the rear door of the manor house behind the footman. Sunrise was nearly an hour away, but Nate made his way through the dim light with the confidence of one who'd traveled the path often. Once outside the ornately trimmed gardens, they set off along a well-traveled road where water stood in the twin ruts, forcing them to take to the shoulders of the lane.

The Surrey countryside looked beautiful in the early morning light. A variety of spring flowers bloomed in the fields, encouraged by May's warmth and rains. Their scents hung heavy on the dew-laden breeze. Despite the pastoral splendor to distract her, Ella could think of little except what Mr. Banks would be like. That and the blister which sprang up on her heel from the ever-shifting green slippers. She wished they could stop for a moment, but that stubborn streak in her refused to give in to the pain. Besides, she didn't want Nate or the other servants to know her aunt had not provided her with decent shoes. Being pitied by the servants would be far worse than blistered heels.

After thirty minutes of brisk walking, they turned down a narrow rutted lane and passed through a small woods. Newland Cottage came into view as they rounded a small curve in the path. The neat red brick building was somewhat nondescript, as were most Georgian cottages. Still, Mr. Bank's residence owned a quaint charm since someone in the distant past had planted roses beside the front door. Over the years the bushes had grown up and over the entry on a wooden trellis. It presently hung heavy with large yellow blooms, which gave the dwelling an inviting quality.

Nate knocked on the front door, and after a few minutes an ancient stooped gentleman whose thinning white hair hung to his collar opened the door and peered out with a decided squint.

"Yes?" His myopic gaze moved from the young man to the young female even as a pair of spectacles were perched forgotten on his head.

Ella wasn't certain he could see either one of them with any clarity, as a befuddled expression remained on his lined face. Yet a lessening of her fear took place due to his kindly expression.

"Harper!" Nate leaned toward the old man's left ear. "This is Miss Luella Sanderson, what was sent by Mrs. Newton to help ye."

The aged valet's beetled brows drew downward as he squinted even harder. "Aye, Miss Sandfordson. Mr. Addison is expectin' you."

"Sanderson," Ella called loudly.

The old man showed no indication he'd heard her correction as he stepped back for Ella to enter. To her surprise she stepped directly into a small parlor. It was an inviting room with cream-colored paper with yellow flowers. Cream and gold striped overstuffed chairs faced one another across a lovely little cherrywood table in front of an ornate fireplace. Ella couldn't help but wonder if her aunt had chosen the paper and furnishings, for it was not a man's room. The only hint of masculinity was the chess set positioned near a window with two worn cane-backed chairs. A game appeared to be in progress, but had been abandoned for other matters.

She turned to thank Nate for showing her the way, only to discover the footman was already halfway back to the woods, headed toward Newton Park. Doubtless, she would be expected to make her way home on her own. Being a servant was not like the daughter of a peer. One could walk wherever one wished without the company of a companion.

Harper closed the door, then stood and stared at Ella as if trying to remember why she was there. After a moment's silence she gently asked, "Will you show me the kitchen?"

"Not yet, child, Mr. Addison wants to greet you." With that the old man shuffled toward a set of double doors. Ella was ushered into a small dining room, made even smaller by the heavy oak furniture and the busy green wallpaper.

Addison Banks sat at a table cluttered with books and paperwork that he'd pushed aside just enough to accommodate a plate of ham and eggs as well as a cup of coffee. On seeing her, he rose. A smile lightened his face. Leona Newton and her brother bore little resemblance. A fatherly gentleman grown stout with age, he still showed traces of his handsome youth. His black hair, heavily grayed at the temples, befitted his sixty years, and smile lines radiated about his twinkling brown eyes.

The cut of his brown coat was more functional than fashionable, and his buff breeches were clean but showed stains in a variety of colors, as if he were a painter. That surprised Ella, for her cousin had made no mention that the gentleman might be an artist, only that he was crazy. Ella knew eccentricity, which seemed common among creative people, was often mistaken for mental incapacity.

A lump formed in Ella's throat. He looked much like her father would have, had the gentleman lived beyond forty. She tamped down the thought, knowing one could not change fate.

Looking into Mr. Banks's sharp cinnamon-colored eyes, Ella knew in a flash that the gentleman was quite sane and that Iris had been facetious. He'd pushed a pair of glasses up on his head, which made two wisps of dark hair stand at angles and gave him the look of some Greek god come to life.

"Miss Sanderson, Harper and I should like to welcome you to Newland Cottage."

Ella curtsied as befitted her lowly position. "Thank you, sir."

"Oh, I'll have none of that nonsense, child. I remember your father well, and while Harper and I shall welcome the help to spruce the place up a bit" — he gestured with his arm to take in the dining room that showed little signs of having been cleaned in a while — "I don't expect you to be bowing and scraping like a housemaid. Come and sit down and share a cup of coffee with me." He rounded the table and pulled out one of the chairs for her.

Still, Ella hesitated. She didn't think he fully understood what her aunt intended. "You know that your sister has sent me to work —"

An arrested expression settled on Mr. Banks's face, then his gaze swept the table. To Ella's amazement, he began to shuffle through the papers in front of him, looking for something. "My sister, Miss Sanderson, is a bit of a pretentious nodcock. Our father was the younger son of a baron and had to earn a living as a clergyman. Leona always resented that an accident of birth kept us from living in the manor. She very much likes to play Lady Bountiful when it suits her purpose." He found what he was looking for and pulled a nub of a pencil from his jacket. After a moment's contemplation, he jotted a notation on a sheet full of numbers, then pushed the paper away from him and smiled at Ella. "Or to put people in their place when she has the opportunity." He leaned over and patted her hand.

"But what did my father or I ever do to her?" Ella was puzzled. Their life had been far harder than Aunt Leona's.

"You had the good fortune to be born the eldest, which entitled you to be heirs."

That made no sense to Ella. Her father had inherited the title, it was true, but also an estate which was awash in debt. All had been auctioned off to pay those debts. They'd been virtually penniless most of her lifetime, forced to live in rented rooms in small villages outside London because it was cheaper. Her father had been reduced to taking money from his friends and working as a secretary for a local squire until his health failed. Then Ella had earned their keep by doing odd jobs for the woman who ran the house where they let their rooms.

Before she could comment about her aunt's whims, Harper entered the room with a plate of food which he set in front of Ella. Her stomach roiled at the sight of the runny eggs and burnt toast. After the servant left, Mr. Banks shrugged. "He does his best, but I fear his eyesight has failed as well as his hearing. I've tried several times to pension him off, but I do believe it would break his heart if I were to send him away. Anything you can do to help relieve some of his burden, Miss Sanderson, I shall greatly appreciate."

Ella smiled. "I am considered something of a respectable cook, Mr. Banks. And as to the cleaning, that shall be no difficulty in a cottage this small." The heavy weight of depression which had been pressing on her since her arrival at Newton Park suddenly slipped away. Mr. Banks was nothing like her aunt and Ella's post as his servant would be no great hardship.

"You cook?" The gentleman's brows rose in surprise. "Why, my dear, you appear to be a remarkable young lady if you've developed such a useful skill. It never made any sense to me to teach young ladies to paint and sew when cooking would be a far more functional skill. Why, my nieces would be utterly useless were Leona to lose her fortune." His mouth puckered a moment before he added, "But you have no wish to hear of my thoughts on Society's ambiguities."

Ella, too, had often thought the Polite World a contradiction. People tended to say one thing and do quite another. Her aunt spoke of kindness yet her actions did not. But Ella was in no mood for a philosophical conversation that morning. "I'm ready to begin my duties, Mr. Banks."

"Shall we dispense with the formalities? I know we aren't related, but we do share a family connection and you are much the age of my nieces. Perhaps you will call me Uncle Addison as they do, and I shall call you Luella if you have no objections."

"Won't you call me Ella? My father did." After that, things seemed less awkward. The pair spent some thirty minutes in pleasant conversation as Mr. Banks walked her through the cottage, while he inquired about her life at Parson's Academy. The place consisted of three bedchambers upstairs, two parlors, a dining room, and library downstairs, aside from the kitchen. Her tour ended back in the dining room. The gentleman gathered a handful of the papers and books that cluttered the table.

"This has been delightful, Ella, but I have work awaiting me. If it would be no problem, I should like a light nuncheon brought to the rear stable at noon, my dear."

Ella smiled. "I shall be there promptly at twelve, sir."

Addison Banks bustled out of the room while Ella remained and began to gather the dirty dishes. When Harper came in, she informed him she was ready to begin.

"This way, Miss Sandlin."

In a near shout she said, "Call me Ella."

He nodded his head. "If there is anything you need just say the word, Stella."

Ella gave up on correcting him and answered, "I'm certain I shall be able to find what I need."

The kitchen proved to be a whitewashed room with cabinets lining one wall and a modern stove which, doubtless, her aunt had installed beside the old fireplace. It was nice to see her aunt did have a heart and showed some concern for her brother's care. However, from the look of the black cast iron, she suspected the valet had never lit the oven. In contrast, the more familiar old-style fireplace was covered in soot and grease. The rest of the room was surprisingly clean when one considered the old valet's poor eyesight. After giving her a quick tour of the main kitchen and adjoining rooms, Harper departed, but not before stiffly informing her that Mr. Banks's room was strictly his domain. "I ain't quite useless as yet, miss."

The first thing Ella did was to kick off the offending shoes by the back door and strip off her stockings. The slate floor was clean and felt good on her abused feet. Next, she found an apron in a drawer, and set about taking an inventory of the larder. She made a list of what would be needed over the next week. When she put her list beside the back door, she discovered a basket of ripe apricots on the floor. With an eye on the clock on the mantelpiece, not wanting to be late with Mr. Banks's meal on her first day, she set about making tarts for the gentleman.

By eleven the tarts lay in neat rows to cool beside the window. That done, she prepared a tray of sliced bread, sliced cold chicken, cheese, a pot of tea; lastly she added one of the newly made tarts. She covered the lot with a napkin, then headed for the kitchen door. She eyed the green slippers with disgust, but slid her bare feet into them and clumped out the door. The stable was some ways from the house, the slate roof visible above the tops of a small copse of spruce trees. A dirt path was easily visible and after several steps in the ill-fitting shoes, she kicked them off in the grass.

The woodsy smell of the spruce brought back memories of her father. They had taken long walks at Sanders Manor during their brief stint in Derbyshire. A sadness she hadn't experienced in years settled on her. Once the estate had been sold, she had few such pleasant memories with her father. He'd done his best, but had been ill suited to earning a living. She tamped down the sad thoughts and reminded herself that life would not be so unpleasant here at Newland Cottage.

A red brick stable came into view as she entered a large sun-washed meadow. She paused to stare at several small platforms which had been built in the open field and wondered what purpose they served. Each had a stairway that led up to a small platform. She'd spent little time away from the village inns and knew little of farm life. Perhaps they were used for storing hay.

From behind the stable, a brown and white spotted dog bounded out to greet her. He didn't bark, only jumped up to put his dirty front paws on her gown and sniff at the tray that was above his head. She laughed and shifted the tray in her arms, then scratched behind one floppy ear. "What's your name? Come, shall we take Uncle Addison his nuncheon?"

The small animal wagged his tail and fell into step beside her, sniffing upward at the linen-covered tray. As she approached the stable, she was amazed at its size. It stood nearly as tall as the cottage. She hesitated when she reached the closed front doors. Should she knock? Somehow that seemed silly.

After a moment's hesitation, she tugged at one warped wooden door. It protested with a loud squeak as it opened. The dog slipped quietly inside and disappeared into the darkened depths. She stepped into the shadowy coolness, then halted. "Uncle Addison?"

A voice called, "Back here, Ella."

It took several moments for her eyes to adjust, but the huge building appeared empty. There was a strange smell of iron instead of hay, and an acrid odor she didn't recognize. As she looked about the cavernous structure she realized there were no horses, cows, sheep, or pigs inside the building — only great piles of something that looked like gray dirt. Rays of light poured in from the rear of the barn that silhouetted another set of large double doors.

She moved toward the light. Suddenly one of the back doors opened and Uncle Addison appeared and gestured to her. "I'm back here, my dear."

She hurried to where he stood, about to announce that she had brought his nuncheon. But she froze at the sight just beyond the stable.

A huge red and blue balloon hovered misshapenly in the large field behind the stable. The base of the balloon was attached to a narrow pipe that came out of the top of a huge wooden barrel, which appeared to be smoking. Four ropes anchored to stakes in the ground were attached to a large net that covered the globe. Clearly, the balloon was in the process of being filled.

Ella had read of aeronauts and ballooning. One of the teachers at the academy still had her Lunardi hat, which had been the rage after the young Italian had made his flight at Moorfield. Most everyone had been mad for flight since Monsieur Montgolfier's first balloon experi-ment in France nearly forty years ago. Ella had even seen one of the contraptions way up in the skies above Islington. Still, she was ill prepared for the sheer size of such a balloon when one stood beside it. Why, it took her breath away. When Mr. Banks had said he had work, she'd thought he painted pictures, built follies, or studied botany like many other gentlemen.

As the dog came up and sniffed her bare feet, Ella remembered her purpose for being there. "I-I brought you something to eat, Uncle Addison."

A grin tipped up his mouth as he noted her dazed expression. "Magnificent is it not, Ella? That was my thought the first time I saw a balloon ascension in Paris as a boy. I was fortunate enough to see Monsieur Charles's early flight from the Tuileries Gardens when I was almost twenty, before Napoleon ran mad all over the Continent. When we returned to England, I helped found The Royal Aeronautical Society in London. I attended many of the early ascensions of Lunardi and those of Mr. James Sadler. I know people lost faith after Monsieur de Rozier's death, but every serious balloonist knows he used a foolish design."

Ella noted the intense glint in the gentleman's eyes as he stared at the inflating balloon. "Is it safe?"

"Why, even ladies are ballooning these days, it's so safe. Madam Garnerin has been flying her own balloon for years. I shall loan you my copy of Mrs. Sage's *England's First Female Aeronaut*." With that he went into a detailed description on how to fill a balloon with hydrogen — a gas he called lighter than air.

Ella was fascinated with the process. "And do you do ascensions in London?"

A line appeared between the gentleman's brows. "Of course not, Ella. I am a scientist, not a showman. Besides, this is the first balloon of my very own. What I hope to do is find a way to propel a balloon in the direction I want it to go. Blanchard claimed he did it. I tell you, balloons can be the future of travel, my dear."

Ella's gaze swept over the thing, and a certainty filled her that most people would prefer the reliability of a team of horses and a responsible driver for a journey. The prospect of being at the mercy of nature would not appeal to travelers with a specific destination in mind, since balloons went where the wind took them. She couldn't help but wonder what it would be like to soar through the clouds on a sunny day. Then she reminded herself she was not here to engage in adventures — her duties were to cook and clean for Mr. Banks. "Where should I put your tray, sir?"

After one more admiring glance at the balloon, Mr. Banks ushered Ella back into the barn to the tack room that now served as his office. The smell of leather and saddle soap still permeated the small space. The chamber no longer held saddles or bridles; instead it was filled with drawings of all types of balloons, artists' colorful renditions of ascensions in London and a quote by the famous artist and scientist, Leonardo da Vinci: "When once you have tasted flight . . . you will always walk the earth with your eyes turned skyward; for there you have been and there you will always be."

Ella put the tray on the table and removed the cloth while the gentleman made an effort to clean up some of the scattered papers. She poured his tea, then asked, "Will that be all?"

"Won't you join me, my dear? I cannot have you working too hard." His eyes twinkled as he gestured her to a second chair.

"I haven't even begun to help Harper with the housework, Uncle Addison. Perhaps another time."

Just then the dog jumped up in the chair Mr. Banks had gestured for Ella to take. "Get down, Mercury." Mr. Banks pulled a piece of chicken from the plate and held it out.

The dog immediately did as he was told. "Lie down." Again the dog obeyed, his eyes never leaving the treat. "Roll over."

Mercury rolled neatly over, then sat up.

The gentleman tossed him the chicken. "Good boy." He grinned at Ella. "Mercury is my helper. I have trained him to untie the ropes when I want to take the balloon up and Harper is nowhere to be found, or the stable lads of the Black Knight are too busy to come. He's much cheaper than most assistants and never fails to show up for work."

Ella laughed and scratched the dog behind his ear, then bid the gentleman goodbye.

"Don't worry about the tray, Ella. I shall bring it back later." With a wave of his hand he settled down to eat as Ella headed back to the cottage. She was going to like working for the interesting old gentleman.

She could hardly wait to write Sarah and Rose to tell them of her new position and the gentleman's unusual occupation.

Within a week, Ella was comfortably settled into the routine of her new life. She rarely saw her aunt and nieces, except on Sunday when she was expected to attend church with the family. The rest of the time she rose early and walked to Newland Cottage where she cooked and cleaned for Mr. Banks. It wasn't an onerous job, for after the initial cleaning of the small home she often found she had time on her hands. Cooking became her favorite pastime. She baked a variety of treats, as well as the daily meals for the men. Uncle Addison and Harper were soon raving about her skill, one preferring her cheesecakes and the other declaring her sticky buns divine.

Sometimes in the afternoons when her work was done, she wandered out to the stable. Mr. Banks loved explaining how things worked. He taught her how to pour sulfuric acid into the barrel filled with iron shavings, the gray dirt she'd seen in the stalls. The combination created the hydrogen gas which filled the balloon, or envelope, as he called it. He brought pails full of the sheered metal which she duly doused. It was a surprisingly long operation to fill the balloon but she was fascinated by the entire process.

Compared to most of her friends at school, Ella's life would be perceived as difficult. There would be no new dresses, no Season in London, no marriage and family. She was expected to work for her keep, but she didn't lament her life. Mr. Banks was a kind man who demanded little and welcomed her help with his fascinating work. Sometimes late at night she might wonder what her life would have been like had her father not been penniless. But she didn't dwell on what would never be. Instead she was thankful for how good her life was in Surrey.

"A garden party?" Gabriel put down his cup of coffee and frowned across the breakfast table at his mother. They'd arrived at Weycross Abbey the following evening, and he'd given little thought to the reason he'd come to Surrey, basking in his delight over once again being in his boyhood home. Somehow it didn't seem real that he would have to take a wife by the end of June, but his mother had just sharply brought the reality home. "I shall be able to find a proper female over the course of the next month without all that fuss and bother."

He hated the idea of a parade of simpering females fawning over him at a party. He rarely attended such affairs in Town for that very reason. Surely there must be young ladies in Surrey who possessed more depth than that.

Across the table and dressed in a simple green morning gown, her gray hair crimped in curls under a lacy white cap, Lady Latimer glared at her son. The daughter of a viscount, she'd always been aware of her station in life. At eighteen she had dutifully wed Latimer as she was told. Her years as a marchioness had only added to her feeling of superiority. Her once pretty face had grown pinched and stern with haughty lines of disdain for most others. She presently looked down her nose at her eldest son as she spoke. "I did not travel out of Town during the Season and leave your sister with her aunt, dear boy, to twiddle my thumbs while you dash about the countryside making sheep's eyes at every pretty female who crosses your path."

Daniel choked on his coffee. "Sheep's eyes! A gentleman would never wish to be associated with sheep. Don't you mean wolf's eyes? He is the predator out looking for prey."

Her ladyship's eyes narrowed as she looked at her younger son. "I'll have my eyes on you, young man, if you do not behave."

Daniel waggled his brows and said in a whispered undertone, "Hawk's eyes, for certain."

The brothers shared a silent chuckle as Lady Latimer went back to her writing. After a moment, she rose. "I am going to pay Mrs. Hyde a morning call. She will know who has returned to their estates, as well as anyone new in the neighborhood of interest."

Daniel picked up a slice of toast. "Also who has the most blunt, who has no suitors, who would sell their soul to the devil to be a marchioness —"

"Daniel! I won't tolerate your facetious comments. This is a serious business which will greatly affect your brother's life and position in Society. I want no more levity concerning this matter. Humor has no place where marriage is concerned." With that the lady departed the room.

As the door to the room closed, Daniel eyed his brother. "That pretty well sums up matters. Marriage takes the pleasure from one's life."

Gabriel leaned back in his chair and heartily agreed, but he didn't say so, not wanting to make his brother feel any more guilty than he already did. He certainly had seen little between his own parents to make him want to rush into marriage. Too often they were like strangers speaking to one another. "I shall do as Father wishes and give some female my name, but that shan't change much about how I live my life."

He rose and tossed his napkin on the table. "Come, shall we ride about the neighborhood and see what changes have been wrought since we were here for Twelfth Night? Lord Barrington was intent on building new stables and Sir Giles mentioned having a racing track installed at the rear of his estate. Let's not worry about females and nuptials for today anyway."

Daniel was all for an outing. He suggested they visit a Guildford inn for a tankard after their ride in the hopes of encountering some of their friends. That would make their banishment out of Town more interesting and pass more quickly.

While Lord Shalford and his brother enjoyed their ride about the neighborhood, Lady Latimer drank tea and ate stale cake with Mrs. Hyde, the village gossip. The gregarious widow had welcomed the marchioness with reserved elation. That emotion rose to ecstasy when she discovered her ladyship's reason for coming home to Weycross before the end of the Season. There was nothing like a gentleman searching for a wife to make life in the community interesting. And a nobleman with a timetable would bring the excitement to a pinnacle.

Mrs. Bertha Hyde duly gave her ladyship a list of titled families currently in residence, as well as the best heeled gentry, for money could never be ignored even when it belonged to mere Quality. With her mission completed, the marchioness returned home to write out the invitations to her party for the following Thursday.

Meanwhile, Mrs. Hyde alerted the neighborhood to the interesting news that the Earl of Shalford, heir of Latimer, was home and in search of a wife by month's end. By the following morning, young ladies from Littleton to Albury were agog with excitement, but none more than Leona Newton. This was the chance of a lifetime for a young lady with the proper attributes. In Mrs. Newton's mind, her eldest daughter's beauty and breeding made her the leading candidate in the vicinity to become the future Marchioness of Latimer.

Yet Ella, settled into her new life, remained happily content and unaware of the Earl of Shalford's quest, or even the gentleman. She was little involved in her aunt's world, and Mr. Banks rarely took note of the happenings on the ground. Few visitors came to the cottage, and in many ways Newland was a world unto itself.

Scarcely a week after arriving at Newton Park, Uncle Addison sent Ella home early due to the threat of rain. With time on her hands, Ella quietly slipped down to the library to find something to read. She hadn't been strictly forbidden to use her aunt's library, but Ella didn't want to take a chance of being caught and reprimanded, or worse, banned from future use of the room. She'd just found Maria Edgeworth's six-volume edition of *Tales of Fashionable Life* and had pulled down the first book when the door to the library opened. Ella slipped behind the brown velvet curtain, fearful that Aunt Leona would take exception to her niece's liberty.

Her aunt's voice sounded low and urgent. "Iris, this is for your ears only, child. I have hopes for Daisy, which your father's fortune will see to fruition, but you are the family beauty. You may look as high as you like for a husband."

Ella could imagine Iris preening at her mother's compliment. A sudden guilt flooded her that she was eavesdropping on a private conversation, but it couldn't be helped.

"Thank you, Mama. But do you not think this yellow muslin makes me look a bit —"

Leona Newton interrupted. "Never mind about your finery, girl. We cannot miss this opportunity that Mrs. Hyde has presented us with. How fortuitous that I should meet her at the linen draper's scarcely an hour after Lady Latimer's visit. Lord Shalford must have a bride by the end of the month. To capture the earl's interest would be the triumph of a lifetime."

"Oh, Mama, I should adore being the Countess of Shalford."

"And future Marchioness of Latimer, don't forget. But you won't be the only young lady in the neighborhood out to gain his attention. Mrs. Hyde's tongue shall be running on wheels, as usual. Once word gets about that he's looking for a wife, the gentleman will be inundated with eligible females. So you, dear Iris, must gain the upper hand."

"How, Mama? I have never before met the gentleman. Can we not merely ride over to Weycross Abbey —"

"Gads, child, and be thought the most pushing females in Surrey and ruin forever your chances with the gentleman? I am ambitious, true, but not a fool. Sadly, we are unacquainted with Lord and Lady Latimer, so I have come up with another way to make the gentleman's acquaintance."

"How, Mama?"

"What do most gentlemen do every morning?"

After the briefest of hesitations, Iris asked, "Is he handsome?"

"Handsome! What does it matter? He may be as ugly as a baboon's hind end, my girl, for he shall be a marquess and a feather in any lady's cap. Use your head, child."

"A baboon?" Iris gasped. "Papa showed us one of those ugly creatures at the fair in Plymouth. Mama, I cannot even consider —"

"Don't be a goosecap, Iris. I only used the animal as an example. I am certain he is quite presentable. Back to my point, do you know what most gentlemen do every morning?"

There was a long pause. "Break their fast."

"Heaven grant me patience." The lady took a deep breath. Her tone clearly showed her exasperation when she resumed. "What use is it to you to know he dines on steak and ale? I refer to a gentleman's morning ride. You must be up early and ride in the direction of Weycross Abbey. What better than a chance meeting with Lord Shalford on horseback? Gentlemen admire a woman who can sit on a horse with style."

The sound of her aunt's voice drew closer to where Ella stood hidden. It seemed in her excitement over expectations for her daughter the lady had begun to pace. Ella held her breath, fearful she would be discovered. After a moment, the lady's voice again echoed from the center of the room.

"You must manage a meeting on the morrow."

Eagerness for the plan filled Iris's tone. "You are a genius, Mama. I shall be the first to meet him. Which habit shall I wear? The blue with the red frogging or the new green with the gold buttons. I think —"

A hint of indulgence tinged Mrs. Newton's voice. "It does not matter. What does matter is that you are dressed and at the stable by six o'clock."

"Six o'clock! Mama, even the hens are not up then. I shall look a fright. Can I not wait until ten?"

An urge to laugh welled up in Ella as she listened to her spoiled cousin, but she stifled it immediately. She wondered how Iris would have coped with life as a poor relation. Not well, it was clear.

"Do you want to be the future Marchioness of Latimer, girl?"

"I do, Mama, I do. But six is very early. Could I not sleep a bit later?"

"Oh, very well, seven o'clock, but not a minute later. Remember, if you do as your mama tells you, you will be saying those words to Lord Shalford by the end of June. I shall inform Barr to have one of the grooms take you to the gates of Weycross, then wait."

In a very calculated tone, Iris cooed, "I know just what to do once I see the earl, Mama."

To Ella's relief her aunt announced, "Come, we must join Daisy in the drawing room or she will be quite suspicious about

71

our absence. Not a word to your sister about our plan. It would only make her want to go, and while I do love her, even I must own the child has the worst seat in Surrey."

A chuckle from Iris was the last sound Ella heard before the door to the library opened, then shut. After several minutes of silence, she peeked out from behind the curtains to find herself once again alone.

She waited another five minutes, then slipped upstairs to her small room. Book in hand, she curled up on her bed to enjoy a respite from work, but the small volume lay unopened on her counterpane as her thoughts returned to the conversation she'd overheard. Were all the wealthy daughters in the neighborhood plotting with equal cunning to snare Lord Latimer's heir? She hated to think that all mothers were quite as devious and ambitious as her aunt, and yet many of the girls at Miss Parson's Academy seemed to think title and fortune the only quality a gentleman need possess to make him an eligible party.

Ella experienced a moment of sympathy for the young man who was likely to be harried by every young lady this side of Guildford, all because of his mother's loose lips. Yet she had to wonder about a man who approached marriage as a business arrangement. One who came to the country with the express purpose of finding a wife at the end of a month could not be very much a romantic. What a cold and disappointing marriage for his bride. Perhaps the Earl of Shalford did deserve someone as shallow as Iris.

On that thought, she opened her book and put her world aside, if only for a moment. Soon it grew too dark, and after lighting her candle she waited until her supper was delivered by Nate, who inquired how she liked her post at Newland. She assured him she enjoyed her work.

After her meal, she wanted to continue to read, but the lone candle her aunt allowed did not provide adequate light. She blew out the candle and settled down to sleep. After all, unlike Iris she must rise at six in the morning.

Three

In accordance with orders, Iris Newton's maid awakened the young lady promptly at seven the next morning. But Mrs. Newton did not allow for the time it would take the vain young woman to choose her attire, dress her hair, and scold her maid for dawdling. First the green habit was tried on, but Iris decided that she might merely blend into the foliage of the countryside and not be remarkable in any way. She determined that the blue was the more striking outfit. A breakfast of hot chocolate and toast was enjoyed before she preened in front of the mirror after her hair was brushed to her satisfaction, which delayed her departure until nearly eight o'clock. Unfortunately for the young lady, Lord Shalford and his brother had ridden toward Guildford at half past seven to meet several old friends.

By ten o'clock that morning Gabriel fully realized that news of his search for a bride was rife in Surrey. To his dismay, during one short stroll down High Street he was accosted no less than three times by old friends of Lord Latimer and introduced to young ladies, who flirted and simpered at him in the worst manner. With his father's demand still ringing in his ears, he dutifully measured each female in his mind and found her wanting, each for a different reason. Miss Stevens was pretty but witless, Lady Diana Newchurch possessed looks but a braying laugh, and Miss Varner was a plain, dull mouse in blue muslin.

His thoughts began to dwell on his impending marriage. As he cantered along the road home with his brother at his side, it struck him that he couldn't continue to be so critical, or he would fail to meet his father's deadline. There was a part of him that wanted to tell his father he wouldn't marry someone he hardly knew. He could buy a commission in the Navy, but that took money, of which he had little. So it seemed he must find a genteel woman to marry.

But surely there was a female out there who wouldn't bore him to death within a fortnight or embarrass him to have on his arm. If marry he must, he would accept nothing less than a diamond of the first water, with a vast fortune, and the most adept social skills. A flawless creature who would be the envy of every man who saw her. He might at last earn his parents' respect by doing his duty for the family.

The two men rode over a small rise that looked over the valley. Suddenly Daniel reined his horse, stood in his irons, and peered westward. Gabriel drew Blackjack to a halt. "What's wrong?"

"Do you see that flash of red and blue there just above the trees?"

Gabriel followed the direction his brother was pointing. "I don't see anything. I think it might have been a trick of the sun."

A grin lit Daniel's face. "No, I saw something. Come on, follow me. Let's go adventuring."

Before Gabriel could protest, his brother was off in a swirl of dust. There could be no denying that too often adventuring was what got Daniel in trouble. Gabriel debated whether to follow as he watched his brother gallop across the meadow in search of heaven knew what. With a shrug of his shoulders, he welcomed the distraction and prodded his horse into action, wondering exactly what his brother had seen to excite him so. In truth, anything that would keep his thoughts occupied and the pair of them away from Weycross Abbey and his mother's schemes would be welcomed.

He pushed Blackjack to overtake his brother. The horse closed the gap, and by the time the two brothers reached the trees they were racing full tilt. When the animals broke through the far side of the woods, the sight that greeted them made both men rein their horses.

Behind a big stable was a red and blue balloon nearly inflated, waiting to have the gondola attached for flight. The two brothers looked at each other and grinned, then without a word they both cantered to where the balloon hovered.

Once they arrived at the site, Gabriel called a hello, but no one responded.

"Do you know whose stable this is?" Daniel asked as he climbed down from his horse and moved closer to inspect the balloon, where his brother joined him.

Gabriel had to think. "It must belong to the old Littlewood estate, but that was bought by a Mr. Newton, a gentleman who made his fortune on the 'Change. But the cottage has been empty for years."

"Not anymore. Clearly it's been let." Daniel's eyes glittered as he walked about the giant orb. "I should love to take a ride in a balloon."

Gabriel eyed the towering globe with interest. A tingle of excitement raced through him, too, and he wanted to experience a flight. He walked to the stable and looked inside, but the building stood empty. As he looked about his gaze fell on a path that led into the woods. Thinking that whoever owned the balloon would welcome a fee for a ride, he said, "Wait here and I'll see if there is anyone at the cottage."

He set out through the woods and within minutes approached the rear of the red brick cottage. As he drew nearer, a young female stepped from the rear door, a heavy caldron in her hands. She poured the steaming water into a washtub, then turned her back on him and began to scrub the wet linens in the water, unaware of his approach.

As he drew nearer, he appraised her shapely figure beneath the plain gray dress and found nothing wanting. Her auburn hair lay in a thick braid down her back and glinted with copper lights in the sunshine. A great many troublesome loose curls had escaped the thick plait. They floated about her head each time she leaned forward to scrub the wash.

As Gabriel approached the maid, one

thing struck him as odd. The servant's feet were bare. Could whoever have taken the lease on the cottage not afford to properly attire her? Or perhaps she was one of those unfortunates who'd never owned a pair of shoes until she was grown, and found them uncomfortable.

Whatever the reason, Gabriel put the matter from his mind, having little interest in his neighbor's servants. Only yards from her, his boots crunched the gravel on the kitchen path and the sound made her start. She twirled round to face him and he was momentarily stunned by her beauty. Wide green eyes stared at him in surprise and she nervously began to tuck errant curls behind her ears. The chit would no doubt attract a great deal of unwanted attention from a certain type of gentlemen. Her lovely face was marred only by a light dusting of freckles across her nose, yet they gave her a decidedly innocent appeal. Her full mouth, a bit wide for current standards, was womanly and immanently kissable. Luckily the girl was only a servant without the worry of fashionable trends.

"W-what do you want, sir?" Her hand fluttered between her hair and the wet pillowcase she held.

"I didn't mean to startle you, miss." Gabriel pulled his black beaver from his head and smiled reassuringly before turning his attention to the old brick building. He'd never dallied with a servant before and he didn't intend to now, no matter how pretty. "I came to inquire who has let this cottage."

Warily she asked, "Who are you, sir?" In her nervousness, she wrung out the small linen cover. The falling water splashed great globs of dirt onto his newly polished Hessians.

In dismay, the earl watched the rivulets of dirty water trickle down his boots, and took a step back to avoid any further carelessness. "Shalford of Weycross Abbey."

When he glanced up he could see recognition of his name change her face. For a moment Gabriel could almost swear there was pity in the little maid's green eyes. But surely he must be mistaken. What could a servant have to pity him for? The look was gone in a moment and he convinced himself it was nothing but a fear of titled persons.

The pretty maid sketched a wobbly curtsey. "I am delighted to meet you, sir. I am Miss . . . er . . ." She hesitated before she continued. "Ella, sir. As to your question, this cottage is leased by Mr. Addison

Banks, brother to Mrs. Newton of Newton Park. But he is not at home this morning. He left before dawn to visit his uncle in London."

As he listened to her speak, he was struck by her cultured tones. Yet he knew that servants often mimicked their betters and could sound quite as haughty as a duchess. This Ella was a strange girl, meeting his eye with a confidence he didn't often find in the serving class, yet with all the fidgety gestures of a typical maid unused to dealing with members of the nobility.

Remembering the reason he'd come, disappointment raced through Gabriel. There would be no ride for him and Daniel today. "Perhaps you can alleviate my curiosity. Does the balloon in the rear belong to Mr. Banks?"

"It does, sir." She smiled, not the coquettish smile of a saucy minx, but a gentle pleasant smile, one that brought a warmth inside of him.

Why was he being so fanciful about a maid? He forced his thoughts back to the subject at hand. "Does the gentleman hire out the balloon for excursions?"

A vexed expression settled on the young woman's face. "Mr. Banks is a serious scientist, sir." Then something seemed to occur to the young woman, for a stricken look came over her features and she looked down at the ground. "But I think you should come back tomorrow and discuss the matter with him. He might be willing to make an allowance for your lordship."

Gabriel resettled his hat and tamped down his disappointment. So she thought he might use his title to get what he wanted. How could he blame her, when so many gentlemen of the *ton* were guilty of such doings? "Then please inform him that I shall stop again tomorrow afternoon."

With one last glance at the lovely young woman, he walked back toward his brother. He informed Daniel that Mr. Banks was gone for the day but they could come back on the following afternoon. Disappointed in their quest for a balloon ascent, the two brothers rode off to visit their neighbor, Sir Giles, which would keep them well entertained throughout the day. A fact that left Miss Newton, who'd missed their departure, cooling her heels in front of Weycross Abbey until well after noon, when hunger forced her to give up the vigil.

For Ella, meeting the earl had been rather unsettling. She listened to the receding sounds of the hoofbeats from where she'd settled on the bench beside the steaming washtub. So that was Lord Shalford. He would have no trouble finding a wife with such dark brown hair, piercing blue eyes, and a tall muscular frame that most young ladies would find irresistible. Her heart was still beating a bit fast even after he had departed, but whether the cause was from her start upon his unexpected arrival or his handsome countenance she wasn't certain. She'd acted as nervous as a silly young girl.

In that moment an overwhelming sense of despair overtook her. For the first time, the hopelessness of her life truly dawned on her. He'd looked at her with that distant stare that people used with servants, as if they weren't there. Penniless, her circumstances removed her from his world, for no earl would take a second look at a young woman who was reduced to doing someone else's laundry.

She eyed the wet soapy linens with distaste, then sighed. Things could be much worse. She could be at the beck and call of her cousins, who would not be so kind as Mr. Banks. She had too much to do to sit there and feel sorry for herself. She rose and went back to her work, but she couldn't keep her thoughts from a certain handsome face with blue eyes.

What the Earl of Shalford lacked in enthusiasm in his pursuit of a bride, his mother more than made up for. Within two days of her visit with Mrs. Hyde, the marchioness and her dresser had addressed all the invitations to the garden party and sent them out. All save one, which she intended to deliver in person. Her ladyship said nothing to her son about Lady Amelia Harris. Wise in the ways of men, she realized there was nothing that would make a gentleman more obstinate than to tell him who would suit him best. Instead, the lady wished to show their neighbor, Lord Hallet, which direction the wind was blowing by her marked attention to his daughter.

She rose early, dressed with particular care, and set out for Hallet Hall with a gift for Lady Amelia, who'd only just turned one and twenty. She had missed her come-out for the past two years with the untimely deaths of both her grandmothers, and had only recently come out of half-mourning for her grandfather. She was to make her bow during the Little Season in the fall.

A smile tipped the lady's mouth at the thought of such an alliance for Gabriel. True, the girl was a bit young, but they couldn't afford to procrastinate. Viscount Hallet's talent for investing wisely had left him a very wealthy man with only a daughter as his heir. She would have suitors stumbling over one another if she were allowed to make her bow to Society.

The visit went as her ladyship planned. Lady Amelia, a petite blonde with dimples, accepted her gift with all the proper expression of thanks, then sat demurely on the sofa, her gaze on the rug, throughout the remainder of the visit. She was polite and unassuming, rarely joining in the conversation. The girl seemed not the least pert or pushing to the marchioness, the perfect daughter-in-law.

When a household matter required attention, Lady Amelia offered to handle it and excused herself prettily, which gave the adults the time needed to come to an understanding. It soon became evident to the marchioness that the viscount had great aspirations for his child, wanting both title and money in a prospective husband. Her eldest son would provide both. By the time Lady Latimer departed, it was generally understood that Lord Hallet would welcome a visit from the earl, which his mother would strongly encourage. One thing was emphasized by the marchioness — this plot would be their secret.

Satisfied with her morning's work, Lady Latimer set out for Weycross Abbey. She had set matters in motion that would end with her son marrying the ideal bride. That done, she turned her thoughts to the first task facing her — the garden party. Even as the carriage returned her to the Abbey, she jotted a list of foods to be served and where the tables would be positioned in the garden. Her ladyship lamented to her maid that Lord Latimer had kept their chef, Monsieur Alain, in Town with him. Mrs. Greenwood would have to serve as cook for her party. It was unfortunate, for while the lady was good enough to suit the family, it was not what her ladyship would have wanted for her guests. But she would have to make do.

Her concentration fully on the garden party, she screeched in alarm when the carriage suddenly veered to the left, then made a hard jolt as the damaged vehicle settled to one side like a sinking ship.

"John!" the marchioness called. "John! What has happened?"

The door to the carriage opened and a

footman with his white wig askew appeared. "The wheel's busted a spoke, my lady."

The marchioness sighed impatiently. She had too much to do to be stranded on a country road. "Well, have John Coachman fix the wheel and let us be on our way."

The servant looked as if he feared for his job. "But — but, my lady, it can't be fixed. Leastwise not here on the pike."

At that moment, John Coachman stepped into view. He was a burly man with long graying brown hair pulled back in a queue who looked more like a prize-fighter than a driver. Having been with the Crowe family for years, the man well knew Lord Latimer wouldn't take exception to an accident, even if her ladyship did. "Lady Latimer, I fear the wheel is done for. I can 'ave the lad 'ere run for 'elp back at the Abbey but likely it'll be near an 'our for 'im to get there and back."

"Well, man, don't just stand there, help me out. You cannot think I shall sit here in this carriage and swelter while we must wait."

The coachman awkwardly helped her ladyship to the roadway. After a disgusted glance at the collapsed wheel, she looked about for somewhere to go out of the sun.

Her gaze locked on a stand of trees and she pointed. "There is a cottage. Come, escort me there so I might rest until a coach arrives to take me back to Weycross."

Inside Newland Cottage, Ella licked a bit of glaze off her finger after she finished icing the tray of orange currant rolls. The baked buns sat beside a tray of macaroons and a plate of almond crumb cakes. She had told Uncle Addison about his visitor the day before, and he seemed delighted that the young man would return today. He'd asked her to prepare plenty of good things to eat, in case the young man wanted to join him for tea. That had surprised her, but perhaps the old man was lonely for masculine company of his own class.

When the knock came at the door, Ella's heart began to race at the prospect of once again seeing the Earl of Shalford. She hurried through the tiny hallway, stopping long enough to inspect her hair in the looking glass beside the door. Even Uncle Addison had complimented her on her looks that morning. She'd taken the time to pull her hair into a cluster of curls on the back of her head instead of the usual braid she wore. She had no illusions that Lord Shalford would take a second glance at her, a servant in Mr. Banks's house, but every woman had that feminine trait that made them want to look their best in front of a handsome gentleman.

Ella, about to open the door, realized she'd left the hated green slippers outside the kitchen door. About to hurry to retrieve them, a second knock came with a great deal of insistence in its cadence. Afraid he might leave if she didn't, she drew open the door and her heart nearly stopped at the sight of the dignified female in a purple morning dress. The lady wore matching purple kid gloves and a white high-crown bonnet with purple flowers. Her gaze swept Ella and her expression grew even more frosty.

"Don't just stand there gaping, foolish girl. Where is your master? Tell him the Marchioness of Latimer's carriage has broken down and I must seek shelter here. And be quick about it." The woman gave the building a quick survey and her expression spoke volumes about her opinion of such a modest abode.

Ella was certain she would never get used to being treated with disdain. A flame of anger ignited deep within her, then she remembered her position. Still, her chin rose and in a quiet, dignified manner she said, "Won't you come in, Lady Latimer. I shall summon Mr. Banks at once and bring you some refreshments."

The marchioness stepped into the tiny drawing room and looked about her. Her nose lifted and twitched, no doubt from the aromas coming from the kitchen. She harrumphed, then moved to one of the striped chairs. She sat down and drew off her gloves even as she inspected the painting of a woodland scene over the fireplace.

Ella hurried back to the kitchen, where she discovered Harper putting firewood in the box. She informed him of their visitor and he offered to go to the stable and summon Mr. Banks while Ella prepared refreshments for the lady. There was a part of Ella that didn't want to give the arrogant old woman anything more than a glass of water, but she knew that servants had been subjected to such treatment for years and had taken it in stride. She would do no less.

By the time Addison Banks appeared at the rear door of the cottage, a flush of exertion on his cheeks from having run all the way, a silver tray lay on the table filled with a variety of cakes, currant rolls, and macaroons, as well as teapot and cups.

"So!" He paused to catch his breath at the sight of Ella pouring hot water into the teapot. "Harper tells me" — he gasped — "we have an unexpected visitor." In his hurry to come back to the cottage, the gentleman had quite forgotten his coat. His amber damask waistcoat was unbuttoned, his cravat askew, and a gray smudge ran the length of his cheek. "I should like to meet my neighbor, albeit rumor has her as being a great dragon." He winked, then started toward the drawing room, but Ella stepped into his path.

"Decidedly a dragon. I have a few scorched hairs already myself." She straightened his cravat, then wiped the grime from his face with a towel. "Do you not think you might want to find a jacket, Uncle? One should never face dragons in shirtsleeves."

He looked down and laughed, immediately beginning to button his waistcoat. "I do suppose one should greet a marchioness in proper attire." Then a frown darkened his features. "Was she very rude? I cannot like that, especially since you are Lord Sanders's daughter."

Ella shrugged. "Her rudeness was no

more so than what most servants experience. Don't give the matter a thought."

His frown deepened. "That won't do, Ella. In the truest sense you are not a servant. You only help me out. Allow me to present you to her, my dear. I would —"

"No!" Ella's tone came out more forceful than she intended. Her gaze moved to her hands, which were growing steadily more rough with each passing day of labor. "I have no wish to be pitied, Uncle Addison. My circumstances would far outweigh my pedigree in the lady's eyes. Besides, my prospects are not likely to change. I am very happy here." She looked back at him then stood on tiptoes and kissed his cheek. "Do not worry. I am content."

He started to say something, but she held up her hand. "The dragon awaits."

The gentleman laughed, but there was a sadness in his eyes that his own situation was such that he could do little to help her. She made a shooing gesture and he hurried up the rear steps. Within minutes he returned dressed in a neat blue coat that Ella had never before seen. "Do I look more the thing, my dear?"

"You are very handsome, Uncle."

Addison Banks led the way into the

drawing room and Ella followed with the full tray. As the marchioness and the scientist made their greetings, Ella began to prepare plates for them and pour the tea. Lady Latimer scarcely acknowledged Ella's existence, instead pressed Mr. Banks for his family history. On learning that he was the nephew of a baron, she unbent enough to ask if the baron resided nearby and had eligible daughters.

Finished with her duties, Ella headed toward the door to the kitchen.

"Oh, Ella, would you open one of the double doors to the garden? It smells of smoke in here. That fire last night, no doubt." Addison winked at Ella, who nearly laughed since there had been no fire. The dragon image returned to her mind. Fortunately Lady Latimer had her attention on the almond cakes which she had just sampled.

"Why, these are quite the best crumb cakes I have ever eaten. Who is your cook, Mr. Banks?"

"Ella," Mr. Banks announced as he picked up one of the cakes and took a bite.

Her ladyship's gaze swept over the slender young girl at the door and a sly look came over her. "Is everything she does as excellent as this cake?" She took a bite from an orange currant roll and nodded her approval. "Excellent!"

"She is quite the best cook I've ever had." Uncle Addison beamed at Ella with such pride, she blushed.

"Come here, girl." Lady Latimer picked up a macaroon and sample it while she waited for Ella to come and stand before her. Her opinion of the girl's abilities confirmed, she announced, "I should like to hire you for a day to cook for my garden party."

Mr. Banks's face grew stormy and he sputtered, "But . . . well, one simply does not hire a gently —"

With visions of a new pair of shoes from the money she earned, Ella interrupted, "I accept." Then she remembered her role and added, "My lady."

Seeing the dark look on Mr. Banks's face, Ella added, "I could use the funds, sir."

Addison sighed, well familiar with tightened circumstances. He'd just been to see his uncle about an increase in his allowance for his scientific work because Leona cared naught for his work. She willingly provided the cottage, but nothing else. "Very well, if you wish you may cook for her ladyship."

That settled, Ella was about to depart when Lady Latimer said, "I shall send a gig for you on Thursday morning. Be ready by six sharp. You will be cooking for one hundred." With that the lady returned to her enjoyment of the refreshments.

Ella's heart sank. That meant she would have to be up especially early to make the walk to the cottage, since she could not have the carriage pick her up at Newton Park. "Very good, my lady."

Nearly an hour later when her ladyship's carriage arrived, Lady Latimer duly departed, issuing Mr. Banks an invitation to the party, which he politely declined, citing business. After he closed the door he went straight to the kitchen to speak with Ella, who was making lamb stew for his dinner.

"My dear, do you not want to reconsider this plan to cook for the marchioness? You should not be going to Weycross except as a guest. Why, your father would turn in his grave if he knew you had been reduced to such circumstances."

Ella put down the carrot she was peeling. "Uncle, I cannot keep looking back at my former life. I should adore to go to Lady Latimer's party as a guest, but that is not to be. So I shall go and make money, which is a much more sensible pursuit. As you know, Aunt Leona feels that I owe her for her *kindness* in taking me to live at Newton Park and my work for you pays for my room and board only."

"Great heavens, Ella. I can scrape up a few coins to pay you if it's money you need."

Ella held up her hand. "That won't be necessary. Besides, you know that I enjoy cooking." He barely had the money he needed for himself and Harper; she didn't want to add to his burden.

But Mr. Banks, disturbed by a young lady working at the Abbey, pursued the matter. "Have you thought about what Leona will say if she learns that you have taken such a post, even a temporary one? Harper tells me that her girls received invitations to the party. She will be fit to be tied if it were to come out that you were Lady Latimer's cook."

Ella bit at her lip. "The Newtons won't know where I have gone that day. They will think I am here helping you as usual. Lady Latimer won't suspect there are any ties, and I should be finished with everything they will need by twelve. I cooked at school for large numbers and shall manage quite well. I'll be back here long before Iris and Daisy arrive at Weycross."

About to protest, a look of relief came into Mr. Banks's eyes. "Back here by noon and the party begins at two. That is excellent." Without another word on the subject, the gentleman made for the back door. "I shall be at the stable should Lord Shalford arrive."

Ella chuckled as the door closed behind him. She still hadn't become used to the gentleman's odd starts when he got an idea about his balloon. After the stew was set to cook, she would slip out to the stable and bring him lemonade, for the day had grown warm.

Leona Newton and her daughters were in a frenzy of preparation since the arrival the previous day of an invitation to Lady Latimer's garden party. The lady decreed that her daughters were to spend their afternoons in their rooms with their maids. They were not to quit until they found the perfect coiffure for a party outdoors. But Mrs. Newton still had not given up on her plan to have Iris accidentally meet Lord Shalford, despite the girl's failure the previous morning.

She duly had her daughter awakened each morning at seven. A grumpy Iris set out for the front gates of Weycross, and again it proved to be for naught as the gentleman did not appear. What did appear were carriages full of females that streamed into the gates of the Abbey.

Still Iris waited, her mother's strictures ringing in her ears, but this time she'd been wise enough to have Cook pack her a light nuncheon. From a position in a small wooded grove across from the Abbey's ornate gates, she watched the carriages come and go until at last the road remained empty of visitors for nearly an hour. By noon she grew tired of waiting and started to pack the remains of her meal.

"Well, Lester," she called to the groom dozing under a nearby tree, "I don't think the gentleman is riding today."

Lester opened his eyes. "Not on the road anyway, Miss Iris. He might 'ave decided to stay within the estate boundaries."

The young lady rose and brushed the leaves from her habit. "I have wasted another day here. Mama's plan is foolish, and I haven't even been able to ride except to come here and back, which is no ride at all."

The lad scrambled to his feet and hurriedly brought the young lady's horse to her from behind a stand of small bushes. "Nothing says ye can't take a good gallop afore we go back, miss. Mrs. Newton won't be any the wiser. She'll think we was sittin' 'ere the whole time."

A cunning grin lit Iris's face. "An excellent suggestion, Lester. We can ride on the back side of Newton Park and she won't be any the wiser. Perchance if we ride the boundary between the two estates we might have the good fortune to see his lordship."

Lester gave a mere bob of his head as he cupped his hands for her booted foot. He lifted her easily to the back of the mare before he jumped on his horse. She was a neck-or-nothing rider and he had to be on his toes. Without another word the young lady set out toward the Park, determined to gallop a bit before she went home.

Gabriel's day began badly. After a late night with Daniel and their friends in Guildford, he'd risen later than normal to discover his mother already departed on morning calls. Worse, she'd left instructions for him to receive any callers who came to welcome them back to the neighborhood while she was out. And come they did, in droves. Every marriageable female from fifteen-year-olds with spotty skin to ape-leaders of thirty, and whose family had even a nodding acquaintance with the Crowes. It was any eligible man's nightmare. But Gabriel had smiled politely until he thought his face would crack.

Daniel gamely stood by his brother's side to face the onslaught. But a younger son, no matter his handsome countenance, held little attraction to a flock of ambitious females with a title on their minds. By noon, when their mother still hadn't returned, the steady stream of visitors had all but ceased. Gabriel decided to risk a trimming from the lady for abandoning his post. He and Daniel set out to visit the owner of the balloon at Newland Cottage. Daniel looked for adventure, but Gabriel had reached an age when he thought adventure much overrated. He merely needed something to distract him from the bevy of females who vied for his name. What better way than a balloon ride?

Worried he might come face-to-face with another carriage full of hopefuls, the pair set out across the pasture behind the Abbey's stables. Daniel chattered about a balloon ascension he'd witnessed in London several years earlier when he'd been sent down from Oxford. He complained the crowds had been so great he'd been unable to get within fifty feet of the balloonist and his vehicle. To be able to meet Mr. Banks and possibly take a ride left him too excited for words.

"Hurry, Gabe, I'll race you to Newland Cottage."

Before Gabriel could protest, his brother set out at a mad gallop. With a nudge of his heels, he set off after Daniel. Gabriel's black soon closed the gap with Daniel's smaller gray. The pair were neck and neck as they sailed the animals over the fence and onto the road to Newland Cottage, which lay on the far side of Newton Park.

The only traffic they passed were hay wagons and a stagecoach headed for London with several men on top, who shouted encouragement at the racing horses. As they approached the fork in the road, they dropped their speed to a more sedate pace, declaring the race a draw.

With their horses at a walk, the brothers came to a rise. Daniel reined to a halt and looked cross-country. "Look, Gabe. The balloon's fully inflated today. You can see it clearly over the treetops."

The red and blue top of the balloon, the rope web which held the orb to the basket barely discernable from this distance, stood exposed above the elms. Gabriel's enthusiasm began to grow at the sight.

"Let's hope Mr. Banks is amenable to taking passengers for a ride."

Before Daniel could comment, the sound of hoofbeats drew their attention. To their left, inside the boundaries of Newton Park, they spied a female and her groom riding full tilt toward them. The unknown lady waved as if they were old friends and continued in their direction, fully intent on approaching the brothers.

"Can I not escape marriage-minded females even on a ride?" Gabriel asked in frustration.

"Ignore her, Gabe. We don't know her and she shouldn't pretend that she knows us. It ain't the thing. Come, we must go." Daniel sprang his horse to a near gallop down the road.

Manners and self-preservation warred in Gabriel's thoughts. At last realizing that the young lady had breached etiquette by approaching them, he made as if he hadn't seen the woman and put Blackjack into a fast canter after his brother.

Even as the wind tugged at his hat, he wondered how his father could have put him in such an untenable situation. How could his mother have been so foolish to have blatantly announced his obligation to the neighborhood? Why had he been such a fool to take the blame for his brother? But he knew the answer to the last question. He loved Daniel and would risk even the stricture of marriage to keep him from harm's way. Besides, it wasn't as if he engaged in romantic notions about marriage. His parents' match had been arranged and they seemed to think that was the way things should be. Yet there had to be something more to matrimony than money and position, didn't there? He pushed the matter from his mind for the present and set his sights on Newland Cottage and Mr. Banks's red and blue balloon.

Gabriel rode hard to close the gap between him and his brother. He had little doubt that the female from Newton Park had continued to follow, as the sound of hoofbeats echoed behind him. Still, he refused to acknowledge her presence. He pushed his Arabian to lengthen his stride and soon galloped at top speed. Daniel proceeded along the road for some ten leagues until the curve of the road obscured them from their pursuer's view. With only a backward glance to make certain they were unobserved, Daniel jumped the stone fence and Gabriel followed. The brothers cut cross-country to Newland Cottage at a full gallop, disappearing into the thick foliage of the countryside.

When Daniel slowed his horse to a walk, Gabriel drew up beside him.

"I think we lost her."

"We can only hope."

The men walked their nearly spent animals to Mr. Banks's stable. Even from a distance, Gabriel could make out the pretty young maid from the day before seated inside the odd-shaped gondola beneath the balloon. But she looked different to him. Strange, but he could almost imagine her a lady of Quality with her hair dressed in that fashion. Then his gaze moved downward and he recognized the same plain gray gown from the day before.

"Who is the lady?" Daniel asked with interest.

"Not a lady, Danny. She's Banks's maid."

Disappointment settled on the younger man's face. "Pity. She's lovely."

That hardly described the girl in Gabriel's mind, but he turned his attention to Mr. Banks, well aware that no good would come from gaping at a maid. One thing they didn't need was for Daniel to add dallying with servants to his list of vices.

Four

At the sound of horses, Mercury, who'd been lying on the ground, rose and barked a warning. Mr. Banks turned from where he stood tightening the shaft on a makeshift propeller he had designed. He took note of two gentlemen on horseback cantering toward him.

"We have guests, my dear. Which one is Shalford?"

Seated in the gondola, Ella's heart began to race at the sight of the gentlemen on horseback. As Mr. Banks awaited, she peered closely at the pair, for they looked so much alike. She quickly surmised that the younger man must be the earl's brother.

"The one on the left is the earl, Uncle."

Reluctantly she went back to tightening the handle of the rudder as Mr. Banks strode over to greet the gentlemen. Unable to hear the conversation, curiosity got the better of her and she watched the meeting through her lashes.

"Lord Shalford?" Mr. Banks extended

his hand to one of the two men who sat their horses. "Addison Banks, at your service."

The young earl dismounted and shook hands. " 'Tis a pleasure, sir. Allow me to introduce my brother, Lord Daniel Crowe."

The young man climbed to the ground to shake hands. Mr. Banks beamed at the pair. "Miss Sanderson told me of your visit yesterday. I'm always delighted with visitors who take an interest in ballooning."

"Miss Sanderson?" the earl asked, baffled. He'd met no young lady the previous day, only the pretty maid who sat watching them.

Addison Banks gestured to the same girl. "Miss Luella Sanderson, daughter of Viscount Sanders and my assistant."

Gabriel stared at the young woman, stunned to learn her far more than the gentleman's maid. "You mean the . . ." He struggled for the right words. He'd admired her countenance, but blast, she'd looked every inch a servant yesterday, up to her elbows in soapy water and barefoot, as well. Who would have thought her genteel? A strange tingle of interest burned in his chest, then he reminded himself he'd set standards which went along with what his parents expected — beauty, fortune, and composed elegance. The last two traits Miss Sanderson sorely lacked, despite more than amply fulfilling the first. His thoughts returned to the scene outside the cottage the previous day. Timbers had been forced to take champagne to his boots after what she'd done. Her situation made it evident that she was not the beloved daughter of a wealthy gentleman, but a poor relation forced to work at menial tasks.

"Sanders?" Daniel's question interrupted Gabriel's musing. Both men's notice was drawn to the girl with eager interest. "I don't seem to remember having met his lordship in Town. Have you, Gabe?"

Shalford shook his head.

Mr. Banks shoved his glasses up on his nose as he turned toward the young lady. "You wouldn't have. Her father hadn't a feather to fly with from the day he inherited. After settling his father's debts, he spent most of his life living in country inns or let rooms before he died some years ago. The current viscount is some penniless cousin who lives in the north. As to Miss Sanderson, she recently returned from school to live with my sister at Newton Park."

His suspicions confirmed, Gabriel still couldn't resist another encounter with the lovely female. After all, it was only a simple meeting. "Er, I fear I failed to properly greet her during my visit yesterday, Mr. Banks. Won't you present the lady?"

Ella looked up to see the gentlemen approach. She experienced no great swell of excitement, for she realized the balloon was the draw back to the cottage. To her dismay, Mr. Banks presented her by name. Under the circumstances, she had wanted to remain the anonymous maid of the day before.

Lord Daniel came forward first. "Pleased to make your acquaintance, Miss Sanderson."

He was a likable young man with a wicked twinkle in his eye. Lord Shalford greeted her more coolly, then his gaze began to rove over the design of the balloon's gondola. She knew she must be wary of not getting caught up in girlish dreams about either of the young gentlemen. Manners dictated that they be polite, but neither would seriously pursue a penniless female.

To Gabriel's surprise, the young lady appeared almost piqued at the introduction. Her lovely cheeks flushed pink and she glared at her uncle for several moments before she rose and curtsied. When she stood, the balloon bobbed up and down, which drew Gabriel's attention to the ropes which secured the vessel. It reminded him of a ship, only it had that strange device attached to one end. Excitement grew in him at the thought of an ascension.

"Welcome to Newland, sirs." The young lady sat back down and bowed her head as she returned to her task, as if dismissing them from her thoughts.

Gabriel's gaze once again rested on her. It was refreshing not to be the object of some young woman's matrimonial quest. But her disinterest sparked his curiosity. He'd been pursued by every single lady he'd met since he'd turned fifteen, a fact he attributed to his situation and nothing more. Yet here was a woman who had, if not the money, the pedigree to deem herself suited to be the future Lady Latimer. Had he done something to offend her? "You must forgive me, Miss Sanderson. When we spoke yesterday I had no notion that you were Mr. Banks's niece."

"There was no reason you should have known, sir," she replied coolly. She lashed a small cord to a curved handle whose function Gabriel imagined involved steering the heavy flat board at the rear.

Daniel began to eagerly question Mr. Banks about ballooning. "Have you been an aeronaut for many years, sir?"

"Since I was your age, Lord Daniel. I took my first ride in a Montgolfier balloon when I was scarcely one and twenty. But like most of my fellow balloonists, I have switched to a lighter than air gas. Hydrogen, as Monsieur Lavoisier has deemed to name the gas. With hydrogen, one can use a smaller envelope, as one calls the silk orb, and seal the gas inside. One can fly longer and at higher altitudes, then open the valve when you wish to descend without the inconvenience of all that smoke."

Gabriel looked up at the bright red and blue balloon and noted the sealed valve at the bottom. He'd read that fire was always a danger with the heated air balloons. So much so that the authorities had banned such balloons from taking flight from London's main parks years earlier. Sealed gas balloons were the choice of the modern balloonist.

It soon became clear to the brothers that Addison Banks was no amateur in the science of flight, nor was he a glory-seeking showman. He was a scientist interested in furthering the capabilities of balloons for travel. The older gentleman spoke of his years of studying not only the successful flights of Lunardi, Blanchard, and Sadler, but meteorology as well, a must for any balloonist.

While Daniel pressed Mr. Banks as to how he acquired the hydrogen, Gabriel's gaze was drawn to Miss Sanderson, still seated in the balloon. She listened as intently to the old gentleman as they did. Had she, too, become an experienced balloonist?

Mr. Banks offered to show Daniel the process of making the gas in the stable, but Gabriel lingered beside the basket. "Have you had the opportunity to fly, Miss Sanderson?"

She looked up from her task and shook her head. "I haven't, sir. The process of filling the envelope is so time consuming that Uncle Addison hasn't taken the contraption up since I returned here from school. But I am looking forward to a flight."

Gabriel's brows rose. "Pardon my saying so, Miss Sanderson, but you appear older than a miss just home from the schoolroom. Have you been teaching?"

A smile tipped her mouth as the breeze

grabbed an errant auburn curl and brushed it across her face. "Quite the compliment, sir. 'My, madam, you look old.' That must charm all the ladies."

Gabriel was struck silent by her remark until he noted the amusement in her green eyes. Not the simpering type at all. He returned her smile. "I have always been a trial to polite society, Miss Sanderson. If you took offense at my careless remark, I do apologize."

"There is no need, Lord Shalford. I was merely roasting you. I am older than most young ladies who end their schooling. I shall be twenty in a few months." She tucked the curl back into place. Her cheeks grew a bit pink as she explained. "There was little reason for me to leave school without home or family to return to."

There was sadness in her voice, but no self-pity. It was a simple statement of fact. Yet Gabriel knew an urge to take her in his arms and comfort her. Thinking himself nonsensical, he said, " 'Tis fortunate that Mr. Banks was here when you needed him."

She looked in the direction of the stable and smiled with genuine affection. "Most fortunate. He is a kind and intelligent man." She returned to her task without further explanation.

Sensing her situation was not a subject she wished to discuss further, Gabriel changed the subject. "Do you think your uncle would be willing to take my brother and me up in his balloon, for a fee, of course?"

Ella felt herself all thumbs as Lord Shalford stood beside her, watching her wrap the handle Mr. Banks wanted installed. His lordship appeared even more handsome than she remembered from the previous day. The dark green hue of his morning coat only emphasized the blue of his eyes, which watched her with interest.

"I-I think he would willingly take up anyone who had a true interest in flight, sir. But first I believe he has several experiments he wishes to perform, and he tells me he must await the proper winds."

The balloon shuddered slightly in the strong breeze. At that moment, Daniel and Mr. Banks came from the stable.

"Gabe, Mr. Banks has offered to take us up on Monday next." The young man's eyes twinkled with excitement.

Addison Banks lifted his hand, holding his index finger erect to stress his point. "That is, if the fine weather holds and I receive the delivery I have been expecting from Kingston Upon Thames."

Gabriel eyed the gondola in which Miss Sanderson sat. "Will there be room for us all, sir?"

"Oh, I shall have finished with all this" — he gestured at the rudder, windmill device, and handles — "by Monday. If you should like, I intend to fly on Thursday morning to test my theory. Come round and watch."

Daniel nodded eagerly. "We should love —"

"Have you forgotten we have an obligation on Thursday, brother?" The earl frowned at his brother's forgetfulness. Then a thought occurred. Would not Miss Sanderson enjoy such an affair as his mother's garden party? Young ladies loved such social events, and she would be the one female there who wouldn't throw herself at him.

Before Gabriel could say anything, Daniel glumly announced, "We cannot come on Thursday, sir."

Not wanting his kindness misinterpreted by the young lady, Gabriel turned to Mr. Banks. "We have an obligation, sir, but there is no reason why you cannot join us after your flight. We should love to hear about your experiments. My mother is having a garden party at the Abbey at two on Thursday. Won't you and Miss Sanderson join us?"

Ella and Mr. Banks's gazes locked. She held her breath and prayed that he wouldn't mention that she was to cook for Lady Latimer's party. The humiliation would be too great. What did come out of his mouth, however, left her speechless.

"I am certain that Ella would love nothing more than to attend your party. She knows so few people in Surrey." The old gentleman winked at her.

Daniel stepped forward and took the lady's hand from where it rested on the gondola gunwale and gallantly kissed it. "Then we shall look forward to seeing you there, Miss Sanderson."

Mr. Banks, completely oblivious to Ella's glare, invited the young gentlemen to stay for tea, but they declined, insisting they had a prior obligation to meet friends in Guildford. As they rode away from Newland Cottage, Daniel remarked, "While Miss Sanderson is quite the looker, I do not think she was what our parents had in mind for your future bride."

"Bride! Not you, too, Danny. I've enough of Mother's matchmaking without adding you to the chorus."

His brother laughed. "Do acquit me of that crime. I was only thinking that Mother might take exception to your inviting every Tom, Dick, and Hopeful Harriet that you meet to her party."

Gabriel scowled. "Miss Sanderson is only one young lady. Besides, adding a single female to the squeeze Mother has planned will hardly make any difference."

Daniel, a wicked twinkle in his eye, asked, "Can one have a squeeze outdoors? I think not. It would have to be called a legion on the lawn. Or better yet a legion of ladies looking for love on Latimer's lawn." He waggled his brows as his grin widened. "Why, I should write poetry."

"Put one word of that on paper and I shall darken your daylights, brother."

"You would blight my budding talent?" Daniel pretended to be wounded, but his brother only shot him a quelling glance. "See, I was right. The mere prospect of marriage and you are out of humor."

"Stubble it!" Gabriel barked as he put his horse into a canter.

Daniel watched his brother ride away. Guilt still ate at him, but Gabriel had made him promise not to tell their father the truth. Perhaps if he needled his brother enough, Gabriel would come clean with their father and save himself from this burden. On that thought, Daniel kicked his mount into a hard gallop and followed his brother.

"What do you mean you cannot go?" Uncle Addison took the cup of tea Ella offered him, then gestured for her to be seated. They had returned to the parlor for refreshments after the Crowe gentlemen had departed.

Ella sagged back into the wing chair, but left her cup of tea on the tray. "Lady Latimer is expecting me to bake cakes and tarts for her, not to be in the thick of the guests. She thinks me a maid."

"But, my dear Ella, she is wrong. Besides, you were invited by her son. She can have no objection, especially once she realizes who your father was. You must go or the young men will be so disappointed."

Nervously plucking at the buttons on her gray gown, Ella bit at her lip. She couldn't deny that she would love to attend the affair. Not that she had any illusions about pleasing Lord Shalford or his brother, but such a party was the kind of event most young girls dreamed of attending. Yet she couldn't totally discount the brothers. While she liked the charming Lord Daniel, it was his brother who made her knees grow weak. She would have to deal with her attraction rationally, and accept that while she admired him there was no hope of any alliance. Otherwise it would only bring on heartache. She looked up to see Uncle Addison watching her hopefully.

"It is not to be considered, Uncle. I shall be in the kitchens all morning. What would I say if one of the maids recognized me in the garden? How would I explain?"

"The maids will be too busy to pay attention to you, my dear. Simply do not go near the tables where they are serving refreshments. Do go to the party for my sake."

His encouragement tempted Ella. Then another difficulty occurred to her. "What about Aunt Leona and my cousins?"

Mr. Banks's brows flattened as he hummed thoughtfully. "Don't worry about my sister. She would never make a scene in public, and if she does ring a peal over you for going, I shall have something to say to her." He leaned forward and took Ella's hand. "Please go. It would make an old man very happy."

The sad shadows in the gentleman's eyes touched her heart. Why did he wish her to go? She sensed some mystery behind his insistence. She sat in silence a moment, but he didn't explain why it was he pushed her to go.

If it meant so much to him she would attend — then she remembered her lack of attire. "I should like to accommodate you but . . . well, I have nothing to wear, sir."

"That problem, my dear, I might well be able to solve. After our tea, I shall let Harper take you to the attic." The gentleman said no more; instead he asked for a macaroon and munched happily. Without further reference to the garden party, he turned the topic of conversation to wind currents at altitude and the bone-chilling cold, and all the while curiosity ran rife in Ella.

Some thirty minutes later, after Uncle Addison had eaten his fill, he put his plate back on the table, brushed his hands, and announced, "I must return to work, my dear. Let me summon Harper."

Ella waited in the parlor, brimming with questions, until the valet arrived. "Come with me, Miss Bella."

A smile tipped her lips. She'd grown quite used to the forgetful old man and answered to any variation on her name that he could bring to mind.

He led her up to the tiny attic. Light

poured in from two dust-coated windows at either end of the slant-roofed room. The small space was filled to overflowing with boxes, broken furniture, and old paintings. It took the old servant several minutes to find the trunk he wanted. It was very large and scuffed, with brass nails trimming the top. For just a moment he paused and ran a hand over the trunk as memories made his face grow melancholy. After a deep breath, he turned the old key in the lock. He pulled open the lid and removed the silver paper to reveal a treasure trove of colorful dresses, neatly folded in rows.

Sadness lay in the depths of his eyes when he turned back to Ella. "These belonged to Mr. Banks's daughter, Adele. She died nearly six years ago when she was six and twenty."

Tears welled up in Ella's eyes and she stepped back and shook her head. "Oh, I couldn't wear those gowns, Harper. Would it not break Uncle Addison's heart to see me dressed in his beloved daughter's clothes?"

"Miss Adele hadn't even worn most of these things when she got sick. Besides, it would make the master happy to think that someone was gettin' some use of this stuff. Miss, your being here has been like a breath of fresh air at Newland. Mr. Banks says it's good to hear a young lady's voice in the house. He said so the other evening after you left." The old valet's face grew solemn, and he added, "As for me, I cannot hear thunder bouncin' off the walls, but when you make the old gentleman happy, you make me happy, miss."

Ella wiped the tears from her cheeks. If Mr. Banks wanted her to use the clothes, she would do as he wished, for he had been too kind to her to be churlish and refuse. "Very well, Harper. I shall choose a gown for the party."

The old servant smiled and nodded his head as Ella stepped back to the trunk and fingered the lovely fabrics. The dresses were clearly made for a young girl, for the colors were all soft pastels of pinks, yellows, greens, and whites.

"Miss Bella, I fear they won't be the first stare of fashion. Still, if you are as skilled with a needle as you are a cook, you might be able to rework one of them in time for the party."

Tears again threatened. Ella knew very little about the man who'd befriended her. She hadn't realized he'd been married and had a child, for there were no portraits of such in the house, but then she hadn't been in the gentleman's bedchamber per Harper's instruction.

As she hesitated, the valet encouraged her. "Go ahead, miss. Pick one. I should like to see you in that pink one with the lace."

Ella stood on tiptoes and kissed his cheek. "You and Mr. Banks are too good, sir."

The valet's cheeks flushed pink. "No, dear, your cinnamon buns are too good for my figure." He patted his middle, which was as thin as the first day Ella had seen him.

They both chuckled. "Now, child, you go through this lot and choose whatever you wish. I must return to my work." He gestured toward the left wall. "In these boxes there are also female . . . er . . . unmentionables" — he blushed — "hats, gloves, and" — he looked down at her bare feet — "shoes in a variety of colors. Mr. Banks said you are to take whatever you need."

"Thank you, Harper." She picked up the pale pink silk dress with white puffed sleeves trimmed with matching pink ribbons. She'd never owned anything so lovely.

She lifted the dress high in front of her

by the sleeves and gave it a shake to help it fall free of the folds. To her surprise, the gown was quite large.

Obscured from view by the gown, Harper said, "Miss Adele was like a fairy to us."

As the width of the dress unfolded, Ella had a hard time imagining something tiny and fairy-like wearing this gown. She lowered the dress to peek at the old man's face over the top of the bodice.

At the questioning look in her eyes, he half smiled. "Well, a plump fairy. She always had a fondness for sweetmeats."

Ella smiled. "I think I shall take this one, Harper."

"An excellent selection." He gave a satisfied nod and headed down the stairs, leaving Ella to rummage through the boxes to complete her ensemble. The first order of business was a pair of slippers. As she opened the crates on top, she found white stockings. She set them atop the gown, then discovered a box of lawn shifts. She chose one which could be altered and added it to the stack. There was a box of bonnets of all shapes and fabrics, but Ella settled on a lovely gypsy straw with yellow flowers and a pink ribbon. At last she came upon a trunk full of shoes. She gasped in delight at the sight of so many styles and colors. She plucked a pair of blue calfskin slippers from the stack and sat on a nearby box. She held her breath as she slid a shoe on her foot. It was smaller than Iris's slipper but still not a good fit. She lowered her foot and the shoe fell to the floor. Could there be any doubt that she had the smallest feet of any grown woman in England? It was a curse.

She tugged a lace handkerchief from her apron pocket, tore it in half, and stuffed it into the end of each slipper. She slipped them back on and walked around.

"They will have to do, for I won't wear those dreadful green shoes to Weycross."

That settled, Ella found a basket and folded up the dress, stockings, and shift, then she wrapped the shoes in a piece of muslin she found and put them in the basket. She covered the lot with an old wool scarf she found. About to depart, she went back to the carton with the shoes and picked out a pair of half boots. Thanks to their lacings, she would have something reasonable to walk back and forth to Newland in. She lay the boots atop the scarf, and with one final look about, headed back downstairs to begin supper. The rest of the day excitement and a bit of fear coursed through her at the prospect of her first party.

"Where have you been?" Lady Latimer demanded as her sons entered the drawing room that evening.

Gabriel quirked a brow at his mother's tone, but walked to the drinks table. Daniel, ever the mischief maker said, "Making sheep's eyes at all the marriageable females, Mother."

"That's not the least humorous, Daniel." She turned her back on her youngest, but after a moment she looked at her eldest, a worried expression on her face. "Who did you meet and where?"

Gabriel ignored her question and asked, "Claret, anyone?"

Both accepted the offer. Daniel settled on a blue damask settee, stretching out his long legs. "You will be pleased to learn that we have made the acquaintance of Lord Sanders's daughter today."

"Sanders? Sanders?" The lady fell into a brown study while she tried to remember where she knew the name. Her eyes suddenly widened. "You cannot mean Viscount Sanders. Why, only the title must still exist. I believe it was the seventh viscount who squandered the fortune, and the eighth was forced to sell everything and retire to the country. I read in the paper he died years ago. Was there a daughter?"

Daniel couldn't resist teasing his mother. "A very lovely daughter. Miss Luella Sanderson. It must be the same Lord Sanders, for it appears she hasn't a feather to fly with —"

Lady Latimer's nostrils flared as she turned to Gabriel. "I should hope that you would not waste your time on a penniless female when I have invited the wealthiest daughters in this part of the county to our party."

Gabriel gave his companions their drinks, then strode to the window to look out at the setting sun. "We only met Miss Sanderson, Mother. I did not propose marriage to her or anyone, nor do I intend to until I must. I well know what a future marchioness must be."

Her ladyship relaxed back into her seat. The air hung thick with tension.

Daniel looked from his brother's stony expression to his mother's indignant one. It was going to be a long night unless he did something.

In an effort to soothe everyone's ire, he struck up a conversation about their friends in the neighborhood. He gave the list of gentlemen they'd met in Guildford, and his mother, her face relaxing as she listened, duly asked what news he'd gleaned of their families.

Ever so slyly, the marchioness looked to where Gabriel stood in silence and announced, "I met an old friend today, as well. Lord Hallet. He and Lady Amelia are in good health." There was little response from Gabriel, as if he hadn't heard.

Daniel's face softened with memories and a bemused smile touched his mouth. "How is Silly Millie? My, how she used to scream when I would put a frog in her pocket."

A frosty look settled on Lady Latimer's countenance. "You will refrain from referring to Lady Amelia by that horrid childhood name. She has grown into a lovely young woman and I won't have her humiliated by you."

"Humiliate? I would never do that to Millie. I liked her, for she was the only female in the neighborhood who didn't carry tales about me to her parents. Will she be at the party?" A hopeful look settled in his blue eyes.

"Of course." Lady Latimer glanced to where Gabriel stood at the door, but he seemed not to be listening. She must be subtle in promoting the match. She might have to search out this Miss Sanderson and let her know that her presence was unwelcome at the Abbey, but then it seemed that Daniel was the one more interested. Her mouth puckered in thought. Or was he only tormenting her by using this penniless girl? He was such a trial.

At the window, Gabriel's thoughts dwelled on the coming party. He must have committed some great offense in a former life to have to endure the torture of a garden party full of females, all come to bedevil him. He drained his claret and refilled his glass, quickly draining that one when the butler arrived to announce the arrival of Freddie and her new fiancé, Lord Marlin, along with Lady Latimer's sister, Mrs. Ambrose Chitwood, who carried a small black Yorkshire terrier in her arms named Fi Fi.

There was a good deal of gushing over his lordship on Lady Latimer's part, a good deal of complaining about the journey on Mrs. Chitwood's part, and a good deal of champagne imbibed by everyone in celebration. It wasn't until after the late arrivals had gone up to change for a much delayed dinner that Gabriel got the chance to ask his sister if Marlin was what she really wanted.

Lady Freddie answered in a breathy voice, "Oh, yes, Gabe. He is quite everything I have dreamed about all my life."

Gabriel watched his sister smile at the young lord across the room and get a responding smile. In a flash he reached a startling revelation. They were in love, not just marrying to please their families. In almost the same instant, a twinge of envy overtook him. He shoved the thought aside. Love was important to females, and he was glad Freddie had found hers, but he had higher expectations for a wife — or should he say, his parents had higher expectations. She would be the future marchioness and mother to his sons. How could he be so foolish to think the whims of the heart should guide such a decision?

A knock at her door made Ella prick her finger on the needle she'd threaded. Putting the wounded member into her mouth a moment to ease the sting, she shoved the pink silk gown under the covers of her bed. She looked about to make certain the basket was hidden, then called for her visitor to enter.

Cilla stepped into the room with a smile.

"Evenin', Miss Luella. I brought ye your supper since Nate ain't feelin' quite the thing."

"Is he ill?" Ella gestured for her to put the tray on the table. Despite Aunt Leona's orders, Nate had slipped away each night to kindly bring Ella's supper to her.

The girl chuckled. "Too much gin at the Angel last night."

"Then I thank you for taking his place."

The little maid slid the tray onto the table. "I was happy to slip away from all the fuss the young ladies are makin' 'bout this here party they're goin' to. One would think that Lord Shalford is the only titled man in England, the way they're actin'."

"A fuss? Surely they have everything they would need for the party." Ella glanced at the counterpane and wished she had someone who could help her, for she wasn't certain she would be able to redo Miss Adele's dress before Thursday. "What has been the fuss?"

"Oh, the usual. Cilla, iron this, wash that, sew this flounce, do my hair in this new fashion. Cilla, be faster."

Ella opened a drawer in the small table beside her bed and drew out an old pottery cup she had made while at school. "Do sit down and have a cup of tea before you return to more endless demands. You sound as if you could use the moment's rest."

A smile lit the little maid's face. "I'd be happy to, Miss Luella."

The girl pulled up the room's only chair beside the little table as Ella sat on the bed. The maid poured out two cups of tea and handed one to Ella with a smile. With little shyness, the maid questioned Ella about her position at Newland. Was Mr. Banks as crazy as the young ladies said?

Ella's cup clinked down on the saucer as she angrily denounced her cousins. "Uncle Addison is *not* crazy." Seeing the startled look in Cilla's eyes, Ella softened her voice. "He is quite brilliant, in fact. I do all the cooking and housework, but he lets me help him with his balloon, as well. He has taught me a great deal about balloon flight."

"Have ye been up in the air yet?" The maid's eyes grew round with excitement.

"Not yet, but he's promised to take me as soon as he finishes with the experiments he has planned."

"I would do near anything to go flyin' through the sky in a balloon, miss." There was a hopeful expression on the girl's face.

A thought occurred to Ella. "Would you be willing to help me with some sewing I have? In return, I will ask Uncle Addison if you can go up with us one day next week. What is your day off?"

"Wednesday." Cilla's excitement almost made her spill her tea. "I'll sew you a ball gown, miss, if you can wrangle me a ride in Mr. Banks's balloon."

Ella laughed. "That won't be necessary. Mr. Banks has given me an old dress that belonged to his late daughter." As she spoke, Ella rose and tossed back the blankets, then pulled out the pink gown to hold up for the maid to see.

"Why, it's beautiful, miss, but frightfully large."

"I know. I have to take it apart and trim all the sections, then sew it back together, and I don't think I will be able to manage it by Thursday."

"Thursday!" Cilla's eyes widened. "Miss, are *ye* plannin' on goin' to the garden party at the Abbey."

Ella nodded and watched the maid's reaction to the news. "Lord Shalford invited me, himself, this afternoon."

"Ye've met one of them gents from Weycross. Wouldn't that just singe the hairs on Miss Iris's head — no wait, I already done that with the curling yesterday, and every day since that cursed invitation

132

arrived. And got duly slapped for it." A large satisfied grin grew on the girl's face. "Why, I should be delighted to help you get ready for the party. Goin' to parade yerself for his lordship, are you?" Then Cilla sobered. "Don't be lettin' Mrs. Newton or the girls see ye or there'll be hell to pay, miss."

That brought the number to four that should not see Ella at the party — Aunt Leona, Iris, Daisy, and Lady Latimer. Ella was taking an awful risk, but if she was careful and stayed on the fringe of the party, she could slip into the shrubberies at the least sign of danger. "I am not going to parade myself, as you call it, Cilla, but I shall be careful."

The maid gave a nod of her head and a wink, then she took the dress from Ella and began to explain how they could reduce the time required to alter the gown. With a pair of scissors, Cilla made short work of splitting the seams. She held the parts up to Ella and determined how much needed to be cut. Within some thirty minutes, the gown lay upon Ella's bed in sections, each piece trimmed to the smaller size.

"You work on the skirt and I shall start with the sleeves." Cilla handed Ella the straight lines of the pink skirt, then settled to begin the detailed work of sewing one white sleeve back to the bodice.

A silence grew in the room as they each worked diligently. For the first time since she'd returned from Newland, Ella sensed that she would be able to remake the dress in time.

Then the door to her room flew open without a single knock. Iris Newton stood with her hands on her hips. "So this is where you slipped off to, Cilla."

The little maid rose, but not before she pushed the bodice she'd been sewing under the blankets. "I came to bring Miss Luella her supper, miss."

"Mama told you not to be waiting on Luella. She is my uncle's maid, not some treasured guest. Daisy needs you to iron her yellow gown. It was wrinkled this afternoon while we were trying on our dresses."

Cilla bobbed a curtsey and made to depart, but not before she cast Ella an apologetic glance. After the girl was gone, Iris stepped toward her cousin, her gaze taking in the pink silk fabric crumpled in the girl's lap.

"What have you there, cousin?"

Ella glared back defiantly. "A gown."

"It looks like silk. Where did you come

by such a fine garment?" Iris moved closer to examine the material.

Ella's chin rose. "Uncle Addison gave it to me. It belonged to your cousin, Adele."

"Adele?" Iris laughed cruelly. "Then it's not a gown but a silk tent." Her eyes narrowed. "What need have you for such a garment?"

There could be no doubt how Ella's cousin would react if she heard of the invitation to the Abbey. Her gaze dropped to the silk and she smoothed it with her fingers. "Am I not allowed any new clothes, cousin?"

Iris's mouth twisted unpleasantly. "I shall inform Mama that you have been stealing from Uncle."

Ella's gaze flew to her cousin. "Uncle Addison asked Harper to give me the gown."

"Why would he . . . ?" The girl's brows drew together as she puzzled out the question, then her eyes widened. "Are you thinking that you can attend Lady Latimer's party?"

"I was invited to go."

"You were *not* listed on the invitation!" Iris's face flushed pink.

"No, but your uncle and I were invited by Lord Shalford this very afternoon."

Iris's pink cheeks flamed a mottled red and tiny tremors raced through her body. Ella didn't know about the snub her cousin had experienced at the hands of the gentleman that very afternoon. She grew concerned for her cousin's state of mind as the shaking continued. Without the least bit of warning, the girl stepped forward and snatched the skirt from Ella's hands.

"We shall see what Mama has to say about this!" On that note, Iris dashed from the room, shrieking for her mother.

Ella slumped back against the oak headboard. So much for her dreams of attending her first party.

Five

Leona Newton stormed up the stairs, outraged that her niece had succeeded where they had failed in meeting the young earl. The swatch of pink silk clutched in her hand, she marched into Ella's room. "So this is how you repay my kindness to you! You sneak around behind my back, trying to insinuate yourself into our circle of friends, pretending to be a young lady of means."

"But I didn't —"

"Silence!"

Ella drew back in fear at her aunt's uncontrolled rage and waited silently.

Satisfied she'd cowed her niece, the lady continued. "I have not finished speaking. There is no reason for a penniless girl to attend such a party. Lord Shalford's mother has made it clear that his wife must be a female of beauty and *fortune*. How do you think he would react if I were to tell the gentleman that you are my brother's maid?"

Ella turned her face away from her aunt. She stubbornly refused to cry despite the disappointment mounting within her.

Her aunt smugly folded her arms. "On Thursday you are not to leave this room, do you understand?"

Ella's heart sank. She had promised to go to the Abbey the morning of the party and prepare desserts for her ladyship. "What about Uncle" — she suspected her aunt would hate that she called the old gentleman by such a familiar name — "er, Mr. Banks? Am I not —"

"You needn't worry your head about Addison. He can manage for one day without you." Aunt Leona stepped to Ella's chest of drawers and grabbed the Bible on top. She shoved it into her niece's hand. "You can spend all day Thursday learning to be thankful for what you have, girl."

Mrs. Newton gathered up the pieces of the unfinished gown and went to the door. "Ungrateful girl." She slammed the door shut.

Alone, Ella allowed her true feelings out. Angry tears of frustration rolled down her cheeks as she listened to her aunt's footsteps recede down the hall. It wasn't until the chance to attend the party had been removed from her grasp that Ella realized just how much she truly wanted to go, despite all the complications.

What was she to do about her promise to Lady Latimer? Ella rose and went to the tiny window that looked out over Newton Park's well-manicured grounds. She lifted the sash, hoping to find some breeze to cool the stifling little room. Darkness had fallen and she couldn't see the cottage in the distance. That ugly little brick building had become her sanctuary from the unkindness she experienced at the Park. She leaned her head against the pane and breathed in the cooler night air.

Something would have to be done to get her aunt to change her mind, if not about the party, at least about allowing her to go to Uncle Addison's on Thursday. She desperately needed the money that cooking would bring. Besides, she didn't want Uncle Addison to have difficulties with the marchioness if Ella didn't show up as she'd promised.

With a sigh, she went back to her bed and took note of her supper, now grown cold. Her appetite gone, she undressed and climbed into bed. There had to be a way for her to go to Weycross Abbey on Thursday, if she had to sneak out and walk the entire way from the Park before dawn, but then her aunt would probably come up to make certain Ella was following her orders.

She tossed and turned much of the night. The following morning she went about her duties as normal, but it wasn't until Uncle Addison arrived in the kitchen, worry in his eyes, that she realized he'd taken note of her listlessness. After some prodding from the old gentleman, she poured out the tale of her encounter with her aunt. He raged against his sister's pettiness for some ten minutes, then he ordered Ella upstairs to choose another gown from the trunk. When she tried to protest, he shook his head. "You are going to that party, my girl, if I have to go to Newton Park and lock my sister and her daughters in their rooms."

A strange look settled on his face and he stared out the window in thought. A chill of fear raced down Ella's spine. She was well aware that he was dependent on his sister for financial help in his experiments, as well as this cottage. As much as she wanted to go, she couldn't allow him to risk his future comfort. "You wouldn't do that would you, Uncle?"

Mr. Banks started at the sound of her voice, almost as if surprised to find her still in the room. "Oh, child, don't be silly. I am not such a fool. Besides, Leona would batter down a door with her bare hands if she thought it meant her daughter could catch an earl. A waste of good wood. Go along with you, now. You have little enough time to rework your gown."

Relieved that he meant his sister no harm, Ella hurried back to the attic. She opened the trunk and rummaged through the old gowns. She settled for a pale blue cambric with white lace sleeves trimmed with dark blue ribbons. She found several bands of white ribbon to change the ties on her gypsy bonnet. By the time she returned downstairs, she discovered Mr. Banks had departed from the house, she assumed to return to his work.

Ella settled into the small parlor at the back and began work on her new dress. She had managed to split all the seams when the sounds of a carriage drew her to the window. To her amazement, there was Mr. Banks tooling a small gig up the drive to Newland. In the carriage beside him sat a small wizened old woman with a reticule large enough to carry a week's worth of clothing.

Some minutes later, Addison Banks strode into the parlor. "I have brought you Mrs. Clifton. She makes all my shirts and she's agreed to help you, my dear."

The old woman never acknowledged

Ella. Instead she opened her reticule and took out a tape measure, scissors, and a cushion filled with pins. She picked up one section of the cambric and announced, "Very nice."

Mr. Banks winked at Ella. "I shall leave you ladies to it. I have to go have a few words with my sister."

Ella rose. "What do you intend to say to Aunt Leona?"

"Never fear, my dear. I'll simply tell her I need you with me on Thursday. If all else fails, I'll tell her Harper is ill."

He departed, leaving Ella not overly confident that his plan would work no matter what it entailed. Beside her, Mrs. Clifton held up the dress bodice in front of Ella. "So Mrs. Newton thinks my work is not fit for even the tanner's daughter. Well, I'll show her. Come, Miss Sanderson, there is work to be done."

A smile tipped Ella's mouth as she realized what Uncle Addison had done to garner the old woman's help. Poor Aunt Leona probably didn't have any idea who Mrs. Clifton was, for her girls were dressed by a French modiste from Croydon.

Of Mr. Banks, there was not a sign for several hours. When he returned, he smiled broadly at Ella, then announced,

"My sister has agreed to allow you to be my assistant on Thursday."

"However did you manage that, Uncle?"

A rather enigmatic expression settled on his face. "I have my ways of dealing with Leona, my dear. Make certain you are here early on Thursday, for her ladyship's carriage will be here by six." With that he announced he had matters awaiting his attention in the stable, leaving Ella perplexed by his success. She could allow herself to dream a little longer. Dreaming helped her escape from the lonely future that faced her. But she'd been disappointed too often to allow herself to believe her dreams could come true.

Gabriel tapped softly at his sister's door at seven o'clock the following morning. When there was no sound, he cracked the door ajar and called, "Freddie?"

A soft groan emanated from the pile of pink and white covers and pillows on the four-poster with the massive canopy.

"You said you wanted to ride over to see the balloon this morning." Daniel had informed his sister and her fiancé about Addison Banks's red and blue balloon the previous evening. All the younger members of the family had agreed to pay the gentleman a visit that morning.

Another groan came from the bed, then a tousled blond head appeared from the mass of covers. "You didn't say you were going in the middle of the night. What would Mama say to your making a call at this hour?"

Gabriel chuckled. "A great deal more than I should want to hear, my dear, but I do assure you that Mr. Banks won't take offense. Come, my girl, the sun has been up for nearly an hour. If you want to go, we will be in the breakfast parlor for the next thirty minutes. After that we shall leave without you."

Her head disappeared once again among the pillows as she groaned, "Uh-huh."

Gabriel made his way downstairs. Lord Marlin and Daniel were already partaking of a hardy meal of eggs and kippers. The plans for the visit to Newland Cottage had been made the previous evening after Lady Latimer retired to bed. Surprisingly, it had been Gabriel and not Daniel to suggest the excursion.

Scarcely five minutes before they were to depart, a sleepy-eyed Freddie wandered into the parlor dressed in an elaborate maroon riding habit, her blond hair tied by a ribbon in the back. Their departure was delayed another ten minutes while she partook of tea and toast. But after a few dainty nibbles, she swore she couldn't eat another bite at such an ungodly hour.

The party set out from the Abbey heading south, but within a short distance they left the road and galloped cross-country. As they approached the balloon, Mr. Banks appeared from the stable doors in his shirtsleeves and waved at the approaching riders; Mercury stood by his side with his tail wagging at the sight of visitors.

"Welcome back, my lord." The old gentleman sketched a handsome bow.

Gabriel found himself looking for Miss Sanderson, but she was nowhere in sight. He introduced the new members of his party to the gentleman. Before he could question the lady's whereabouts, Freddie eagerly asked if she might climb into the balloon's gondola.

Lord Marlin demanded to know if it were safe for them. When the old gentleman assured them it was so, the young viscount helped his fiancée down. The affianced pair climbed the stairs attached to the balloon, which was safely tied to five sturdy stakes.

The young lady leaned over the gunwale of the gondola and teased, "I should dearly love to fly away. Can you not accidentally untie the ropes, Daniel? You are quite good at accidents."

At the words 'untie the ropes,' the little dog's ears perked up. The animal dashed toward one of the ropes and began to tug on the hemp. Mr. Banks called, "Heel, Mercury!" The dog obediently returned to his side.

"See, even the little dog wants me to fly." Freddie smiled.

Daniel frowned at his sister. He disliked the idea that she might get to go up first. He turned to Mr. Banks. "Do you think you will be able to complete your experiments on Thursday, sir?"

Addison Banks looked up at the light clouds streaming across the sky. "As long as the wind is low. I fear I am at the mercy of the weather, always."

Gabriel moved from the back of the gondola, where he had been inspecting the propeller. He had read that similar devices were being used to propel ships with steam; perhaps Mr. Banks was on to something by putting one on a balloon. "Did you receive your shipment from Kingston Upon Thames, sir?" Their flight on Monday was contingent on several factors, that being one.

The old gentleman's brows rose. "I quite forgot." He pulled out his pocket watch and gave a nod of his head. "Perhaps, my lord, you might do me a favor."

"Of course."

"Can you escort Miss Sanderson to Graham Farm? 'Tis just a short walk down the road. The lads should be ready to be brought here, and Mr. Graham is leaving for Guildford at nine."

"It would be my pleasure." Gabriel jumped at the chance to once again enjoy Miss Sanderson's company. He wondered what lads Mr. Banks had hired, but he suspected he knew why they had been hired. There was always a need for strong men to hold the ropes when a balloon was released.

While the others were busy inspecting the gondola, Gabriel headed toward the cottage. As he came to the kitchen door, the smell of fresh cinnamon hung enticingly on the air. He knocked, and within moments the young lady opened the door. Her lovely green eyes widened at the sight of him.

He drew his hat from his head. "Good morning, Miss Sanderson. Your uncle requested that I escort you to pick up the lads at Graham's."

"Did he? Are you certain that you wish to go?" She arched one delicate auburn brow as she reached behind her and untied the white apron which covered her plain gray dress. A smile played about her mouth, and he couldn't help but think she might be pleased that he'd agreed to accompany her — or was it that he wanted her to be pleased?

"It would be my honor to be your escort." He bowed with a great flourish, then set his hat on his head again.

Miss Sanderson was barefoot, as usual, but she slipped her feet into a pair of brown half boots which sat beside the kitchen door. His sharp eyes noted that the shoes looked larger than the tiny feet being put into them. After quickly doing the laces, she grabbed an old chip straw bonnet. " 'Tis not your honor that I was thinking of, sir, but your dignity." There was a twinkle in her eyes as she donned her bonnet that piqued his interest.

Uncertain what she could mean, he gallantly offered her his arm. "Dignity? Do you think I am rather high in the instep?"

"Not at all, it is only . . . did my uncle not explain to you about his lads?" She slid her arm through his and gestured toward the road.

Gabriel set out in the direction of the main road at a moderate pace. "Miss Sanderson, do you think I shall be intimidated by some burly farm hands? Or is it that you think I am some park saunterer who cannot walk above a mile without summoning my carriage?"

She smiled up at him, and a strange tightness settled in his chest.

"I do acquit you of either of those failings, sir. It is only . . . well, I shall allow you to see for yourself." On that, the lady fell silent on the subject. Instead she commented on the lovely countryside through which they passed and the pleasant summer weather they were enjoying in Surrey.

The conversation became general, as it often does with people who are scarcely acquainted, and they discussed points of interest in the county. At last curiosity got the better of Gabriel. "Do you plan to attend my mother's party on Thursday? If your uncle is not going, I can send my mother's carriage for you." He felt a slight twitch in her fingers, then she shook her head.

"That won't be necessary. I shall be there and I have transportation." She then changed the subject, asking about a lovely estate visible on a distant hill.

Within twenty minutes they arrived at a small stone cottage with a barn that dwarfed the snug building. Miss Sanderson directed them to the larger structure in the rear. The chatter of chickens and turkeys filled the air as they approached. "Mr. Graham?" she called.

A tiny fellow with leathery features appeared through the open door. His face split into a grin. "I was beginnin' to think Mr. Banks 'ad forgot today is me market day. Ain't nothin' like an angry flock of cockerels when the grain bins grow empty."

"Lord Shalford, this is Mr. Graham."

The old man bowed dutifully. "Heard ye was back in Surrey for a bit of huntin', my lord." The farmer gave him a knowing wink, then eyed Miss Sanderson and nodded his head as if approving the lady as a choice for his bride.

Gabriel had little doubt the entire neighborhood had heard why he had returned home. He hated that everyone seemed to know his private affairs.

Hurriedly the lady asked, "Are the lads ready, sir?"

Gabriel was grateful for her interceding so he didn't have to respond to the old man's innuendo.

The farmer snorted. "I done what Mr. Banks wanted, but between us, miss, I'm thinkin' the old gent has less brains in his box than most of these 'ere birds. They're a flighty lot." Mr. Graham laughed heartily at his own pun. "They don't take direction well."

Gabriel frowned. He didn't understand what the old man referred to. "I'm sure Mr. Banks knows what he is about."

The farmer shrugged. "Well, as to that, I'm one what thinks that if God had meant man to fly, he'd 'ave given us wings, my lord. Follow me."

The farmer led them around behind the barn. As they turned the corner, the sounds of honking rent the morning air. Gabriel came to a complete halt as they rounded the final turn. There, scratching about in the dirt inside a paddock, stood four huge white ganders wearing small leather harnesses similar to horses. Two long leads extended from each goose and were tied to the nearby paddock rail.

Miss Sanderson calmly announced, "My lord, may I present you to the lads." She ticked off the names. "North, South, East, and West." After a brief hesitation, she added, "Or maybe that one is South and that one West, or is it East?" She shrugged as she smiled up at the gentleman.

Whatever their names, Gabriel found himself speechless for a moment before he began to laugh with gusto. After a moment, he inquired, "Mr. Banks's steeds of the sky?"

"Precisely!"

After his amusement dissipated, he pondered the situation. "We are supposed to *drive* them to Newland Cottage?" Gabriel surveyed the leather collars with interest. Mr. Graham had devised a small version of a yoke which fitted the animals snugly without impairing their wing movement. The long leather lead attached to the harness just behind each bird's head.

"Drive?" Ella's tone was doubtful. "I think you are being far too optimistic, sir. I suspect a better word would be *drag* them back to Newland."

Gabriel shook his head in disbelief. "I shall be lucky if I am not permanently banned from the Four-in-Hand Club should one of my friends see me attempting to tool this lot."

"On the contrary, sir." Ella grinned. "You would be deemed a true Knight of the Road if you manage to drive the lads to Newland in under a day, in my humble opinion, and so I would tell your friends."

Ella's predictions of difficulty proved prophetic. The geese, while docile enough tethered to the fence, took exception to being piloted about on leashes. Each had a direction he wanted to go that had nothing to do with returning to the cottage. At first Ella took two reins and Gabriel took two, but the young lady proved not strong enough to manage the honking ganders when they resisted her gentle tugs. The large fowl were determined not to leave the comfort of Mr. Graham's paddock.

After several minutes of flapping wings and distressed honking, the farmer disappeared into the barn. He returned with a small wooden pail. Over the din, he called, "My lord, I suggest you be the drover" — the old man grinned to be calling an earl such — "and take all the reins. You, miss, must go in front and drop a few bits of grain. These greedy lads will be after you in an instant. Lead 'em back home."

After a nod from the earl, Ella handed her reins to him.

"Lead the way, Miss Sanderson."

She took the pail of grain from Mr. Graham, who urged, "Give a whistle and rattle the grain in the pail, miss, each time you drop the food, and they'll come." He opened the paddock gate and Ella passed through. She walked about ten paces then turned and shook the grain. She wet her lips and blew. She made several attempts before emitting a halfhearted sound loud enough to attract the squawking geese's attention. Once the white birds were turned in her direction, she spread a bit of the grain.

Gabriel found his gaze strangely locked on the lady's lovely mouth as the pink tip of her tongue moistened her lips to whistle. Something intense flared in him and a desire to kiss her coursed through him. The sudden tug of the hungry geese on their leads snapped him out of his stupor. Where had that come from, he wondered. Miss Sanderson in no way fit the qualities he'd determined a wife of his should possess. She might be in unfortunate circumstances, but she was a respectable lady and he shouldn't be having such thoughts of her.

For the next thirty minutes, the earl had little time to contemplate Ella Sanderson's merits or anything else as he struggled to manage the team of geese, each with his own direction in mind. As to the human side of the affair, they worked together, enticing the uncooperative fowl down the road toward the cottage.

By the halfway point, they had developed something of a rhythm: Ella rattled the grain in the pail and Gabriel made a soft clicking noise, so that the geese moved forward at a steady pace toward their proper destination.

Then the sounds of an approaching vehicle drew Ella's attention. "Oh, goodness, it's my aunt's carriage." Her tone was full of panic. "I cannot allow her to see me away from my household duties or she will be furious."

Before Gabriel could say a word, she darted toward the stand of trees they'd just passed, then she halted. "She will see me there."

"I don't understand." Gabriel struggled to keep the geese in check when they saw the lady with the food change directions. Why was she afraid her aunt would see her?

Frantically the young lady looked about, ignoring the gentleman. Her gaze fell on the stone fence and she raced to the barrier which separated the road and the meadow. With a flash of petticoats, she climbed over and hid. Unfortunately, the geese, aware that the rattling pail she carried contained the food, were hot on the young lady's trail. Each thinking to catch the food first, they darted here, there, and everywhere in their attempt to get to the grain. Half went left and half went right, and when the lady disappeared behind the fence, the fowl began to run about wildly, unable to discern where their food had gone.

By the time the carriage drew level, the leather reins were completely entangled around Gabriel's legs, which left him stranded. As the ladies in the carriage peered out, he gallantly tipped his hat as if he were on an ordinary walk in the park.

Inside the passing carriage, Mrs. Hyde, invited to Newton Park for nuncheon, said, "Why, I do believe that was Lord Shalford."

Leona Newton, who had been too busy picking her guest for more information on Lord Shalford to pay attention as they drove past, leaned toward the window to take a look. With only a faint glimpse of a man surrounded by a bevy of white birds, she settled back and frowned. "Are you certain? What would the Earl of Shalford be doing on the road with a lot of geese?" Her frown deepened. "Were they wearing harnesses?"

Across the aisle, Daisy said, "Perhaps they are his pets. I have always wanted a little cat or dog —"

Ignoring her sister's rambling, Iris interrupted. "Did you think him handsome, Mama?"

But Mrs. Newton was still perplexed by the geese. "I cannot think what he would have been trying to do with geese in harnesses." The lady's brows drew together. "Have you heard of any . . . well, mental irregularities in the Crowe family, Mrs. Hyde?"

Having received no response from her mother, Iris pressed her sister. "Did you see him, Daisy? I fear I was looking at the geese. Was he handsome?"

Daisy's eyes widened at her mother's question, her sister's unheard. "Do you think him mad, Mama?"

Mrs. Hyde gave a trilling laugh. "Oh, my dear Mrs. Newton, upon my word. Mental irregularities, indeed! You can be certain it is some foolish wager that has him leading about a gaggle of geese."

With a stamp of her foot, Iris demanded, "But was he handsome?"

The three others in the carriage stared at her in surprise at her fit of pique. Mrs. Newton folded her hands and glared across at her daughter. "What will Mrs. Hyde think of you for such indelicate conduct?"

"But Mama, you said he might be as ugly as a baboon's —"

"Iris!" Mrs. Newton shrieked, fearful her daughter would continue. "I said no such thing. Do consider what you are saying and where you are saying it, child." The lady managed a wan smile for their guest, whose gaze sparkled with malicious delight.

As silence fell over the ladies, the old gossip tittered behind her gloved hand. What a day she was having! First the earl and his geese, and then Miss Newton's improper conduct, and Mrs. Newton's having called the earl as ugly as a baboon. She couldn't wait to tell the ladies of the neighborhood her news.

Ella poked her head above the fence and peered in the direction the carriage had disappeared. "Are they gone?"

"They are, and I would appreciate your immediate assistance," the earl implored.

A laugh bubbled up inside her at the sight of the gentleman completely entwined with leather leads, the ganders quietly scratching in the dirt at his feet. "Oh, I am so sorry to have abandoned you with the lads, sir."

"Lads! I think Mr. Graham might have

the right of it when he questioned Mr. Banks's wisdom to be attempting to use these winged fiends."

Ella climbed back over the fence, chuckling at the sight of the gentleman and the geese. The earl busily unwound the leather straps, being careful not to spook the geese by talking to them in a soft voice. Unfortunately, at the sight of the bucket of grain the birds all rushed at Ella, nearly toppling Shalford, who'd lifted one boot to bring one of the straps from behind him. She closed her eyes, fearful of an attack. But the gentleman tightened his grip on the reins and the birds were brought up short only a foot from her.

"Whoa, you feathered fools!"

Ella opened her eyes to see the birds once again properly positioned for the jaunt back to Newland Cottage. "I think you have the knack for driving geese, sir."

The earl rolled his eyes and shook his head, then gave a mock bow. "Shall we continue this traveling raree show, Miss Sanderson, before another one of your relatives passes by and you are forced to flee, which will once again create pandemonium among our feathered friends?"

"A raree show? More a circus act, sir." Her mouth trembled as she struggled not to smile. "You were the perfect maypole. No doubt your mother might wish you to recreate the performance for her party."

The gentleman laughed. "I don't think we could keep the lads away from the food long enough to perform."

At the mention of the food for the garden party, Ella grew uneasy. She still didn't know how she would work out going first as the cook, only to arrive later as a guest. Mr. Banks would tell her to enjoy her day and let tomorrow take care of tomorrow. It was good advice, she thought as she once again set out for Newland, leaving a grain trail that the geese followed.

On arrival back at the cottage, Mr. Banks had them take the geese to the stable, and all the while Lord Daniel and Lady Freddie teased their brother and Ella. Once at home, Gabriel was glad to seek the solitude of his room, the joke having worn thin. Why had he not found Miss Sanderson's roasting annoying, when he wanted to strangle his own siblings into silence? Because the lady had not belabored the point. He realized he had enjoyed his morning with Miss Sanderson. It was certainly a pity that her situation removed her from consideration as a proper wife, for he thought her an appealing young woman.

As he changed from his riding clothes, he paused a moment at the window. The gardeners were giving the lawn one final going-over for the party. He must put thoughts of Ella Sanderson aside and concentrate on finding a suitable female with fortune and birth to recommend her. Yet that thought only made him feel decidedly downcast.

Six

Ella arrived at the kitchens of Weycross the following morning long before the sun's rays lit the sky. The Abbey's cook, Mrs. Greenwood, obviously had her nose out of joint that her ladyship had brought in someone else to cook pastries for the party. Not only someone else, but a mere slip of a girl.

With a dismissive sniff, Cook turned Ella over to one of the undercooks to be ushered to the pastry room. Four young maids stood waiting in crisp white aprons amid rows and rows of empty worktables. Ella could see the doubt in their faces at the sight of her. Behind the servants flames were visible through the open doors below the heating ovens. Good, she wouldn't have to start the fires, which would only delay her. Time was her enemy this morning.

Her nerves wreaked havoc with her stomach, but she gamely set to work. After a quick survey of the pantry's stock, she ran down a list of things needed. The Abbey's stores were in abundance so her options were unlimited.

By half past six, Ella had all the maids busy. One peeled apricots, pears, and apples, one was hard at work blending the pastry dough as another mixed a basic yellow cake, and the last maid Ella set to shredding coconut for the macaroons — a staple at any party. After inspecting the ovens and determining they were fully heated and ready, Ella began to chop dates and nuts for her walnut sugarplums, which she usually made at Yuletide. She thought they would do well here for Lady Latimer's garden party.

Within thirty minutes, ten trays of individual tortes were baking in the top row of ovens and ten sheets of almond macaroons were in the lower ovens. Ella set two of the girls to rolling out the pastry dough for tarts while the freshly sliced fruit simmered with sugar and spices to fill them.

By nine o'clock, the wonderful smells of cinnamon, almond, and caramel filled the entire lower level of the Abbey. The vast expanse of tables were partially covered with cooling trays of macaroons, tarts, fruit tortes, caramel rolls and iced cakes.

Despite the help, Ella's energy flagged. She paused to look at the clock as she brushed an errant auburn curl from her cheek, inadvertently smudging herself with powdered sugar. She hoped she would have time to rest once she returned to Newland or she would be too tired to enjoy the party. Doubts still lingered about the wisdom of attending, but she didn't want to disappoint Uncle Addison and she couldn't deny her own curiosity about such an affair.

"Miss Sanderson?"

Ella started, and looked to the door to see Lord Shalford's brother, dressed for a morning ride, staring at her in surprise.

"Lord Daniel, w-what are you doing here?" Her heart sank at the sight of him.

"Everything smelled so wonderful I came down to cozen a treat from Cook. Imagine my surprise when I discovered you are Cook for the day. May I ask how that came to be?" He stepped into the pastry room and surveyed the rows and rows of baked goods.

All the maids watched the pair with eager interest. Ella brushed the sugar and flour from her hands and stepped to the doorway where the gentleman stood. She lowered her voice so that only he could hear. "Your mother visited Uncle Addison and tasted my pastries. She hired me to supervise the food for the party."

His dark brows rose as an angry flush flooded his cheeks. "Mother hired a viscount's daughter to cook at the Abbey? Great heavens, her audacity knows no bounds."

Ella's own cheeks warmed as she looked at her hands. "Well . . . in truth, sir, she didn't know I was Lord Sanders's daughter. She thought me Uncle Addison's maid."

The young gentlemen stood speechless for a moment, then a deep laugh erupted from him. "Oh, Miss Sanderson, you must allow me to present you to her at the garden party. I should —"

"You cannot." Ella gripped his arm. "I shall not come if you intend to do so. I would not wish to stir the lady's wrath."

Lord Daniel sobered, his hand closing over hers. "Do not distress yourself. If you don't wish it, I shan't force you to meet her as your true self. I cannot say I blame you, for Mother can be quite the tyrant when she is displeased. But you must allow me to tell Gabe of Mother's —"

"I wish that you would not. It would only make him uncomfortable." Seeing the questioning look on the young man's face, Ella stammered, " 'T-tis only that I think your mother would not like that Lord

Shalford had invited me without her approval. I should not wish her to take him to task, nor would I want to be embarrassed by being asked to leave." She knew there was far more to her not wanting the earl to know her secret than she stated.

"Asked to leave? I'll not allow it, nor would Gabe."

Ella smiled at his vehemence, and found a measure of comfort in his assertion that Shalford wouldn't be angry, as well. Then she sobered. "If my understanding of the party is correct, I do not think your brother will have the time to have any say about anything."

An angry glint settled in the gentleman's blue eyes. "If your understanding is this party is a fashionable cattle drive of eligible females for my brother, then you are correct." A thoughtful expression transformed Daniel's handsome face as the memory of his mother's tirade against the young lady the previous evening returned. There could be little doubt that the marchioness would make no noisy scene. But anyone who knew the lady would know she was not above pulling a guest aside and demanding they leave. He would never want Miss Sanderson subjected to such an indignity.

A wicked twinkle in his eyes, he took the young lady's hand. "Then I shall make certain that Mother is too distracted with the rest of the herd to take note of you, Miss Sanderson — only, do promise you will come."

"I shall, if I may return to my task here" — she swept her hand toward the half empty tables — "so that I may be finished by noon."

Daniel's gaze roved over the assortment of treats, then he sniffed the air. "I shall leave you to your work under one condition."

"What is that, sir?"

"That I be allowed to sample some of those wonderful pastries."

"Come, eat your fill, then away with you."

Daniel followed her into the room, calling a greeting to the maids who stopped their tasks to curtsey, then continued to covertly watch as he sampled one of the small caramel cream cakes. "Oh, Miss Sanderson, this is wonderful. The best confection I have tasted in ages! Why, even the shops in London —"

"Daniel!" Lady Latimer's voice boomed from the doorway. "What are you doing down here disturbing the servants?" The lady's frosty gaze settled on Ella.

Her heart skipped a beat when that mischievous twinkle returned to Lord Daniel's eyes. He picked up an almond macaroon and winked at Ella, then strode to the door. "Mother, the aroma of these wonderful pastries lured me to the kitchens. Your party will be judged a success if food is the measure."

With that, he stepped behind his mother, then twisted his expression into one of terror as he looked at the stern lady before he winked and slipped away, leaving Ella struggling between laughter and trying to maintain her dignity in front of Lady Latimer.

The marchioness, unaware of her son's antics, entered and passed by each table to duly inspect the product of the morning's labors. As the sights and scents of the pastries met her approval, the lines of her face relaxed. "This looks very good, Ella. You have done well. Do you think this sufficient for one hundred guests?"

Ella curtsied before she spoke. "I do, my lady, once the last of the cakes are taken from the oven."

"Very well, when you have finished, inform Mrs. Greenwood. Once she approves, she will inform my housekeeper, and Mrs.

Jenkins will see to your payment. I shall have one of the grooms drive you home." Before departing, her ladyship picked up a walnut sugarplum and took a bite. "Excellent."

There was another thirty minutes of hard work in which Ella had the maids ice the final small cakes with orange or cherry glazes, then top each with a sliver of fresh fruit. It was almost noon when Mrs. Greenwood was duly informed that Ella was finished. Cook marched into the pastry room and sampled several of the variety of desserts. After a few nerve-wracking moments for Ella, Cook grudgingly gave a nod of approval. This had been perhaps the hardest task, for Ella knew that Mrs. Greenwood would be the toughest judge. Yet she unwound enough to inform Ella that if she needed a recommendation, she might rely upon Cook to provide her one.

With that high praise, Mrs. Greenwood departed to inform the housekeeper. Once paid, Ella began to thank the four maids for their hard work. She was about to depart when the sound of Lord Shalford's voice could be heard in the lower hallways.

Ella's eyes widened. "Oh great heavens, I cannot be found here by his lordship."

Jane, the eldest of the girls, asked, "Why ever not, miss? His lordship ain't the least high in the instep."

Meggie nodded her head. "And he ain't one of them toffs what dallies with the help."

"Unfortunately," Jane sighed, and the other maids tittered, calling her a wicked girl.

At the sound of heavy footsteps, Ella grew frantic. "You don't understand, I know the gentleman and he invited me to the party."

A dawning came on Jane's face. "Quick, miss, hide behind us."

The four maids formed a line so close that their skirts touched, and Ella stooped behind them and prayed. Shalford poked his head inside the door only moments after she'd disappeared. "Good morning. Have you seen that rascal of a brother of mine?"

Jane boldly answered, "He was here, my lord, to filch pastries, but her ladyship sent him on his way. Is there anything I can do for you?"

The earl's gaze roved over the tables of deserts. "You have done a wonderful job." He stepped into the room. "May I taste something, as well?"

The maids stood frozen, uncertain what to do. If they moved, he might see Ella. He stood waiting, an expectant look on his face.

"Of course, my lord." Jane eyed the other girls, then locked her arm with Meggie's and tugged her in the direction of the table. In a strange movement, the entire group edged to a laden table nearby. Behind them, Ella crawled on her hands and knees, wishing she were anywhere else.

Jane grabbed a sugarplum and the maids all edged forward, where she handed it to the earl. "Try this one, my lord, 'tis my favorite." She dimpled up at him coquettishly.

"Is something wrong?" Shalford's brows rose as he watched the four maids baby-step back and forth as if they were glued together. The gentleman suspected them of having sampled a bit too much of the cooking liqueur.

"Oh," Meggie said, her cheeks flaming pink, "you mean this odd moving about. We hear they are lookin' for a chorus line at the new playhouse and they pay very well. We was practicing, my lord."

As the earl bit the sugarplum, he stared at them as if they'd lost their minds. At the taste, he looked down at the treat then back to the girls. "My advice would be to stick with the cooking, girls. The hours are better and this is very good." He bid them good day and departed.

As the sound of the earl's footstep's faded, the maids crowded round Ella as she rose and brushed off her hands. "Thank you, you saved me a most embarrassing moment."

Jane eyed her thoughtfully. "Who are ye, miss?"

"Let us merely say I am not a real cook." With that, Ella went to the door and looked left and right before she slipped from the kitchen, leaving the maids full of speculation about who Miss Ella Sanderson might be.

Ella rode back to Newland Cottage in a small gig driven by a young groom who tried to flirt with her, but received so little encouragement he soon fell quiet.

As she stood on the front porch of Newland Cottage and watched the gig disappear down the road, Ella sighed with fatigue. She must be crazy to be thinking about returning to Weycross as a guest. But deep down inside, she wanted to wear the gown Mrs. Clifton had helped her rework, to attend a party like a proper young lady, and to meet Lord Shalford along with all the other eligible young ladies in the county. For her, this might well be the one and only social affair of her life.

While Ella spent the morning at the Abbey, Mr. Banks had been busy as well. He'd risen early to see Ella off. After testing all his ropes and equipment at the stable, he returned to his breakfast parlor to enjoy the orange buns Ella had baked the day before and await the arrival of the Black Knight's stable hands who would release the balloon. As he savored the re-warmed buns, his thoughts turned to Ella and what her arrival had meant to him. Nothing would replace his dear Adele, but just having a young lady in the house again brought joy back to his life. In all ways, he and Ella were good for each other, having lost everyone in their lives who'd truly meant anything to them. Although Leona wasn't aware of it, she had done them both a favor.

Pouring himself another cup of Harper's mud-like coffee, Addison sat back and smiled despite the bitter liquid. He had no illusions as to why Leona had sent the girl to him. Not to make his life easier, but to put Ella in a position of menial work. The woman still harbored a dislike for the viscount's daughter despite Ella's misfortunes.

Worry took hold of him and refused to let go when he thought about the afternoon affair. What would Leona do if she discovered her niece at the party? It had taken all he could manage to convince his sister to allow Ella to come to the cottage today. For some strange reason, where Ella was concerned the woman bordered on irrational. He suspected it had more to do with jealousy and less with any flaw in Ella's character. Leona's own offspring could in no way be called remarkable in looks nor temperament, whereas Ella possessed looks, a sharp mind, and a lively wit.

He brooded on the matter for some twenty minutes more. It would be utter disaster for Leona to encounter Ella at that party. What could he do to protect her? He rose and went in search of Harper, who always seemed to have solutions for problems. On finding his old butler, he confided his worries. "After due consideration, I cannot be certain that Leona will not take revenge on Ella should she see her at the party this afternoon. Should I convince the child not to go?"

The old man's eyes took on a look of

cunning as he cleared away the gentleman's razor from the dresser. "The lady can't see anythin' if she don't make it to the party."

"What do you have in mind?"

"The stable lads from the Black Knight are comin' this morning to hold the lines of the balloon, are they not?"

Addison looked to the clock on the mantelpiece. "Aye, they are due at seven."

"Remember Jacob?"

A tiny furrow appeared on the gentleman's forehead. "Do you mean the lad Leona tried to have fired because he flirted with Daisy at my first balloon ascension? Or, more correctly, should I say the lad who Daisy admired excessively?"

"The very one, sir. He's no great love for Mrs. Newton. Works with carriages at the inn, he does, and he would know how to —"

Banks raised his hand. "I don't want to know. That way, if Leona asks, I can truly say I haven't a clue. Only make him understand that the ladies are not to be harmed."

A smile tipped the valet's mouth. He owned a decided dislike of Mrs. Newton and her daughters for past grievances. He had never forgiven them because the ladies had been unduly cruel to Miss Adele during her lifetime because of her weight, her lack of suitors, and her timid nature.

Some thirty minutes later when the strapping young ostlers arrived, Harper sent them all to the stable, where Mr. Banks awaited them. All except young Jacob, whom the valet invited into the kitchen and plied with orange buns while he explained what he wanted.

A handsome lad of twenty-three with brown hair and gray eyes, Jacob worked hard at the Knight to support his mother and two sisters. It took little to convince the young man to do a favor for Mr. Banks, especially once he learned that the target was the much disliked Mrs. Newton.

Gabriel stood in the yellow drawing room and watched as the maids and footmen set up the tables in rows in the gardens. As the line of tables formed along the yew hedge in the rose garden, it seemed more that they were building a fence round him than setting up for the party. A feeling of doom settled over him and somehow the party's significance grew in importance. It would be his last day of true freedom. By tonight he would be expected to put a name to a female that met with his parents' approval or be prepared to live in poverty along with Daniel.

In the room behind him, his mother and her sister, Mrs. Chitwood, a smaller, younger version of Lady Latimer, chattered about what best to do next, to follow the afternoon party and forward the courtship of Shalford's chosen lady.

"What about a musical evening?" his aunt suggested.

"A waste of time and money, Belva. One cannot get to know someone when one must sit and listen to music. Besides, there is not a decent Italian singer to be hired in all of Surrey and only the best will do for my parties. No, I think once Shalford meets all the young ladies, if one does not stand out, he must make a list of, say, five who are good candidates, and we shall have them over to dine and afterwards a bit of dancing. Not a ball, mind you, something more intimate."

Mrs. Chitwood clapped her hands like a child. "Oh, I do so love dancing. I should adore an opportunity to wear my new gown from Madame Cherise, with its yards and yards of yellow tulle. I designed a special pair of navy slippers with yellow flowers to —"

"Yellow tulle?" The marchioness sniffed

with disdain. "Good heavens, my dear, you are a widow of almost forty. Leave yellow tulle to milk-and-water misses about to make their come-out."

Mrs. Chitwood, despite her lesser standing in Society, was not the least cowed by her sister's arrogance, and was the only person brave enough to refer to the marchioness by her childhood name. "Ambrose has been dead these five years, Becky. I may be forty, but I'm not dead, and if some eligible gentleman were to take notice, I should be quite happy. Yellow suits me nicely."

Had Gabriel been in a lighter mood, he would have laughed when his mother snapped, "We are here to find my son a wife, sister, not a new husband for you. And my name is Rebecca."

The sounds of an arriving carriage made the ladies fall silent, keeping Mrs. Chitwood's retort unspoken. Gabriel looked at the clock. It was almost one o'clock. Who could be arriving a full hour before the party? When his gaze shifted to his mother, there was such an intense look in her eyes as she watched him, he grew suspicious. Who had she invited to come before the main body of guests?

That question was answered within five

minutes as the Abbey's resident butler, Falworth, opened the doors and announced, "Lord and Lady Hallet and Lady Amelia."

Gabriel had only vague memories of the young lady who'd tagged along behind a much younger Daniel whenever there had been any social event at the Abbey. She had been a skinny, freckled gamine, all blond pigtails and large gray eyes which had looked at his brother like he had hung the moon. He hadn't seen nor spoken to the child since before Daniel went to Oxford.

The years had been kind to Lady Amelia. Petite without a single imperfection on her ivory complexion, her guinea-gold hair dressed in a cluster of tiny curls at the rear of her head, she was quite lovely in a pale pink afternoon gown in the last fashion. Beside her, Lord Hallet tugged nervously at his cravat when his gaze locked with Gabriel's. The viscount's wife stared about the room as if she were measuring the place for new furniture.

Her ladyship rose and welcomed the pair. She introduced her sister before she reminded the viscount they'd met Gabriel years earlier. Lord Hallet stepped forward and shook the earl's hand, then laughed heartily. " 'Tis good to see you looking so fit, Shalford, now that we are thinking about merging our two families."

Gabriel's gaze shot to his mother whose face was a study in fury as she glared at their neighbor. "Are we doing that, sir?"

The older gentleman leaned in and winked, then said in a lowered voice, "Ain't no need to be coy on the matter. We have brought our Amelia over to be inspected, and who could find anything wanting in a beautiful, wealthy chit like our Millie?"

It was obvious that the young lady heard her father, for her cheeks flamed pinker than her gown as her gaze remained locked on the intricate design of the Oriental carpet. Gabriel didn't know what to say as anger at his mother burned within him. "Who indeed, sir?"

The older man, oblivious to the glaring expressions of his wife and the marchioness, continued on. "I have often thought that a union between our two families would make for —"

"Lord Hallet!" Lady Latimer angrily called, then continued in a more normal voice, "Would you care for a tankard of ale before the other guests arrive?" The woman was desperate to put something in his mouth that would silence his loose tongue.

The viscount's face brightened at the prospect of something other than the cakes and lemonade that he was expecting at the party. "A capital suggestion, Lady Latimer."

Wanting nothing more than to be gone from the old man's outrageous match-making, Gabriel knew no force in heaven or that room would allow him to leave while his mother still breathed, unless . . . He looked to the young lady, who appeared to be suffering as much as he. "Perhaps Lady Amelia would like to inspect the Crowe family portraits in the long gallery?"

In a rush, Lady Latimer said, "Yes, yes, I think that an excellent notion."

Without giving her opinion one way or the other, Lady Amelia duly rose and gave a silent nod of her head. She followed Gabriel across the room and he ushered her into the hall, then closed the door. Without looking up, Lady Amelia wrung her hands, and in a voice scarcely above a whisper said, "Lord Shalford, I do apologize for my father's pushing manner, but after Lady Latimer's visit the other day, he has it in his head, well . . ."

"My mother came to Hallet Hall?" Gabriel's brows flattened. A knowing light settled in his blue eyes. "I fully understand the fault is not with you, Lady Amelia. It would seem that our parents have taken it upon themselves to . . . matchmake."

Before Lady Amelia could comment, the sounds of footsteps echoed in the hall. Gabriel turned to see Daniel coming down the stairs at a rapid pace. Fearful he was late, the young man tugged to straighten his cravat, as if he'd dressed hurriedly.

He spied his brother at the drawing room door and called, "Gabe, you will not believe what mother has done! But I cannot tell you —" Daniel's countenance lit, and he halted midsentence and midstep. "Millie, is that you?"

For the first time since Lady Amelia had entered Weycross Abbey, her gaze lifted from the floor. "Danny." She breathed his name with delight and took a step in the direction of the stairs, then seeming to remember herself, she folded her hands neatly in front of her and waited for him to come to her. "You are looking well, Lord Daniel."

The young man hurried to where they stood, knowing no shyness at meeting his old friend, and took Lady Amelia's hands.

"My dearest Millie, what is this Lord Daniel nonsense?" He held up her arms. "Why, you are quite grown up and a beauty to boot." His gaze scanned her face as an appreciative gleam glinted in his eyes.

A shy smile tipped her mouth. "Time has a way of passing without us taking notice. Changes are inevitable."

Gabriel watched the pair with avid interest as they gazed into each other's eyes with a rapt expression that he'd never before seen on his brother's face. There was a bond there which seemed to transcend mere friendship. After a moment, the couple laughed and began to speak at once. The affectionate bond seemed to reignite inside them as they began to reminisce about their long-ago follies, and Lady Amelia's timidity fell away. It was like watching a flower bloom before one's eyes as the pair put their heads together and began to whisper.

Gabriel suddenly suspected that his mother, Lord Hallet, and Daniel's little opera dancer were about to be disappointed about the meeting of these old friends. For the pair it might well be a life-changing encounter.

Daniel and Amelia might not understand what was happening, but Gabriel did. Daniel had that same look on his face that Freddie did when she looked at her Lord Marlin. He was utterly smitten with his old childhood companion.

Thinking to give the pair some time to themselves, Gabriel cleared his throat. "Pardon my interrupting this reunion, but perhaps you might escort Lady Amelia to the long gallery to view the family portraits."

A startled expression altered Daniel's face. "Never say you asked to see a bunch of our fusty old relations, Millie?"

"Well" — Lady Amelia's cheeks flamed pink — "that is . . . I should not object if you took me."

Gabriel chuckled. "Do place the blame where it belongs, my dear. 'Twas I that forced the lady to suffer such a trial. I was fearful that one or the other of us were about to be embarrassed by our parents. It seems that no matter how old one grows, mothers and fathers continue to be a trial."

A smile tipped Daniel's mouth as he gazed raptly into the young beauty's lovely eyes. "No boring old portraits for us. I know Millie would much rather go down and walk beside the River Wey with me. I have a great deal to tell her."

The young lady smiled back at him with equal captivation. "Have you been staying out of mischief in London?"

Daniel looked at his brother and winked. "Mischief? Who, me?"

Lady Amelia laughed and shook her head. "You cannot play the innocent with me, Danny. Remember, I have known you for years. I do believe Mischief is your middle name."

The young man leaned in, and in a whispered undertone said, "Not Mischief, dear Millie. Everyone knows my middle name is Devilment."

Their gazes locked, and for a moment Gabriel thought his brother was going to forget himself and kiss Lady Amelia. He hurriedly said, "At last you admit it, dear brother."

The young couple started as if they were surprised Gabriel was still there.

He gave Daniel a speaking look. "I believe you were going to escort the lady to the river. Do not linger long, the guests shall begin to arrive in" — he looked at the longcase clock — "thirty or so minutes." About to depart, he asked, "What were you going to tell me before your reunion?"

Daniel's brows puckered a moment, but he was too distracted by the young lady's presence to remember. "Who knows? It has slipped my mind." Without another glance at his brother, Daniel drew Lady Amelia's hand through his arm, then called over his shoulder, "We won't be late."

Heads together, the pair disappeared out the front door. As the door clicked shut, a twinge of envy filled Gabriel. Could he not find a female whose very presence would befuddle his wits like his siblings?

The image of an auburn-haired chit with flashing green eyes rose in his mind and he immediately pushed it away. Miss Sanderson might be lovely, amusing, and close at hand, but she was in no way what he and his parents would consider a future marchioness. He'd spent too many years trying to gain his father's approval to wed against everything that Society deemed important. His spirits decidedly low, he turned and headed for the library. He would need all the privacy he could get for the next half hour to be able to endure the three hours of torture ahead.

While Ella dressed for the garden party, events occurred at Newton Park that were for her benefit but without her knowledge. The three Newton ladies were fully dressed and ready to go by noon. After

186

carefully inspecting her daughters and finding them to be in looks, Leona drilled them in all the important points of polite conduct with a marchioness. Soon the girls lost patience with their mother and informed her they knew how to conduct themselves in public. Still, her nerves were jangling, so Leona paced the Aubusson rug until the drawing room clock struck one. Then she sent word for the carriage to be brought round.

Iris glanced at the clock. "But Mama, 'tis only ten miles to Lord Latimer's estate. If we leave now, we shall be there before two."

"There is nothing wrong with being the first to arrive, girls. It gives one time to spend with the host until the others arrive." She avoided looking at her daughters, for the advice was the exact opposite of what her mother had told her.

She herded her girls into the carriage and ordered the coachman to make haste for Weycross Abbey. He set out at a modest pace, not wanting to jostle the young ladies, but the mistress soon thumped on the carriage roof and shouted an order for him to "spring 'em." They bowled along the road to the Abbey chattering about the coming party. Unfortunately, the vehicle had traveled no more than a mile from Newton Park when the right wheel slid off the axle. There was a great deal of hysteria on the young ladies' part, but Mrs. Newton did not lose her head. She straightened her bonnet, told the girls to hush, and climbed out to send the coachman back to the Park for the old barouche while the footman remained to calm the pent-up team.

The Newton's coachman, Rollins, was a beefy man of fifty-five years with a penchant for ale and Cook's treacle pudding. Despite knowing the urgency of his mistress, his pace slowed after the first half mile. By the time he reached the gates of Newton Park, he was forced to stop to catch his breath. Strangely, as he stood resting in the shade of the stone pillars, he heard a noise in the empty gatehouse. Pulling his hat from his grizzled gray head, he wiped the sweat from his brow with the back of his sleeve and peered at the grime-coated windows of the small building. It had never been in use as long as he had worked for Mr. and Mrs. Newton, but he swore he could hear a female crying inside.

He edged closer to the building and listened. Definitely a female voice, calling for help. He tried the door and it opened, but the small front room stood empty except for one broken chair.

"Who's there?" Rollins called, but got no answer, only the continual cry for help. Following the sound, he went down a narrow hallway. The door at the end was closed, but he was certain that was where the woman was. On reaching the door, he opened it, only to discover that it was a room without a window. The overwhelming darkness forced him to step inside.

"Are ye hurt, miss?"

The door slammed behind him and the sound of a bolt being slid home echoed in the empty room. The coachman hammered on the door. He heard the sound of running feet and then silence. He pounded and shouted but realized there was no one about. After some ten minutes, he settled on the floor, where he found a jug of cider which he gladly sipped. Occasionally he would call out and pound the door, but mostly he sat and rested, hoping whoever had pulled this childish prank would come and set him free. It would be well after six that evening when one of the grooms on his way to a night of drinking at the Black Knight would hear pounding on the door and let the poor man out.

As for the Newton ladies, by the time they realized Rollins wasn't returning, nearly an hour had passed. Ill-equipped to walk any great distance in their elaborate gowns and delicate slippers, it took another hour for them to make the trek back to the Newton stables. They arrived hot and sticky, with their hair wilted by the afternoon heat and exercise. To the ladies' horror, there was not a single groom about to hitch the second-best team to the barouche. They had been given the afternoon off since the ladies were to be gone. Mrs. Newton ranted furiously; Iris cried and stamped her foot. Only Daisy remained calm. She professed herself to be hungry. Without regard to anyone's sensibilities, she suggested, "I say we forget about going to Weycross this afternoon. The party will be over by the time we arrive. Shall we go to the kitchens and see what treat Cook has?"

"After all," the youngest Miss Newton announced, oblivious to the killing looks from Iris and her mother, "Lord Shalford is not the only gentleman of wealth and title in England."

"Take me back home." Ella made the announcement to the stout young ostler as he

190

tooled the Black Knight's gig through the gates to Weycross Abbey. The scent of wild lavender hung heavy on the afternoon air as they rode up the graveled entry. Rows of empty carriages could be seen lining the drive in front of the gray stone abbey in the distance.

The blue dress Mrs. Clifton had refashioned suited Ella perfectly, the bonnet was neatly tied, and she had the blue shoes stuffed full of handkerchiefs so they would remain on her feet. She'd seen herself in the looking glass in the front hall of Newland and knew she looked as any young lady about to attend a party. But suddenly, with the event imminently before her, she lost her nerve. What was she thinking to be coming to Lady Latimer's party without her knowledge, no matter the invitation from her son? To make matters worse, Ella was over an hour late, having fallen asleep after returning from her task.

The lad turned and looked at her as if she'd utterly lost her mind. "Are ye dicked in the nob, miss? A party at the Abbey is a grand occasion, and there'll be the best peck and —" He halted on seeing the befuddled look on the young lady's pretty face. "What I mean, miss, is that there will be a grand spread of eats. Ye don't want to miss that, nor visitin' with yer friends."

"But I have no friends in Surrey, so what am I to do at a party? Stand about by myself for three hours. I was an utter fool to come."

Fitch knew what he would do if he were going to such a gathering — make a dash for the food, not stand about yammering to his mates. But females didn't care about such things, did they? Especially not gently bred ones like Miss Sanderson. "That won't happen, miss. Why, I'm thinkin' that no sooner than you arrive and everyone's gonna want to make yer acquaintance."

Ella's eyes widened. "Oh good heavens, you don't think that the butler will be introducing people, or that there will be a receiving line? I cannot go in the front door. Do take me home, Fitch."

The ostler eyed the young lady with doubt as he slowed the carriage to a near halt while she tried to make up her mind. Who was this strange female that old Harper had hired him to drive to and from the Abbey? He was beginning to think her jingle-brained. Why, every other female in the county was agog about attending this party. Besides, he was hopin' to snag a few eats himself, so he best convince her she did want to attend. "Now, miss, it's just yer nerves talkin'."

"You don't understand. I cannot enter through the front to be seen by everyone."

The ostler pursed his mouth a moment, contemplating what he must do. "Shy, are ye? Well, if ye ain't wantin' to go in through the front, I'll show ye a shortcut into the back garden. I was sportin' with the Abbey's pantry maid last fall and I always came and went that way. Ye can slip in, see if there aught ye want to do, and no one'll be the wiser, miss."

"No one will be able to see me?" A hopeful look settled on her countenance.

"Not if ye don't want 'em to, miss." He veered the gig down a narrow path that angled off from the main drive. The trees closed in on the tight lane, but Fitch kept driving at a spanking pace with little fear. At last he came to a long set of stone stairs which climbed the hill, then cut through a yew hedge. "Here ye be. At the top is a gate which ain't locked. Just follow the path and it'll take ye through the various gardens until ye reach the manor house."

Ella did so want to at least take a look at the most important social event in Surrey. If she didn't feel comfortable, she wouldn't have to reveal herself. Taking a deep breath, she announced, "Don't go far, Fitch. Likely I won't be long."

The ostler slumped back onto the worn leather seat and looked about the dark woods. He wouldn't even get a chance to pass the time talkin' with the other drivers. As the young lady disappeared from sight, he called, "If ye happen to pass one of them tables of food, grab me a bite to eat, miss."

Seven

Parties at Weycross Abbey were never dull, and the grounds were so extensive that many of the gardens were often never seen by visitors. Like most hostesses of her class, Lady Latimer wanted every guest to declare her affair to have been a triumph. Her son's party was no different. All her guests would be fed and entertained to the fullest. An archery tournament was planned, as were games of bowls, and shuttlecock, the latter being more for the gentlemen and not the young ladies. The long doors to the gold drawing room were opened onto the rose garden, and inside were tables for whist, casino or any other card game that suited the guests' fancy.

Despite his reluctance, Gabriel did his duty and welcomed most of the guests alongside her ladyship, but when the constant stream of arriving families slowed to a trickle, his mother ordered him to circulate. He managed to slip away from her watchful eye and spend nearly ten minutes of peace in the library. He watched the colorful crowd mill about on the lawn and was reminded of market day in Guildford, where everyone came to buy or sell wares. His parents had put him in the unhappy situation of looking for a wife as one did a turnip. A bitter laugh rumbled within, as he realized that many of the ladies he'd met had no more conversation in them than the average tuber. Many of today's female guests had stood with inane smiles upon their faces while one parent or the other listed their accomplishments.

Every type of female had been paraded past him, yet not a single one had taken his fancy. Oh, there had been girls with enough beauty to stir a man's interest, but he found himself comparing each one to a certain young lady at Newland Cottage, and all had come up short. Yet if he were honest with himself, he would own that were one to measure prospective brides, Ella Sanderson would certainly not top the list by Society's standards.

It suddenly dawned on him that Miss Sanderson had not passed through the front door while he stood duty. Had she changed her mind about coming? Or had something happened to Mr. Banks during his balloon ride that morning? More likely she simply hadn't wanted to waste an afternoon at a boring party. He certainly would not have attended had he any other choice.

The clock on the mantelpiece chimed the hour of three. Gabriel sighed heavily, knowing he could no longer shirk his duty. He squared his shoulders as if preparing to do battle.

No sooner had he entered the rose garden than a swarm of females descended upon him to ask his opinion on everything from the weather to the color of gown he preferred. He was polite and answered what questions he could, but did not single out anyone with special attention. His gaze kept returning to the door through which the newest arrivals entered the garden, but he saw no auburn-haired young lady descend the steps.

After some forty-five minutes of females pressing in on him, he encouraged his companions to join in one of the activities his mother had provided. For the determined young ladies who hung on his sleeve, he even went so far as to hint that he admired females who engaged in the more physical sports, like archery. Within minutes, a cluster of girls were clamoring for their turn with the bows and arrows.

Finding himself momentarily unencumbered and beside one of the long tables of food, Gabriel picked up a plate on which he put a variety of items, for he'd had nothing to eat since the lone sugarplum in the pastry room. He ate while he surveyed the teeming lawns in search of his brother, whom he'd not seen since Daniel had slipped away to the river. Gabriel could have used some of his brother's humor to lighten his mood.

"What are you doing idling here by the tables?" Lady Latimer said, approaching her son from the rear. "I didn't invite all these people here just to eat their heads off and play games."

Gabriel determinedly reached for a macaroon on his plate as he responded, "I did my duty. I spoke to most of the young ladies at least once, and some even twice, madam. It would not do to single one out when I haven't decided if there is a particular female I prefer among your guests. Besides, as I told you before, I am fully capable of finding myself a wife without this kind of boring affair." He bit into the coconut biscuit and ignored his mother's expression, which had darkened at his announcement. After chewing, he remarked, "I must say that Mrs. Greenwood has outdone herself for the party, though. Would that she could do so well for our normal meals."

Lady Latimer picked up one of the few remaining sugarplums, then turned and searched the garden for someone as she distractedly said, "Cook had nothing to do with this spread. I hired Mr. Banks's little maid to prepare the food."

Gabriel nearly choked on coconut. "Who?"

"Oh, you likely do not know the man who leases Newland Cottage. His maid, Ella, is a divine cook, so I hired her for the party. I am thinking of offering to pay her twice what she makes with Banks to see if she might come here permanently."

Speechless for a moment, Gabriel suddenly realized why Ella hadn't come to the party. She'd already been to the Abbey that morning and likely was exhausted. "Mother, have you any idea —"

But before he could inform the lady what she had done, the marchioness interrupted him. "Where is Lady Amelia?"

Gabriel's eyes narrowed as they rested on his parent. He well knew what she was about after his conversation with the young lady. "Daniel took her to walk beside the river. Mother, about this cook."

"He did what?" Lady Latimer rounded

on her son. "What can he be thinking? He should be here entertaining the other guests, not wasting his time on a female whose father has bigger plans than a mere younger son."

Suddenly all thoughts of Ella being used as a servant by his mother flew from Gabriel's mind, and his anger flared. "Mother, I strongly suspect that Daniel has a *tendre* for Lady Amelia. Are you telling me that Lord Hallet will not even consider his suit?"

"A *tendre!* What nonsense is this? Lovely though she is, he hasn't seen the chit in nearly four years." Her ladyship sniffed, then added, "Your brother is hardly fit to be asking anyone to be his bride, falling from one scrape to another like he does and with little but his allowance to live on. Besides, Lady Amelia is a sensible girl. She will marry where she is told."

Gabriel hoped that wasn't true for his brother's sake. While his mother continued to search the crowd for the missing couple, he stared at her in disbelief. Did she really care so little about her own son and what he wanted? About what would make Daniel happy? She, like their father, had never been a doting parent. In truth Gabriel and his siblings had been raised by nannies and governesses, with little contact with either of their parents until they had been old enough to come to London, but surely she owned some affection for her children.

At least he had always thought she had. Yet here she was plotting against one son and helping her husband force another into a loveless marriage of convenience. In a tone edged with dawning enlightenment, he asked, "Do you not even care if we are happy in our lives, Mother?"

"Oh, there is Lady Hallet. I shall keep her distracted while you go and escort Lady Amelia back to the party." She glanced up, and her brows rose at the sight of distaste on her son's face. "What were you saying? Something about happiness. Don't be a fool, my boy. Happiness is fleeting at best. Wealth and position are constant. An advantageous marriage on your part will not only increase what we have but our standing in Society. Do hurry and find Lady Amelia before Daniel's foolish imaginings sets Lord Hallet against us."

Without waiting for Gabriel's response, she hurried in the direction of Lady Hallet. He stared after her in complete astonishment. In the past two weeks the scales, as it were, had dropped from his eyes. The true nature of both his parents had been revealed. Somewhere along life's journey they had ceased to feel true emotion for the things that mattered. Or was it that they had allowed unimportant things to become too crucial in their world? They were willing to send Daniel to the Indies rather than risk a snub by royalty. They would force Gabriel into marriage without the least thought of his future happiness — only of how such an arrangement would increase their wealth and power.

As the full weight of the revelation settled on him, Gabriel ran a hand through his hair. How could he have wasted most of his life trying to gain the approval of people who didn't truly care about anyone?

He shoved his plate back on the table, too sick at heart to eat another thing. He couldn't face any more of the hopeful young ladies, nor would he drag Daniel back from his stroll with Amelia to face a trimming from their mother.

Without a backward glance, Gabriel slipped through the hedge and strode through the small outer gardens, hoping to put as much distance as possible between himself and the circus his mother was running in her rose garden. He didn't know what he would do about this cursed marriage his father was trying to force, but one thing was for certain: he would do all in his power to see that Daniel's life wasn't utterly ruined by his parents' apathy. If Lady Amelia was what his brother wanted, then he would have her, even if Gabriel had to drive the pair to Gretna Green to accomplish the union.

On entering the Abbey's grounds, Ella paused at the top of the rise. She was some distance from the house and scarcely able to see the chimney stacks. From her vantage point she could make out a number of interlocking gardens. A single path cut through the hedges almost like a maze. It had been her intention to go straight to the party, but as she entered the unlocked gate she was drawn to inspect each of the unique gardens.

The first garden she entered was a knot garden with a simple fountain in the center and a baroque design of tiny boxwoods trimmed low to the ground. It created a rather stark place, more gravel than greenery, but the honeysuckle that ran up the rear stone wall filled the small space with a pungent, sweet odor that Ella quite liked. The tiny rocks in the garden crunched beneath her borrowed slippers as she passed through the gate into the next terraced space.

To her surprise she discovered this flower garden to be occupied by a gentleman. He sat on a bench at the far end, a beatific expression on his face as he watched a wren splash about in a small marble birdbath.

Ella hesitated a moment, then approached the gentleman whom she recognized from her weekly visit to church. He was the Reverend Mr. Sims. A smile lit his face and he rose, which frightened the bird, who took flight.

"Miss Sanderson, how delightful to see you again. Are your aunt and cousins here as well?"

Ella hesitated a moment before she merely said, "It was their intention to come, sir. I came directly from Mr. Banks's home where I help out."

"Ah, yes, I do believe your aunt mentioned that to me. Well, child, don't let me keep you from the party. I slipped away to enjoy Lady Latimer's lovely tulips. I fear I am too old to enjoy these affairs, except for the food and the fauna." He gestured at the wren, who watched them from the garden wall. "Keep heading in that direction and you will find the rose garden where everyone is."

Ella thanked the gentleman and followed the path through several more small gardens that were a riot of colorful delphiniums, hollyhock, foxglove, and geraniums. As she continued, she entered more formal gardens in which the shrubs were neatly trimmed into the shapes of wildlife. Fascinated, she walked about inspecting the topiary birds, deer, and boars. She noted that wire frames had been shaped like the animals, coaxing the plants to grow within the frame.

After looking her fill, she once again headed for the party. She climbed a small set of steps, which led her to a lovely oriental-style garden complete with a wooden pagoda and a pond with a narrow arched bridge. She was totally enchanted. There were small evergreen trees, as well as orchids intermingled with lilies, whose scent added to the exotic feel of the garden. Several benches sat at angles to the pond so that one could come and enjoy the solitude, but Ella was far more intrigued with the pagoda and the delicate bridge.

Knowing she shouldn't be there, she looked round and determined that no one was about, not even a gardener. She mounted the bridge and walked to the center. Beneath her, schools of goldfish swam about in their never-ending search for food. The sunlight reflected on their gold scales, making them sparkle like magical creatures. She leaned against the narrow wooden balustrade and watched them circling, and her mind was drawn back to her youth when her father used to take her fishing for trout. She could have wished that all fish came so near the surface for one to see, for very often she and her father had returned home without a single specimen to give to the landlady for their dinner.

"Miss Sanderson, you came." A masculine voice echoed loudly in the small hedge-enclosed garden, making Ella straighten. The little bridge shook at the sudden movement, then held firm. She realized she'd been foolish to venture onto such a delicate structure. Despite the danger, her gaze was drawn to Lord Shalford standing in the opening between two well-trimmed hedges. He looked disconcerted to see her, and a bit disheveled, his hair tousled. Her cheeks warmed as she realized she was in a part of the outer gardens to which the guests were clearly not invited, for she had discovered only the vicar and he had claimed to have slipped away.

"My lord, I do apologize for wandering about your grounds, but I must ask, why so many gardens?"

Distracted, Shalford's gaze seemed to lock on her feet. "The monks had nothing better to do when the Abbey was still a Cistercian monastery. Never mind that, Miss Sanderson. It's that bridge on which you stand. It's rather old, and I am not certain the wood has been replaced since I was a small boy. Walk slowly to me."

Ella looked down at the old bridge. It had recently been given a coat of black paint, which had fooled her into thinking it wasn't so old. But on closer inspection she could see the irregular grooves where the rotted wood had been covered over.

"Surely the water is not very deep?" She didn't know how to swim, but no fear gripped her. Somehow she knew in her heart if the bridge gave way, Lord Shalford would save her.

"Only a foot or two, but I shouldn't want you hurt in the fall. No sudden moves." He reached out his hand to her.

She walked slowly back to where the earl stood at the edge of the bridge. It swayed only slightly, so she kept edging toward the steps. She was almost safe. But when she went to take the first step down, her borrowed shoe slid off her foot. It bounced on the wooden plank, then the handkerchief she'd stuffed inside fell out, before both splashed into the water.

Ella's cheeks burned at the humiliating event, but it was as if his lordship hadn't seen a thing. He reached forward and grabbed her by the waist and lifted her safely to the ground. For just a moment, the very air in the garden stood still. She couldn't catch her breath as she stared up into a pair of blue eyes that seemed to devour her. The heat of his hands still holding her seemed to do strange things to her pulse. It was as if they both were under some enchanted spell in the small garden.

A large frog jumped from a lily pad into the water with a loud plop, and seemed to break the spell. The gentleman's hands fell away and he took a step back, then turned to the pond. "It would seem that I need to do a bit of fishing to recover your shoe, Miss Sanderson." He took off his jacket, which he tossed to a bench, then he rolled up his sleeves.

"Oh, there is no need for that, sir." Ella began to look about. She found a small dead limb beneath one of the trees. It was angled like a vee. She broke one end short, then held up her tool. "The poor man's fishing tool. My father taught me how to do this."

"You went fishing with your father?" There was a hint of envy mixed with admiration in his question. "I don't think I have ever done anything other than dine with mine."

She came back to kneel beside the pond with his assistance. "It was one of the few things we could do that didn't cost money. Besides, my father was a very good angler. Many a night the landlady used our catch to supplement her meager meals." Ella dipped the limb into the water and tried to snag the toe end of the shoe, but it was just beyond her reach.

"Here, let me do that." He knelt beside her on the stones and took her makeshift tool. Within minutes he captured the slipper and lifted it out of the pond. Blue dye dripped back into the pond. The water had not been kind to the delicate fabric of the slipper. He set the misshapen shoe on a nearby rock.

Ella turned around and sat beside him on the rock wall. There was a moment of silence as they stared at the soggy shoe, then they both began to laugh, long and hard.

At last getting their mirth under control, the earl said, "Oh, Miss Sanderson, I needed a good laugh."

"Did you? Are you not enjoying your party?" At her question his face grew grim.

"No." He didn't elaborate and she didn't press him. They sat in silence for a moment, then he cocked his head and smiled at her, and her stomach seemed to do a flip-flop. "How did Mr. Banks's experiment go today?"

Clearly he didn't want to dwell on the party. Her uncle had not been at the cottage, but Harper had given her a thumbnail sketch of the morning's events. "I do believe we are having North — or perhaps it's West — for supper on Saturday, if that tells you how badly things went."

"That bad. Well, Mr. Graham did warn us." Lord Shalford picked up her shoe. "I fear this is quite ruined."

Ella held out her stockinged foot and wiggled her toes. "I fear I am destined to be forever barefoot, sir. That is the second pair of shoes I have lost since arriving in Surrey, and I have yet to find a replacement pair that fits properly."

"Well, never let it be said that a party at

the Abbey was unable to provide a guest with every amenity. Give me the other one and I shall see what I can do."

Ella took the other slipper off, sheepishly pulled the handkerchief from the toe, and handed it to the gentleman. "Have you a cobbler in residence?"

"Cobbler, no, three females with more shoes than Wellington's army, yes."

Before Ella could protest, the gentleman, shoes in hand, hurried to the garden opening. "Wait here. I shall find you a replacement pair."

A silence fell over the small garden as Ella rose and padded in her stockinged feet to a nearby bench. While she waited, her thoughts revisited the moment when Lord Shalford had lifted her from the bridge. She tried to tell herself there was no significance to that moment, but she knew in her heart that, for her at least, she'd had a dawning revelation. Lord Shalford was more important to her happiness than he should be.

Nearly ten minutes passed before the sound of rapid footsteps approached and sent fear through Ella. How would she explain being here and barefoot, if it were anyone but the earl? But there was no need for an explanation when Shalford appeared at the opening arch, a pair of slippers in his hand. "I gave one of the maids your shoe and orders to find a pair of similar size. She came back with these." He displayed a lovely pair of blue satin slippers with yellow flowers worked on the front.

"Are you certain that no one will object to giving up such a lovely pair?"

He frowned as he looked at the slipper. "I believe my aunt mentioned them earlier today, and my mother declared they would not do, for some reason. Don't worry, I shall reimburse her should she protest."

To Ella's surprise, he knelt on the gravel. "If you will allow me?" he asked, and at her nod slid a shoe on her foot. Like the one that had tumbled into the water, it was a bit too large. "It doesn't fit, sir. Perhaps you should take it back." She wasn't comfortable accepting slippers from one of the ladies from the Abbey.

"Nonsense." Shalford pulled his handkerchief from a pocket, and before she could protest, ripped it in half and removed the shoe, stuffed the slip of fabric inside, then resettled it on her foot. "There, I do believe that will suffice." He fixed the other shoe and slid it on her foot. "That should hold you until you are able to purchase a new pair. There is an excellent cobbler in Guildford on High Street. My sister Freddie frequents him when she's here. I do believe he keeps a full selection of sizes at all times."

Ella lifted her foot with the new slipper. "Even elf sizes."

The gentleman laughed. "Perhaps no elf sizes in stock, but no doubt he could make a pair within a day."

The sound of approaching footsteps sounded behind them, then Lady Latimer's voice penetrated the thick shrubbery. "Shalford, is that you? Did you find Lady Amelia?"

Ella's heart skipped a beat. She didn't want to encounter the marchioness and have what she suspected would be a very ugly scene, with his lordship needing to defend himself for having invited her. "I must be going." Before the earl could protest, she dashed back in the direction she had come, hoping that Fitch was still waiting for her.

About to leave the oriental garden, she looked back to see her ladyship staring after her. She could only hope that the marchioness hadn't recognized her, dressed as she was. Ella hurried along the path to the gate, this time not stopping to admire the gardens, nor to bid the vicar good-bye. Within minutes she was through the gate, running down the stairs.

Fitch lay asleep on the ground, the horse and gig nearby. She shook his shoulder. "Wake up, man, we must go." Ella didn't think she had been followed, but she didn't want to take a chance. She wasn't quite sure what she was afraid of, but she could think of nothing worse than being utterly humiliated by her ladyship in front of Lord Shalford.

Within minutes they were turned around, headed back to the safety of Newland Cottage. Ella had never made it to the party, but she would always treasure the memory of the time she spent with the earl in the tiny garden.

Lady Latimer stood frozen. Had her eyes deceived her? "Who was that?" As her gaze moved to her son, she didn't like the angry look directed at her. What had happened? "Why I would have sworn it was Ella, the maid that I — no, that's not possible."

"It *was* Ella. But she is the late Lord Sanders's daughter, Mother, not a maid." Gabriel folded his hands behind him, making no other comment.

A stunned silence followed as the marchioness grew pink with indignation that she'd been duped, or worse, made a fool by the chit. She made a harrumphing sound. "Well, it makes no difference. Penniless maid or penniless lady are all the same to me. The point is, I didn't invite her to the party. Did she —"

"Daniel and I invited her when we met her at her uncle's house, madam. You do remember Mr. Banks and Newland Cottage?"

There was such a challenge in his eyes, her ladyship knew no purpose would be served by taking him to task for inviting the chit. But she would not stand by and allow him to make a cake of himself over the girl. She turned the matter over in her mind a moment, then knew how best to rein in her eldest son's defiance.

"I think your father and I have made it clear what we expect of you. You know that this penniless creature is not suitable. If you continue to defy me, Gabriel, I shall tell your father the truth. That it was Daniel in that brothel and not you." She raised a finger to halt his words. "Belva had it from her nephew, who was there that night and knows you both well."

"I did it to keep Daniel from being sent away." Gabriel turned and looked in the direction the girl had disappeared as if he were hardly attending to what she was saying.

"Gabriel!" Lady Latimer practically shouted his name to gain his full attention. "You will do your duty and marry Lady Amelia as her father and I would like, or I shall send word to the marquess at once to have Daniel sent to the East Indies."

Gabriel rounded on his mother in anger. "You would do that to him?"

"Of course. Younger sons must make their way in the world, and what better place than the Indies. It will do the boy good. Too much levity is Daniel's problem. A few years working in Calcutta might work some of the foolishness out of him. I expect you to follow me to the party within a matter of minutes." Without another word, and convinced that she had won the day, Lady Latimer turned and left her son.

Gabriel stood completely still as the sounds of his mother's footsteps faded into the distance. His anger was so great that he thought he could throttle someone if they were to cross his path at that moment. Did his mother truly think he would marry Lady Amelia when there was a strong affection between Daniel and the girl? It would be better that he risk Daniel's health than to destroy his dreams.

Too disturbed to return to the party, Gabriel headed toward the river walk where his brother had taken Lady Amelia. He had to speak with Daniel, to know what was in his brother's mind and heart. If Lady Amelia was the one, there had to be a way to make it happen. While Gabriel had been perfectly willing to enter into a marriage of convenience, he would never take a woman his brother cared for. Nor did Gabriel want an unwilling bride.

When he came to the rise above the River Wey, he spotted the pair through the trees, seated on a marble bench at the riverbank. There was an intimacy about the pair as they leaned toward one another that confirmed Gabriel's suspicions. Then his brother lifted a hand to the young lady's cheek and her arms slid round Daniel's neck. Their kiss was full of passion.

Gabriel turned away, feeling like a voyeur. As he strode back toward the Abbey, there was little doubt in his mind which of the two brothers the lady preferred. The problem now would be to outwit both of their parents so that the pair could wed, if that was what they both wished.

Gabriel stopped at the opening to the oriental garden. And what would he do?

Marry someone his parents chose to buffer their wrath about Daniel and Lady Amelia. After all, for his brother the lady was a prime catch. But he would make no plans until he spoke with Danny. His gaze fell on Miss Sanderson's misshapen shoe abandoned beside the pond. If only things were different, he reflected as a pair of twinkling green eyes rose in his mind, then pushed the thought away. He would see Daniel's future safe first, then worry about himself later. For the present he would send a maid to summon the couple from the river to the library. Gabriel needed to know where things stood.

"You . . . marry Millie?" Shock and belligerence were evident on Daniel's face. He took a menacing step toward his brother, who stood at the library window watching the few straggling guests who remained. The earl was either seemingly unaware of his peril at his brother's hands or certain Daniel wouldn't raise a hand to him. "I won't allow it, Gabe. I-I love her." He turned to gaze at Lady Amelia. "I think I always have."

She put a loving hand on Daniel's arm. "But it was never Shalford's plan, Danny. It was our parents. I tried to hint my father in your direction, but in truth, I knew only my own heart and not yours. How was I to know that you had not fallen in love with one of the London beauties I hear about. But my father is adamant that it must be your brother I marry."

Gabriel turned to see his brother stiffen. "No matter what his lordship wants in a husband for his daughter, Daniel, you must do the honorable thing. Go tomorrow morning and ask for the lady's hand."

Daniel gazed into Amelia's eyes. "Adamant, is the old gentleman? And will you do as he wishes if I am refused?"

The young lady put her hand upon her hips. "Do you take me for a ninny, my dear boy?" When he grinned and shook his head, she tugged playfully at his arm. "First of all, your brother has not asked for my hand. Second, I would not accept if he were such a fool to ask without the least encouragement." She blushed and looked at the earl. "I beg your pardon, Shalford."

"I took no offense, Lady Amelia." Gabriel quite liked their little neighbor. She was not at all what she had seemed when he'd first met her in the drawing room. There he had thought her a shy, biddable girl. Clearly in her love for Daniel she found her strength and resolve. She would make him the perfect wife with her calm, sensible approach to things. "I do believe Shakespeare had the right of it: 'A fool doth think he is wise, but a wise man knows himself a fool.' "

Daniel slid his arm round his love's shoulders. "What are we to do if I am refused?"

Gabriel grew thoughtful then asked, "Are you certain your father would refuse permission for Daniel to pay his addresses to you?"

She nodded her head. "My father said" — she blushed and took Daniel's hand — "not to waste my time with the 'spare' when I could have the title and fortune and all that goes with the heir."

As if reaching a painful decision, Daniel stepped away from her, then lifted her hands and kissed them. "He's right you know. I have only a small estate in Yorkshire from which I shall receive a modest income at my great aunt's death. You could do much better."

"There is no better than you for me, Danny." The quiet conviction of her tone was more powerful than any shouted words could ever be.

Gabriel smacked the desk with his open

hand, making the pair jump. "That is settled then."

Daniel looked bemused. "What is settled?"

"That you want to marry."

"Of course we want to marry." Daniel again drew Lady Amelia into the shelter of his arm as she smiled up at him. "But everyone else is opposed."

Gabriel grinned. "But I am not. If you ask Lord Hallet and he refuses, which shall it be, special license or Gretna Green?"

"This from the son who has been a paragon of virtue most of his life? Either way would entail scandal. I won't subject Millie to that." A tortured looked passed between the pair of lovers.

Gabriel strode over to his brother and laid a hand on his shoulder. "Don't make the mistake I have, trying to please others when they neither appreciate your efforts nor your desires. If you love her, damn the naysayers and marry her if she is willing."

Daniel grew thoughtful and looked at Lady Amelia, who nodded trustingly. She left the choice of the decision in his hands. "Then the special license it is. I don't want Lord Hallet chasing after me with his pistol. I don't want to be a groom and a corpse on the same day."

Gabriel nodded. "That would certainly take the fun out of being married." Everyone laughed. He gestured for the pair to come closer. "We must make plans, dear ones." The trio put their heads together and soon realized that they would need a diversion for Daniel to go to London and back without anyone being the wiser.

"If your suit is rejected, I think a picnic on Saturday!" Gabriel arched one dark brow questioningly.

The young man looked as if he were in no mood for such a treat, then a dawning expression lit his face. "I say, Gabe. An excellent notion." He strode across the room to a county map and ran his finger over the town names. "What say you to a visit to Leith Hill, near Dorking? 'Tis the tallest mount in the south of England. It would be a full day's journey. One could ride to London and back in that amount of time."

Plans were quickly made. Gabriel suggested they invite Freddie and Marlin to go with them, while Daniel slipped away to London for the license. A part of him wanted to invite Miss Sanderson, but logic told him he was too drawn to her for his own good. Besides, he had too much to worry about with Daniel to worry about his own future at the moment.

The trio rejoined the party, Lady Amelia on Daniel's arm. Lord Hallet and Lady Latimer exchanged a worried look until Gabriel suggested the picnic. It was soon arranged that the outing would be on Saturday morning. Before the viscount and his family departed, Daniel asked Millie to join him and his brother for a ride the following morning, and she readily agreed, knowing his real intent was to gain an interview with her father.

It wasn't until everyone else had gone to bed that night that Daniel came to Gabriel's room for a private moment. With a half grin he asked, "Have you considered what Father will say if I steal Millie from under your unsuspecting nose?"

Gabriel tugged his cravat from his shirt, not having rung for Timbers yet. "Don't worry about the matter. I strongly suspect he will merely say, 'Lady Who?' not having given the matter a moment's thought."

Daniel frowned. "Do you truly think he cares so little?"

Not wanting to disillusion his brother as fully as he had been, Gabriel walked toward the balcony, making certain Daniel couldn't see the lie in his face. "I think Father's head is too full of government affairs on any given day to have time to give the matter much thought. In the end he will be pleased you have married well and you are happy."

That seemed to satisfy the young man; there would be no repercussions for himself or his brother. He bid Gabriel good night.

As the door shut behind his brother, Gabriel stepped out onto the balcony. He thought himself the fool he'd professed to be this afternoon for not only encouraging Daniel to wed without approval, but involving himself in the arrangements for the clandestine marriage. But Gabriel had had his fill of hypocrisy and avarice from his parents, who treated their children little better than pawns to advance the family's position. He wasn't so certain that things would turn out well, at least for him. If it took a marriage to the lady of the marquess's choice to protect Daniel's portion from the scandal that would ensue after a runaway marriage, then so be it. After all, unlike his siblings, Gabriel wasn't in love. His gaze was drawn to the direction of Newland Cottage, which lay in the darkness. Then why did he feel so low about never seeing Miss Sanderson again?

Eight

The interview with Lord Hallet went much as the Crowe brothers expected. When Daniel departed the library, it was evident by the pinched look on his face that his suit had not prospered. The viscount had refused Daniel's request, albeit kindly, informing the young man that his daughter was destined for more than a marriage with a younger son.

Before the meeting, Gabriel had warned his brother not to argue with the gentleman or to lose his temper, but to accept Hallet's answer gracefully. After all, one didn't want to burn bridges with one's future father-in-law, even if the viscount didn't know he was fated for that role.

Since Gabriel waited in the hall, Lord Hallet reluctantly agreed to Amelia riding with the brothers. "I will trust you, Shalford, to take care of my daughter."

The implication was obvious to all. In the viscount's mind, Lady Amelia was intended for Gabriel and no one else.

"All Crowe men are trustworthy." Gabriel slapped his riding crop on his booted leg in repressed anger. He had hoped for better for Lady Amelia, that her father would care more about her happiness than the Latimer title. Unable to vent his true feelings, Gabriel merely said, "Shall we go?" He turned and stalked from the hall, Daniel and Amelia trailing behind. They mounted and rode away from the hall, each knowing that with Hallet's refusal they were set on a course which would entail scandal and angry scenes with both their parents.

The riding party passed through the gates of the estate, out of sight of the Hall. Gabriel reined his mount and eyed the pair questioningly. "Are you still of a mind to marry even without permission?"

Daniel turned to Amelia as she reached a gloved hand across the distance between their mounts. United as one, they announced, "We are."

"Then you, dear brother, are for Doctor's Common tomorrow to procure a license while the rest of us spend the day at Leith Hill. Lady Amelia and I shall find a vicar near Dorking who will perform the ceremony."

"When can we have the ceremony?" Daniel asked.

Gabriel looked out over the Surrey countryside. "We are supposed to go ballooning on Monday. We shall go to Dorking instead. Come, let us inform Mr. Banks that we have had a change in plans." Disappointment pooled inside Gabriel. He wanted to go up in the balloon with Ella — and the others — but he had to make certain that Daniel and Amelia's future was secure before both their parents tried to force the issue. If his father didn't completely disown him for his role in the elopement, then perhaps he could go flying another time.

Gabriel led the way across the meadows, riding hard. The sight of the red and blue balloon's top, visible above the treetops, drew them straight to the stable, not the cottage. As they neared, he could see Ella seated in the gondola, working at some task, her head bent. An unnamed longing began in his chest. Would that he could spend the afternoon in the lady's company — to watch her green eyes light with amusement, or her lovely mouth moue in disapproval. He sighed, for there was little doubt that Daniel's affairs must take priority at present. Yet there was certainly something about this woman that drew Gabriel despite his responsibilities.

The sun reflected on the silk balloon, making it almost glow in the morning light, but the brisk breeze tugged at the envelope, which made it shudder and dance with the occasional gust. The gondola hovered some five feet off the ground beside one of the staircases that Mr. Banks had built in the pasture. Five ropes extended from the boat-shaped basket to sturdy stakes in the ground. The young lady seemed not the least affected by the balloon's gentle movement.

A need to speak with her welled up in Gabriel, if for no other reason than to apologize for his mother's faux pas in hiring her to cook, for God's sake.

On the ground beneath the basket, Mercury's sensitive ears alerted him to their approach first. The dog, his tail wagging, yipped an excited greeting. The lady looked up. Even from a distance he could see her smile, which set off a stirring of desire inside of Gabriel. What was wrong with him that a mere smile could elicit such a reaction? Had it been so long since he'd been with a woman that he was susceptible to any pretty face?

The trio reined their mounts as they neared the balloon. Daniel waved and called a greeting to Ella.

"Have you come to see Uncle Addison?" she called. "He is at the cottage. I fear his trip yesterday left him a bit blue-deviled, for none of his experiments worked."

The gentlemen dismounted and Daniel hurried to assist Lady Amelia. Gabriel drew off his gloves as he said, "That is unfortunate, but no doubt as a scientist he is used to experiments going awry."

"No doubt." Ella nodded even as she eyed the lovely lady beside Daniel.

The young man drew the beauty forward and made introductions. Ella rose and curtsied, making the balloon rock and dip at what seemed a great height to those on the ground.

Lady Amelia's eyes widened. "Oh, do be careful, Miss Sanderson. Is it safe?"

Daniel walked up to one of the tie-downs. "Quite safe." He gestured at the ropes that ran directly from the bottom of the gondola. Then he stepped back again to eye Miss Sanderson, who'd resumed her seat. "Do you think Mr. Banks would see us if we went to the cottage? I should like to speak with him." Seeing the doubtful look on Ella's face, he added, "Perhaps a few visitors would cheer him up."

"I think you would cheer him up. Knock at the kitchen door. Harper is there ironing shirts. He will take you to Uncle."

Gabriel informed his brother he wanted to speak with Miss Sanderson, then stood in silence as Daniel and Millie disappeared through the trees toward the cottage. He stooped to pat the dog on the head, never taking his gaze off Ella. "May I join you, Miss Sanderson? There is something I wish to discuss."

She looked down from her high position, her green eyes full of questions, but she gestured to the stairs beside the gondola. "Please do, but watch your step. It's a bit windy today, which makes the balloon a bit unstable."

He climbed the platform and stepped down into the gondola with Ella, who was in the process of removing the handle for the rudder. The balloon rocked and swayed, which forced him to grab the sides before it stabilized.

A smile touched his mouth when he noted she wore the blue and yellow slippers he'd given her the day before. He suddenly remembered he'd failed to mention the shoes to his aunt. Taking note of the direction of his gaze, the lady drew her feet back under the edge of her skirt, her cheeks growing pink.

"Is there something I can do for you, sir?"

"May I help you?" he asked, when he realized all the experimental equipment was no longer needed and must be removed.

She pointed to the shaft of the propellor. "We must untie these ropes." Below her, Mercury stood at the command and set to work. Unaware of the dog below, Ella continued, "Everything must go. Uncle said it was utterly useless when he tried to propel himself forward. We will need the extra space on Monday for the ascension Uncle promised."

Gabriel sat on a wicker box and set to work on the rope. "I fear that is why we have come. We cannot come on Monday. Something . . . important has come up. I do apologize."

He noticed her busy hands halted for a moment at his announcement, then resumed their work. A gust of breeze rocked the balloon, which caused him to look up at the towering hydrogen-filled envelope above them. "Are we safe here?"

"You needn't worry. Uncle's helpers secured the rope firmly before they left. The balloon can ride out a storm tied as it is." She hesitated a moment, then met his gaze. "I helped him refill the balloon last night for the ride, but I'm certain he would be willing to delay the flight for you."

As their gazes locked, some intense spark seemed to hold them entrapped in the warmth of the other's gaze. The gondola again shuddered under the wind's onslaught and broke the spell.

They each returned to untying the many ropes. "There was one other matter I wished to discuss." His lips arched upward. "I thoroughly enjoyed your macaroons."

Her gaze flew to his face. "Daniel told you? He promised he would not."

"Daniel? How did he know?" A sudden surge of jealousy raced through Gabriel that she had trusted her secret to his brother. Then he reminded himself that Daniel had Amelia.

She bit at her lip a moment, then gave a shrug that her secret was out. "He stole into the kitchen to filch some biscuits and found me in the pastry room. He vowed to protect my secret."

Gabriel laughed. "In the kitchens? How like my brother. Always into mischief. But I do assure you that he is trustworthy. He wouldn't betray you. I found out from a completely difference source."

At a sudden jolt from a particularly violent gust of wind, Gabriel caught her as they were thrown to the floor of the gondola. He found he liked the feel of her soft body pressed against him in the small space.

His gaze consumed every feature of her lovely face, ending on her full mouth. Before he realized what was happening, he kissed her with a passion that welled up from some hidden depths. She stiffened briefly, then relaxed into his embrace, responding with equal ardor.

After several desire-filled moments, he realized what he was about. He drew back to see wonder and amazement in the lady's eyes and cursed himself for being all kinds of a fool for having given in to his desires.

Realizing he'd taken advantage of the situation, he sat up and drew her with him. "That was a strong gust of wind, Miss Sanderson." His voice was husky with emotion. He looked upward in an attempt to regain his composure. "Do you not think perhaps we should climb down from the gondola until the winds have died a bit?"

Ella's mind whirled with emotions. He'd kissed her. What did it mean? Dare she hope that her deep regard was returned? "Y-yes, perhaps y-you are right." Below them she could hear Mercury barking excitedly. What had the animal in such a frenzy?

He helped her to her feet, but they both

staggered under the balloon's unstable sway. "I'm not certain —" The gentleman froze a moment. He gripped the gunwale and looked down. "Great heavens! Allow me to rephrase that, Miss Sanderson. I *am* certain it's not safe for us to be in here on such a windy day. We are in flight."

As the sun rose, so had the winds. All the while the pair had been conversing, the balloon had bobbed about like a toy sailboat on a pond. But unknown to the pair in the gondola, Mercury had been busy below them. On hearing the command "Untie the ropes," the hound had set about doing as Mr. Banks had trained him for just those occasions when the lads from the Black Sheep couldn't come. He had worked on the outer ropes first, and the slip knots pulled free with only a bit of tugging. Mr. Banks had designed the single tie-stake beneath the balloon in order to keep it stable while Mercury did his job, so the pair inside the gondola hadn't any idea what the industrious and well-trained dog had been about as they spoke.

Stunned to be in flight, Ella looked over the gondola's gunwale to see the roof of Uncle Addison's stable far below. The balloon had been safely tied, even Uncle Addison had said so. Below them she could see Mercury barking and dancing around on his hind legs as she'd seen him do after performing some special trick for Mr. Banks. Then she remembered Uncle had told her about Mercury's ability to untie the ropes. Had he done it? It was the only reasonable explanation.

The inane thought that several shingles were loose on the stable floated through her dazed mind. Still in utter disbelief, she noted three small figures exiting the cottage. They paused a moment, then raced toward the ascending balloon, but a gust of wind wrapped its strong fingers round the gondola and balloon and tugged them easterly at a frightening pace. Yet even as they floated ever higher, Ella found herself awed by the vista below them.

"Miss Sanderson?"

She turned to find the earl staring downward. "Is it not amazing?"

He gave a nod of his head. "Utterly, but unless you want to be in France by nightfall, I would ask, do you know how we make the balloon go down?"

Befuddled at the turn of events and experiencing a slight dizziness, Ella closed her eyes and babbled, "It was Mercury who did this. Uncle trained him to pull the ropes loose when he had no helper. It's all my fault. I should never have told you to untie the ropes. He thought the command for him."

The earl put a finger under her chin and lifted her face. "Don't be afraid, Ella." She opened her eyes and stared into his blue gaze as he calmly said, "Balloons go up and down every day without incident, as will this one. We shall have quite a tale to tell about this someday."

She wanted to believe him, but her gaze drifted to the countryside below. It sped by at a shocking pace. She shook her head in doubt. Without a word, he folded her into his arms. In that moment, his strength of will seemed to flow into her and she felt safe even as the balloon flew eastward.

They stood wrapped in each other's arms for several minutes, before he gently asked, "Ella, time is essential. How do we make the balloon go down?"

His patient tone and strength brought her to her senses. She blushed, then drew back and gestured at the many ropes which hung from the envelope. "One of these releases a valve at the top of the balloon. The gas slowly escapes and you float safely to the ground."

He smiled reassuringly at her. "Excellent. Which one?"

She sighed. "Unfortunately, I don't know. All I do know is that the others release the gondola from the envelope. If you pull the wrong one . . ." Her voice petered out at the possibility that they might tumble to earth, but it was evident by the expression on his face that he fully understood the danger of making a wrong choice. Their situation had just taken a much darker turn.

On the ground beneath them, Daniel and the others watched helplessly as the balloon swiftly moved toward the east, gaining height with each passing minute. "Can they get down, Mr. Banks?"

"Does your brother understand anything about ballooning, sir?"

Daniel shook his head. "We have never before flown. What about Miss Sanderson? Has she the knowledge to bring them safely to the ground?"

Wracked with guilt that he'd never walked her through everything, Mr. Banks wrung his hands. "She has only a rudimentary knowledge of the balloon." His gaze darted to Mercury, who had settled on the ground beside one of the stakes to chew the tie rope. "I have been a complete fool."

"Should we follow them?" Daniel

cupped his hands above his eyes to make out the balloon, which disappeared into the morning sun's glare.

"You would never be able to keep up. The winds aloft are often double what a horse can travel. We shall only know they are down when they send word." The old gentleman's shoulders slumped and he turned his back on the sun. With his head bent, he appeared to be in prayer, which frightened Daniel.

"Gabe will figure out what to do to bring them safely to ground. I have confidence in him."

The old gentleman turned back to the pair, who looked bewildered by the strange events. "Take Lady Amelia home and I shall meet you at Weycross Abbey to break the news to the marchioness after I have informed my sister about Ella."

The old gentleman strode off at once, leaving the young couple alone.

Despite Daniel's brave words, worry lurked in his gaze as he offered his hand to Lady Amelia. "Come, my dear. I shall return you to your father."

"I want to stay with you." She grasped his hand.

"And I should like nothing better, but we cannot know when Gabe will come down . . . nor in what shape they will be. I shall need to be able to leave in a moment's notice."

She sighed. "Very well, but you will come if you should need me."

He took her face in his hands. "It might be some time before I shall see you."

She fully understood that he meant that all their other plans were delayed for the moment. "I shall be there for you whenever you return."

He kissed her, then escorted her to her horse and home.

Unaware of the events happening at Newland Cottage, the atmosphere at Newton Park was decidedly glum that morning. Mrs. Newton and Iris awoke early, still beside themselves about having missed Lady Latimer's garden party. Daisy didn't have an opinion on the matter, too taken up with devouring the sticky buns Cook baked that very morning.

"Oh, Mama, I missed an opportunity to become a marchioness," Iris moaned into her tea. She sat slumped against the table. Her brown curls lay flatly against her head due to her refusal to allow Cilla to dress it that morning, so depressed had Iris been.

"We don't know that, child." Leona sat

back, pushing her half-finished plate of eggs aside. "Who's to say any young lady at the party took his fancy? There really is no female hereabouts who is so very remarkable as to win Lord Shalford's attention in one afternoon."

Daisy looked up from her breakfast. "What about Lady Amelia? Everyone declares her a diamond of the first water."

Leona frowned, but whether it was from her daughter's words or the fact that the girl was licking icing from her fingers was uncertain. "Too shy for the earl, without doubt. Besides, have the Harrises and the Crowes not been neighbors for years? Likely she thinks of them more as brothers than prospects for marriage." The lady grabbed at another straw. "Is she out of mourning for her grandmother?"

Daisy nodded and chewed a bit of bun. As her mother waited not too patiently for her to finish, she said finally, "I saw her in Guildford last week while you and Iris were shopping for ribbons. She and Lady Hallet were trying to escape Mrs. Hyde's wagging tongue. Not a trace of black or lavender on either gown that I saw."

The breakfast parlor grew quiet for a moment. Then Mrs. Newton jumped to her feet. "Why did I not remember? If we

240

want to know everything that happened at the party, we must pay Mrs. Hyde a visit."

Iris straightened. "Mrs. Hyde! Yes, she will know if I can still hope." Showing the first spark of animation they'd seen since the disaster of the day before, the eldest Miss Newton ran her fingers through her hair.

"Hurry, girls. Put on your best gowns. We are for Guildford."

Leona and Iris were out the parlor door before Daisy complained, "Not Mrs. Hyde's. She always serves stale cakes and tepid tea."

Mrs. Newton shouted, "Don't dawdle, Daisy, or there shall be no nuncheon for you, young lady."

Despite her reluctance to go, Daisy was at the carriage a good ten minutes before her sister, and so she reminded her mother. The ladies arrived at Mrs. Hyde's small house within twenty minutes and were ushered into the noted gossip's parlor, where they discovered the vicar's wife. All the better in Leona's mind, for while Mr. Sims preached about goodness, Mrs. Sims enjoyed pointing out everyone's lack of the trait.

Mrs. Hyde rose, her eyes brimming with curiosity. "Ladies, I have been much concerned for your health when you didn't arrive at Weycross yesterday. Whatever happened?"

As the Newton ladies took their seats, Leona used her handkerchief for dramatic effect and pretended to sniffle. "Oh, you cannot imagine all our woes, dear Mrs. Hyde. First, a carriage accident — thankfully no one was hurt. Then my coachman managed to get himself locked in the gatehouse, which I have yet to understand. By the time we walked home to Newton, it was too late to set out. We are inconsolable." All pretense dropped away. "Who was there and did anything of import happen?"

"How dreadful, my dear Mrs. Newton." Mrs. Hyde clucked softly. "But don't fret unduly. Except for the food, there was nothing remarkable to report."

Mrs. Sims, a plain woman with salt-and-pepper brown hair peeking from beneath an ugly black bonnet, leaned forward as she asked, "How, then, does it happen that your niece attended? Miss Sanders, is it?"

It was as if someone had punched Leona in the stomach. She was barely able to correct the mistake. "Sanderson is the family name." A flame of anger lit and roared to a full blaze within seconds. Through clenched teeth she was barely able to inquire, "Are you certain it was our Luella?"

Mrs. Sims tittered, "Oh, well, I did not see her, but Rufus spoke with her in one of the gardens while he was taking a stroll. And I do assure you my husband never forgets a name. He remembered her distinctly from Sunday services. She looked lovely in her new gown, he said. It was really most kind of you to spend money on a girl with few expectations."

Leona's mind was in a whirl. Her niece had gone to the party that they had missed. Not only that, she'd been wearing a new gown. Why, that disobedient chit! Suddenly all of yesterday's events took on a sinister tone. Had Luella managed to sabotage her daughter's chance to meet Lord Shalford? Her ire was so great that she couldn't join in the conversation when Iris asked about the earl's actions.

Even the news that his lordship hadn't singled out any particular lady, and had disappeared from the party for a goodly length of time, did little to redirect Leona's outrage from her niece. Had she not specifically informed Luella she was not to attend that party? This was Addison's fault. He had convinced her that the girl was necessary for his foolish experiments. He had declared the girl invaluable, not only in the cottage but with the balloon. He had no doubt provided her with another of Adele's gowns to rework. Well, he would soon discover he had made a mistake.

At the end of the requisite fifteen minutes, Leona rose, said her good-byes, and hurried her girls back to the carriage. The door had barely closed behind them before she unleashed her wrath about her ungrateful niece. "Why, that conniving little ingrate."

Daisy, gawking out the window at a handsome young farmer come to town for market day, said, "I told you her cakes would be stale."

"Not Mrs. Hyde, you ninny. I mean Luella. Somehow she managed to go to the marchioness's party."

Iris's eyes glittered maliciously. "What are you going to do, Mama?"

"Do?" Leona said, "Exactly what I told her I would do. I shall send her packing."

Daisy sighed as the young man passed from sight. "Packing, did you say? Are we going on a trip?"

Leona and Iris glared back at the younger girl.

"If you cannot pay attention to the conversation, pray do not speak."

"Yes, Mama."

Within thirty minutes of arriving at home, Cilla had reluctantly packed Ella's few belongings and they were waiting for the young lady's return that evening. However, it was Addison Banks who arrived just after noon to inform his sister about the escaped balloon. But before he could utter a single word, his gaze fell upon the packed portmanteau and its significance was not lost on him.

"What is this, Leona?"

"This is the result of you foolishly helping Luella attend a party where she had no business being. You knew as did she that it was my wish that she know her place. Now she shall reap her reward. She is no longer welcome here, so if you have come to plead her case, save your breath."

Addison stared at his sister with contempt. "There are times like this that I often find it difficult to remember that we had the same parents, Leona. Your so-called goodness is a mere facade to mask a truly mean soul."

"How dare you speak to me in that manner? Do you forget that 'tis I who provide the very roof over your head?"

"Then I shall give you notice that Harper and I shall be gone by the month's end." Without informing the lady about

Ella and the earl's plight, he picked up the bag. "I shall inform the child she is no longer living under your roof."

He pulled open the front door and went straight to the waiting gig without a backward glance. But Leona had to get in one last blow. She called from the doorway, "I shan't give the little jade a single cent, nor you."

Addison settled beside the young ostler from the Black Knight. "You needn't worry about Ella. She is no longer your concern."

The carriage disappeared up the driveway. Leona Newton slammed the door with a muttered, "Good riddance. We shall never have to hear of that pushing creature or Addison again."

After the initial fear at finding herself in the sky, Ella found the experience exhilarating. They passed through several large puffy white clouds which enveloped them like gossamer as they floated past. The Surrey countryside below was a mosaic of fields and towns cut into irregularly-sized shapes. "It's lovely. There are the villages of Shackleford and Littleton. They look so small from here."

Beside her the earl said, "They look

small, but that storm does not." He pointed to the north, where dark clouds were gathering on the horizon. "I think we are going to be in for a rather rough ride, unless we can determine how to make the balloon descend."

The sudden events of their flight had taken away any discomfort either had experienced at the earl's unexpected kiss earlier. Ella hadn't forgotten the intoxication of the moment, only put it aside to savor when things were less hectic.

She eyed the storm warily and wracked her brain for what Uncle Addison had told her of his flights. Then a thought occurred. She pulled open the top of one of the small wicker baskets on which they'd been sitting. "Can you perhaps use this?" She held up the small three-pronged grappling hook which was attached to a long coil of rope. "Uncle said he uses this to grab the trees to bring himself to a stop. Mr. James Sadler wrote that the hooks saved his life on his flight from Vauxhall in 1811 when a dreadful storm blew him cross-country."

The earl pulled the coiled rope attached to the hook from the box. "I think we are too high to make use of this at present." He looked up at the sealed valve some ten feet above their heads. "We must reduce the gas."

Ella followed his gaze. The valve hung below the main envelope. Mr. Banks had explained that it was a metal ring sewn into the silk, then closed with a cork and sealed with a thick coat of wax. It was very difficult to open. She'd watched Mr. Banks open and close it during the filling process. They didn't have the tools to do it. Then she raised her eyes to the blue and red silk panels that held the hydrogen. The old gentleman had explained why the silk was best. The very thin threads could be woven to such a tight fabric which trapped the gas and scarcely leaked. The panels were small so if one failed, the gas loss would be slow enough to keep the descent controlled.

But he'd also warned her of the vulnerability of the fabric. Even a single bird could create a tear. She looked at the sharp prongs on the grappling hook, then at the earl, whose attention was on the rapidly approaching storm.

"Perhaps we can tear the fabric with this." She handed the hook to him. "Just a small hole is all that is needed."

He looked up, then back at her and smiled. "Well done, Miss Sanderson."

The earl slid the coil of rope over his

head, the hook hanging in front. "I feel like a mountain climber without a mountain."

"Be careful." Ella's heart was in her throat as she watched him climb first to the gunwale, then hoist himself up into the balloon's riggings. Unfortunately, the storm which was rapidly approaching, roughly buffeted the balloon. Finally he stood at a point where the silk envelope was just above his head. He positioned his feet so that he was stable, then undid a loop of rope to give some length to the hook.

He drew back the hook to pierce the balloon, but a sudden gust pitched the balloon's gondola sideways. Ella was thrown to the floor. As she looked back to where the earl stood, she could see that the sudden shift of direction had thrown the gentleman forward. The hook had not merely pierced the fabric, but torn a long gash. There was no noise as the gas escaped, nor odor, only the sensation in her stomach of descending. As to Shalford, he'd fallen, but managed to save himself among the balloon's netting.

He scrambled down quickly and peered over the edge of the gunwale. "I fear we are going to come down faster than we planned."

They both stood in silence as the balloon lost gas and rapidly sank back to earth. To add to their problems, the storm closed in around them and pushed them easterly at a frightening pace. The ride grew more bumpy, and the earl's arm slid protectively round Ella's shoulders.

Over the howl of the wind, the earl called, "If something happens, Miss Sanderson . . ."

As he paused, measuring what to say, she said, "Call me Ella, sir. I do not wish to die —"

"Ella" — he turned her face up to him — "we are not going to die. Since I met Mr. Banks I have read a bit about ballooning. There have been few fatalities in the last twenty years."

"How many of those balloons had two complete . . . novices piloting them? I would doubt any."

Before the earl could comment, rain began to fall. Even with the balloon above them, there was little protection from the swirling drops. The gentleman pulled off his coat and slid it over Ella's shoulders. As the rain pelted them, the white lawn of his shirt adhered to his skin, revealing his athletic physique. Despite their peril, she found it difficult to draw her gaze from the contours of his manly chest.

Regardless that it was June, a chill invaded Ella's being that seemed to go bone-deep. She had little doubt that the gentleman, too, must be freezing in the downpour. Suddenly, she remembered the emergency boxes Mr. Banks had shown her.

"Look in the box, I believe there are blankets."

He undid the hasp on one of the small wicker boxes. He pulled out a gray blanket and put it over his head and shoulders, then again drew her into the warmth and shelter of his arms. She leaned her head against his chest and stared out into the wall of rain, wondering what would become of them. Would they land safely? And where?

She looked up at the towering envelope and noted it had become misshapen. It looked as if almost a third of the hydrogen might have escaped.

"Look," the earl shouted. "I see trees. We are near the ground."

Ella peered through the downpour and she could see what looked like a hillside. "Look out!"

She'd barely called her warning when the gondola slammed into jutting rocks.

They were thrown to the floor, but Ella experienced no pain in the safe comfort of his lordship's arms. There were several loud pops, then the basket tumbled in a spiraling motion downward, leaving a trail of debris along the hillside, until it came to rest between two rocks.

Dazed and jarred by the fall, Ella lay still, trying to make certain she was in one piece. After several minutes passed, she realized that his lordship's arms, while still around her, had grown limp.

"Lord Shalford?"

Only the sound of the torrential rain hitting the outside of the gondola echoed in the small space where they lay. She lifted herself up to look at the earl's face. He was deadly pale, and a stream of blood poured from a wound at his hairline.

"Sir?" She shook him, but to no avail. He'd been knocked unconscious in the fall. Ella's heart plummeted. She searched her mind for what to do. After several moments, she put her hand to his chest and felt the strong beat of his heart and relief raced through her. Surely that meant all was well.

The only visible injury she could see was his head wound. Yet she knew that being unconscious meant it could be far worse than it appeared. She pulled up her skirt and tore a strip from her shift. As she made a makeshift bandage and bound it about Shalford's head, she prayed that he would be all right.

The storm raged on outside, and she determined that it was best she remain where she was. While his lordship needed help, it would do no good for her to stumble and twist an ankle, or worse, on the slippery slope. Then they would both be stranded. She looked about to see what remained in the basket after their tumble, and found one of the wicker boxes had been wisely tied to the side wall. She looked inside, and to her delight, discovered a second blanket which was essentially dry, and a jug which proved to be full of water.

Covering the earl with the drier blanket, she tugged the earl's coat tighter about her shoulders then settled back to wait out the storm. Once the rain ceased, she must find help. She would worry about sending word to Uncle Addison after she had Gabe safe and dry somewhere.

Her cheeks warmed when she realized she'd thought of him as Gabe and not Lord Shalford. That was what Lord Daniel called him, and somehow it seemed to suit him. Her gaze rested on his face and she couldn't resist the urge to reach out and trace a finger along the strong line of his jaw, up along his cheek to the edge of his bandage. He had taken care of her and protected her during their tumble down the hill. She would do the same for him now that he was hurt and vulnerable.

A sudden awareness that she always wanted to be there for him filled her. She loved him. Then reality seeped into her like the rain. He might dally with a penniless girl, stealing a kiss here or there, but he would do as his family wanted and marry one of the females his mother had invited to the garden party. She laid her head down and a tear trickled down her cheek. She brushed it away with the back of her hand. There was no point in crying for what would never be. She would savor the short time she would have with him. If she were lucky, the memories would last a lifetime. She turned her gaze to the falling rain, hoping it would cease.

The afternoon passed slowly, the storm waxing and waning as only a summer storm can, but continuing nonetheless. Several times during the passing afternoon, the earl moaned and Ella grew hopeful, but still he remained unconscious. She wondered if there would be help nearby.

They had drifted in an easterly direction. Were they still in Surrey, or had they flown into Kent or Essex? She could only hope they hadn't gone quite so far.

The weeks of hard work with little rest caught up with Ella. While the rain pattered on the top of the overturned gondola, she fell asleep despite the cramped conditions.

"Ella!"

A voice penetrated her dreams. But she was so tired she didn't want to come out of the soothing darkness. Then she felt a hand upon her face. Her eyes flew open and she found herself staring into a pair of familiar blue eyes.

"Ella, are you injured?"

The concern in Lord Shalford's voice warmed her heart. She lifted herself on an elbow. "I am unharmed but delighted to see you have awakened. How do you feel?"

"As if Danny had beaten me with a cricket bat." He smiled and tried to sit up, then grimaced. "I seem to have hurt my left ankle and my right knee, as well as my head." His hand came up to touch the bandage she had placed on his head. "Perhaps you can help me stand?"

Ella looked out and noted the rain had stopped. She scrambled out of the gondola, taking note of a few sore muscles of her own. She leaned in and helped the earl as he tried to climb out and join her.

He climbed to his knees, greatly favoring his right one, but when he tried to stand, his injuries kept him from bearing his own weight and they both tumbled to the wet ground.

"Are you unharmed?" the earl asked, his face only inches from hers.

The wind had been knocked out of Ella, so it took a moment for her to respond. "I am unharmed."

It seemed for a moment as if he would kiss her again, but to Ella's disappointment he rolled aside and struggled to sit up. "I fear I am unable to walk." His tone was full of frustration.

Ella sat up beside him. "Then I shall go for help."

The earl's hand clamped over her arm before she could stand. "I cannot let you go." He looked about. "It's not safe. It will be dark in another ten minutes. You might hurt yourself on this slope, or worse, meet some unscrupulous villain on the road at night. I would rather spend a cold night here on this hillside than to risk your safety in the darkness."

About to protest, Ella scrambled to her

feet as rain once again began to fall. "Come, let me help you back into the gondola."

Within some ten minutes they were both back inside the small cramped space. The earl encouraged her not to worry and to get some sleep. She had seen pain in the shadows of his eyes, and she wished there was something more she could do for him. He lay in silence with his eyes closed, but she could tell by his breathing that he wasn't asleep.

Ella watched darkness fall through the mist of rain. It had been a long wet day and would be a longer night. She was damp all the way to her shift, but that didn't compare to what the earl was experiencing. She resisted the urge to stroke away the crease of pain evident on his brow.

Her mind turned to her family. What had Uncle Addison told her aunt about today's events? She knew he would do his best to protect her, but there could be little doubt that Aunt Leona would be furious. She had been livid at the prospect that Ella would meet the earl at his party. What would she be like when she discovered her niece had flown away with the gentleman in a balloon?

Most likely the lady would make good on her threat to be rid of Ella. What would she do? Go to London? Become a companion or governess? The problem was she had no recommendations to supply. Despite his kind nature, Uncle Addison hadn't the resources to provide for her. The best he could do was protect her temporarily until she could find another position, or until Aunt Leona threatened his security at Newland Cottage.

Somehow Ella knew that her first balloon flight would be life-altering.

Nine

"What nonsense is this?" Lady Latimer looked from her son to Mr. Banks. "He flew off in a balloon?"

Mr. Banks, having awaited Daniel's return from taking Lady Amelia home, stepped forward, hat in his hands since he refused to surrender it to Franklin. He had come to reassure the lady, but wanted to return home in case word came that the balloon was safely on the ground. "I fear it was my fault, madam. I trained my dog to release the ropes on the balloon for those occasions when I was unable to hire lads from the Black Knight to come and assist me. Somehow either Ella or your son must have inadvertently given the command to untie the ropes and . . ." He shrugged, not knowing what had truly happened.

The marchioness began to pace. "This is some trick. It must be. No one simply flies off in a balloon by accident." She rounded on her youngest son. "This is something you and Shalford plotted to keep him from having to fulfill his obligation to his father."

259

Daniel's cheeks flamed red. "Do you truly think that I would endanger my brother's life in this manner just to thwart you and Father's ambition, madam? Do you not understand what Mr. Banks told you? Gabe and Miss Sanderson are up in the clouds without the least knowledge of what to do to bring the balloon back to earth. They were swept away by the winds of the very storm which rages outside the house at this moment. We shall be lucky to see them alive again."

Mr. Banks put a calming hand on the young man's arm. "There, there, lad. 'Tis not as dire as that. They were on the winds in front of the storm. Ella knows I have a grappling hook and your brother is strong. If they can get down before the worst of it, all shall come out well."

"Why did you not help him, Daniel?" Lady Latimer snapped, unwilling to see reason.

Daniel threw up his hands and turned his back. Mr. Banks cleared his throat and stepped into the breach of silence. "A balloon can far outpace a horse, Lady Latimer. The balloon was out of sight within minutes of lifting off. We were at the cottage when it happened. It would have been pointless to follow."

"Well, we must do something. We cannot just stand around while he is taken God knows where."

Mr. Banks sighed. "There is nothing we can do until we hear from them. They were headed east last time we saw them, but the winds are unpredictable, Lady Latimer. For all we know they could have gone to the north or south after they were blown out of sight. I feel certain that Ella and the earl shall survive unharmed. Mark my words, we shall hear something by tomorrow afternoon at the latest."

"Tomorrow afternoon!" The marchioness rounded on Mr. Banks. "Are you telling me that my son shall be gone all night with that girl?" Her eyes narrowed as she glared at the old gentleman. "This is some devious plan on your part to force my son to marry that penniless creature."

"Mother!" Daniel returned to his mother and took her by the shoulders. "It was an accident. There was no plot on anyone's part. Can you not understand? You owe Mr. Banks an apology."

"Accident, ha!" She shrugged free from her son's grip. "You are a complete fool if you think it so. That girl lured him into that balloon. She knew that honor would demand Shalford make an honest woman

261

of her if they didn't return tonight. Penni-less females are all —"

"Madam!" Mr. Banks's face flamed red. He jammed his hat on his head. "You need have no fear that Ella will marry your son, even if he has ruined her reputation by failing to return home tonight. Why, I should sooner marry the chit myself before I would force her to call you mother-in-law." He nodded to Daniel. "Good day, lad. You have my sympathies to have to call that irrational creature mother." He turned on his heel and departed.

The door to the drawing room banged shut behind him. But Lady Latimer wasn't cowed by the gentleman's trimming. "What a vulgar little man. As if he could marry his own niece."

"He is no relation to Ella," Daniel said between clenched teeth. " 'Twas the late Mr. Newton who was Lady Sanders's brother. 'Uncle' is a mere courtesy title she uses with the old gentleman."

"Then I won't worry so about Shalford's future." She walked over and sat down. With little sign of distress, she poured out a cup of tea.

Daniel watched her calm demeanor a moment, then strode to the door in long angry strides. He paused before opening the portal. "Did you ever truly worry about any of us, Mother?"

The lady ignored his question. "Where are you going?"

"To send a message to Father. Perhaps he might stir himself to care that his heir is in danger." Without waiting for her response he left his mother alone.

Ella awoke to heavy fog the following morning. The thick mist blanketed the area so thoroughly that she could scarcely see ten feet beyond the gondola's opening. Yet she was certain that the sun was burning off the mist by the sounds of chirping birds further up the hill.

Beside her, Lord Shalford lay in restless sleep, his cheeks flushed. She gently pressed a hand against his forehead, which proved to be hot and dry. Blues eyes opened, heavy lidded and dull. The gentleman gave a wan smile. "I fear, Ella, that I am not better today as I had hoped." He looked beyond the opening. "You shall have to go for help on your own once the fog lifts." His body was wracked by a dry cough.

Ella offered him the jug of water and he drank deeply before he continued. "In the pocket of my coat you will find a small money pouch. You will need it once you find a cottage or inn to secure assistance." He stared out at the fog, then took her arm in a surprisingly strong grip. "If I fall asleep again, promise you won't leave until the visibility improves."

"I promise, and I shall be careful." She took the jug and put it close at hand. "You must promise me that you will try to sleep."

"That is one promise I don't think I shall have difficulty keeping. I feel as if I haven't slept in months." He stared at her a moment, as if memorizing the features of her face, then he closed his eyes.

For Ella, the time passed slowly. When the fog began to lift, she could see wildflowers in clusters dotting the hillside. His lordship had once again fallen into a restless sleep, so she slipped out of the damaged gondola and stood surveying their landing area. They were high above a vale, but the fog still hung so thickly below she could make out little. Above her she could see the torn red and blue silk balloon lying completely deflated among the rocks and trees near the top of the hill. The ropes had become entangled among the small shrubs, which must have kept it from blowing away before the gas had fully escaped. It was plain to see that the envelope was ruined. Her heart ached for Uncle Addison. He loved ballooning and had few funds to replace the damaged silk.

For the present, she needed to focus on finding help for the earl. The sun's position in the sky told her it was nearing noon. As she looked down the hillside she could see that the fog hung more like a sheer veil, so she set off to find an inn. The going was slow in her borrowed slippers on the damp ground. She had scarcely gone a quarter of a mile when the sound of rushing water penetrated the thinning fog. Aware that roads often followed rivers, she moved toward the sound. What she came upon was no river, but a small stream which remained swollen from the previous day's downpour.

She paralleled the water, hoping to find a bridge to help her cross. Some half mile further along, she saw a road in the distance, but unfortunately it was across the deep stream. No bridge was in sight. She removed her slippers, but left on her stockings to protect her feet. She held the shoes in one hand and lifted her skirt with the other. After one more wary glance, she stepped into the fast-flowing water.

It was cold, and Ella shivered despite the

growing warmth of the morning. Still, she waded deeper. She reached the middle of the stream with only her stockings wet. The water whirled around her legs while she picked her way through the rocky bottom, making her stagger on occasion.

She was near the other side when one misstep on a slippery rock sent her tumbling into the water. The small stream seemed to swallow her for a moment as she fell on her bottom, the current tugging at her. In her effort to keep her head above the water, she lost her shoes.

Sputtering, she sat up. "Good heavens, what else can go wrong? I shall be an utter fright by the time I reach an inn."

She sat in the middle of the stream, her gown soaked, and her hair, under a second deluge of water, had finally slipped from its pins and floated on the water. A flash of fear raced through her and she scrambled to reach inside her pocket for the money pouch. It was still safely nestled inside the wet material. With renewed strength and determination, she struggled to rise even as she choked and sputtered at the onslaught of water. But the weight of her soaked gown and the tug of the current worked against her.

"Do you need 'elp, miss?"

Ella sat up to get her head fully above the water. She saw a young farm lad who looked scarcely twelve years old. Behind him stood a chestnut colt on a rope. Relief washed over her like the stream. "Oh, thank you, yes."

He left his young horse and waded into the water to help her, heedless that his pants were soaked. Once she was standing, he climbed the embankment, then turned and helped her scale the slope. At last she stood on the path where the colt waited, not the least concerned with events as he grazed on a nearby patch of grass. She stood dripping and shivering as she asked, "May I know your name, sir?"

"John, miss, John Sparks."

"Pleased to make your acquaintance, John. Do you live nearby?"

"Aye, miss." He pointed toward the south. "Me da is the smithy beside the King's Crown in Hollingborn."

"The King's Crown," Ella said the words with satisfaction. "Can you take me there? There is a gentleman injured up on the hill. I need help to bring him down."

The boy retrieved the colt's lead line and led the lady to the village, which she learned was in County Kent. They had been blown over forty miles cross-country.

The most frightening part came when she learned that the channel was another forty miles east. It hadn't seemed like it at the time, but the encounter with a Kent hillside had been fortunate or they might have found themselves in the sea.

So anxious was Ella to get help for the earl, she paid little heed to the strange looks she received from the townspeople they encountered on their way to the inn. The Crown proved to be a small, half-timbered posting inn that catered more to local traffic than passing strangers.

The lad ran inside to summon Mr. Adams, the owner. Ella thanked her rescuer and tipped him before he led his horse back to the smithy.

The innkeeper surveyed her warily when she stepped into the main hall where the rotund gentleman waited. Ella had tried to brush the mud from her gown, but with little success. Near the cold fireplace in the main taproom, one local farmer looked up and called to the owner, "Core, Mr. Adams, looky what the storm blowed in."

The smell of freshly baked bread made Ella's stomach rumble. But she ignored her physical needs and signaled the innkeeper. At the look on his face, she nervously tucked an errant wet curl behind her ear.

"May I help you, miss?" His gaze spoke volumes about what he thought of her bedraggled state, yet she sensed he would give her a fair hearing.

In a rush she introduced herself, then poured out her tale of a runaway balloon, an injured earl, and a wet night abroad. As a final inducement, she pulled out the coin pouch and poured a number of guineas into her palm.

The gentleman folded her fingers over the coins. "We can worry about that later, miss. First things first." The man was all business: calling for maids to prepare rooms, ordering ostlers to find a cot on which to bring his lordship down the hillside, demanding a doctor be summoned, and insisting his wife see to Miss Sanderson's needs.

But Ella refused. "I must show you where Lord Shalford is, sir. I shall rest only after he is safe."

He eyed her thoughtfully, his gaze moving from her wet curls to her muddy, stockinged feet. A look of respect came to his face for her game determination, yet he inquired, "Are you certain, Miss Sanderson? The smithy's lad can take us back there if he led you here. If the gentleman is on the nearby hillside, we shall find him."

"Quite sure." Ella was determined to return and see to the earl herself. While things were being arranged, she requested pen and paper. She wrote a quick note to inform Uncle Addison where they had landed and that his lordship was injured. She would let him inform Lady Latimer. She sealed the missive, then requested that Mr. Adams send it express to Newland Cottage, Surrey.

In a matter of some ten minutes, a party of men followed Ella as she retraced her path to what she had learned was Hollingborn Hill, the highest in Kent. One of the ostlers kindly carried her across the stream, which had only grown deeper since she had crossed it earlier. She led them up the slope, and when she spied the gondola looking like a broken toy among the rocks, she dashed ahead of the party.

"Lord Shalford?" she called as she approached the overturned basket.

The gentleman was sitting up, but he still had a feverish look to his eyes. "Ella," he said huskily, then his eyes widened as he took in the state of her hair, clothes, and her lack of shoes. "Are you unharmed?"

Ella looked down at her ruined gown. "I tangled with a stream, and as you can see the stream won." She lifted one slipperless foot. "The watery villain stole my shoes, as well, but I am unhurt."

A weak smile played about Gabriel's mouth as he shook his head, his gaze riveted on her muddy stockings. "I come to think that what you need, Ella, are a pair of slippers that can be tied to your feet, like a ballet dancer."

The party of men from the Crown arrived with the narrow cot. Ella moved out of the way while Mr. Adams supervised the mission to move his lordship onto the portable bed. Once the earl was safely settled, the rescue party started back down the hill. The trip back to town was slow; still, the earl's face reflected the pain that each jarring movement of the makeshift stretcher sent through him. The Crown's ostlers were strong, but the task of moving the injured man proved not to be an easy one. By two o'clock that afternoon, Shalford was ensconced in the best rooms of the inn with Dr. Greeley from Maidstone seeing to his injuries.

Mrs. Adams, a kindly woman with round rosy cheeks and a twinkle in her brown eyes, had shown Ella to another room where a bath had been prepared. The woman had had the forethought to send one of the inn's maids to the vicar's house to borrow a proper dress from one of the man's daughters.

It had been a while since Ella had been able to savor such kind treatment; still, she didn't linger in the soothing comfort of her bath. She wanted to see the earl.

Once clean, with her hair washed and toweled dry, Ella donned the borrowed dress, which despite its well-washed appearance was superior to her gray muslin. The green and white striped morning gown was a bit small. Despite the demure cut, she looked nothing like a schoolroom miss in the simply cut gown. The muslin fabric molded tightly about her figure, emphasizing her womanly curves. But Ella was too tired to care about anything but that it was dry and warm. After their adventure a chill had seeped into her bones and she had feared she would never feel warm again. A scratchy tingle at the back of her throat nagged at her, but she pushed it aside for the present.

Mrs. Adams arrived with a pair of shoes which the vicar's daughter had sent later, thinking that the young lady might need them, as well. The black slippers didn't fit, but Ella had grown quite used to managing that difficulty. She borrowed several bits of cloth from the kindly woman and stuffed the rags in the toes.

As she slid the shoes on, she asked, "Have you seen the doctor? What did he say about Lord Shalford's health?"

The innkeeper's wife paused from directing the maids to empty the tub, and shrugged. "He hasn't left the gentleman's room as yet, miss. But he did send word that he wishes to see you."

"Thank you, Mrs. Adams."

Ella hurried to the room where the gentleman had been conveyed. She knocked softly on the door and entered when beckoned to do so by an unfamiliar male voice. Lord Shalford lay in bed wearing a clean muslin nightshirt, no doubt Mr. Adams's. The makeshift bandage she had made was gone, which left an ugly gash exposed just below his unruly dark curls. To Ella's relief, his face looked less flushed. He smiled at her, but his lids appeared heavy, as if he would doze off any moment. "You are well, my dear?"

She blushed at such intimacy of address in front of the stranger. "I am, sir."

The doctor rose from a chair. "Ah, Miss Sanderson. I am Doctor Greeley. I hope you have weathered your adventure unharmed."

"I suffered no injury, sir. How is his

lordship?" Even as she spoke with the doctor, her gaze never left Gabriel's face. There was an intensity to his return gaze that sent a shiver down her spine.

"He has sustained several injuries. Nothing that a few weeks in bed won't right, however. A severely sprained knee and ankle, and it would appear he took a chill. But how about you? Your color is a bit high."

Ella was certain it had more to do with the way the earl was looking at her than her health. Her thoughts returned to the kiss in the balloon and she felt warm all over. She had a difficult time concentrating on what the doctor was saying. "I-I'm fine, sir. Is there" — she forced her gaze from those captivating blue eyes and gathered her wits — "is there anything I need to know about his care?"

The doctor, who seemed to be unaware of the current of attraction which flowed between the pair, picked up a bottle of medicine and said, "I have given him some laudanum to help him sleep and will leave some to use when he is in pain. I would advise you use it sparingly. I'm certain his family will want their own physician to see to him. When he feels up to it, he should be able to travel home without worry."

"Thank you, sir."

Assured that the young lady had survived the ordeal unharmed, the doctor bid Gabriel and Ella good afternoon, then promised to pay a call the following morning before they departed. She moved closer to the earl, suddenly feeling quite shy to be left alone with him. "How are you feeling?"

"Much better." He took her hand, his eyes full of admiration. "You are quite remarkable, Ella, to have survived our flight without harm, and then to hike all the way to this inn, return to the hillside, then back again. I don't know many females who have the stamina or determination to accomplish something that exhausting."

"Nonsense. Anyone would do the same." She smoothed his bedcovers, too embarrassed by his praise to look him in the eye. "Are you hungry, sir? We have not eaten since yesterday."

"Famished. But there are important matters about which we must speak, Ella. The future."

Ella's eyes widened. He sounded so serious. But she misunderstood, convinced he meant their journey home. She could see that he was struggling to stay awake and she thought nourishment best. "There is no rush. You must eat first and then sleep." Ella headed for the door. "When you waken we can discuss whatever you like. I shall have Mrs. Adams prepare a tray for you."

The earl watched her bemusedly — no doubt the effects of the laudanum — then a frown appeared. "Do make certain that she doesn't try to serve me some invalid's meal of gruel and bread. Meat and potatoes, or I shall come down and cook it myself." He paused a moment. "Better yet, I shall request the best cook I know prepare it for me."

Ella laughed. But his praise of her cooking reminded her of home and her amusement faded away. "I have sent word to Uncle Addison of our whereabouts. Mr. Adams thinks that they should be able to arrive in Kent by this evening."

His lordship sat up in bed. He winced a bit with pain and put a hand on his knee. A determined glint settled into the shadows of his blue eyes as he looked to her. "Ella, don't worry. I shall handle matters with my mother and your family, as well. All will turn out well. I promise."

A feeling of well-being surrounded Ella. She didn't know how their families would react to this strange adventure, but she knew in her heart that Lord Shalford would protect her from whatever came to pass. What did he mean about the future? Then her thoughts once again turned to the passionate kiss they'd shared. Dare she hope that he returned her affection? She nestled that thought within her heart and went to see to his meal.

As the door closed behind Ella, Gabriel lay back in bed. He hoped he'd put her mind to rest. There was little doubt in his mind as to how his mother would handle this little adventure, and he wouldn't allow her to take her wrath out on Ella. He closed his eyes as the laudanum began to pull him into sleep. Still, his thoughts dwelled on her. Her aunt would be livid that they had spent the night — Gabriel's eyes flew open and he sat up in bed, oblivious to the pain that shot through his leg and ankle, as the significance of the fact that he'd spent the entire night on the hillside with Ella sank in. He could marry Ella Sanderson with his parent's approval. Honor demanded that he protect her good name.

Marriage! The very thing he'd been resisting since his father had ordered him to find a bride was no long a daunting prospect. A smile tipped his mouth at the thought that Ella would be the one. She wasn't what he'd deemed the standard for a perfect wife, but he'd been a fool to set such cold-blooded criterion for a bride. He could see that now. She was beautiful, brave, and good; what more could a man want? In that instant a dawning revelation overcame him — he loved her.

Gabriel lay back against the bank of pillows, resisting sleep. He truly had been a fool to want only to please his parents and Society. He tucked his arm behind his head. His eyes had been opened to his mother's hypocrisy and unfeeling nature. He'd resisted his attraction to Ella for the sake of the family, but that was no more. He loved her. It was distinctly possible he had since the very day she'd ruined his boots with soapy water. The memory of her barefoot and beautiful that day made him chuckle. Memories of all their encounters began to drift through his mind and he closed his eyes, reliving each.

The laudanum won the day and the gentleman drifted into sleep, despite his efforts to stay awake to see the lady he was about to ask to marry him.

Ella found Gabriel softly snoring when she returned with a tray of lamb stew and bread. She stood a moment and stared at his handsome face. Her heart ached with the magnitude of emotions she experienced. Was she fooling herself that he returned her feelings? Only time would tell. With a hopeful sigh, she returned his meal to the kitchens, knowing that sleep was the best medicine for him at present.

The express letter from Ella arrived at Newland Cottage just after five that same day. Addison Banks broke the seal and read the missive with Harper squinting over his shoulder.

"Thank God they are safe at an inn in Kent." Relief so overwhelmed him, he had to sit down for a moment. His affection for Ella had grown to what any man might feel for his own child.

After regaining his composure, the gentleman wrote a quick note to Lord Daniel to inform him of his brother's whereabouts. Mr. Banks included the scant information he had, which was that the gentleman had been injured and would need transportation back to Weycross.

Harper volunteered to carry the note to the Black Knight and have one of the ostlers deliver it to Weycross. The servant would also arrange for a post chaise. Mr. Banks agreed, then hurried to change and pack a portmanteau. When he set it beside Ella's, which still rested by the front door where he'd left it after his visit to Newton the day before, he realized he needed to make new arrangements. There was little doubt he would have to spend the night in Kent. That very morning he had hired Jacob's sister to act as Ella's companion once she returned, so he would have to take Mary with him to bring Ella back to the cottage. Addison knew that he might think of the child as something close to a daughter, but the rest of the world would not, at least not yet.

Before Harper or the chaise returned, a knock sounded at the front door. To the gentleman's surprise, a second express delivery arrived. Mr. Banks tipped the man, then closed the door. He tore open the letter from London and quickly scanned it, his brows flattening.

At that moment he heard Harper arrive in the hired carriage, so he shoved the solicitor's letter into his pocket. He would deal with the matter later. Banks bid Harper good-bye, then ordered the post boy to pick up the maid. There was a wait of some ten minutes after the old gentleman explained his mission while the excited Mary packed and bid her family good-bye. Then the old gentleman and the servant headed for Kent, hopefully to arrive first.

Unfortunately, the family carriage at Weycross had been pulled from the carriage house the afternoon before and readied for word that Shalford was safe. Lady Latimer and her youngest son, in chilled silence, had set out some ten minutes after the missive from Mr. Banks arrived. They had a good half hour's head start on Mr. Banks. It took the better part of the afternoon to make the journey into Kent. The crested carriage rolled to a halt in front of the King's Crown an hour before the sun set on Hollingborn.

Daniel helped his mother down, then hurried into the inn ahead of her. He introduced himself to Mr. Adams, asking first of his brother's condition. Once assured that his lordship was well and sleeping upstairs, he requested Miss Sanderson's direction. The innkeeper led him to the inn's only private parlor.

Not waiting for his mother, Daniel tapped on the door and entered, going straight to Ella when she rose. "Miss Sanderson, are you unharmed? I am told Gabe is well."

"He is hurt but will recover. I was more

fortunate." Her gaze moved to stare warily behind him when her ladyship appeared in the doorway.

"Daniel," Lady Latimer said in a frosty voice. "Go see if your brother would welcome visitors."

Concern for Gabriel motivated the young man not to protest. He lifted one of Ella's hands and brushed a kiss on the back. "I shall speak with you later. You must tell me all about your and Gabe's adventure."

He departed, and the sound of his boots on the stairs echoed in the hall. Ella's heart plummeted as Lady Latimer stepped inside the room and closed the door. The lady eyed her with a stare that would freeze the sun. Worse, Ella felt dreadful. As the afternoon had worn on, her throat had grown sore and scratchy. She recognized the symptoms of a cold and prayed she would be home before the worst overtook her.

"Well, Ella, you have been quite deceitful with me. Lord Sanders's daughter, are you not? I must ask myself if there was a purpose behind such deceit? What have you to say for yourself?"

"Lady Latimer." Ella nervously clenched her hands at her side. "I meant no harm in keeping my identity from you. In truth, I needed the work you offered and I knew you would never hire a viscount's daughter to cook for you. I never thought . . . well, that we would ever meet again."

The marchioness began to remove her gloves with great deliberation, but never took her steely gaze from Ella's face. "So the girl I hired to cook at my party thinks to marry my son. Have you any idea what you have done to Gabriel?"

"Marry? I-I have no such plans." Ella knew that wasn't true. The thought had crossed her mind, but mostly in wishful fantasy. What could the marchioness be thinking? Ella suspected that the lady had taken leave of her senses, so determined was she to marry off her son. Ella held a slender thread of hope there might be some affection on the gentleman's part, but she wasn't a fool. Why would a gentleman marry a penniless girl when the county was full of wealthy young ladies? Faced with that reality, Ella suspected he would do what was expected of him.

"Don't play the innocent with me, girl. You must know that he will be forced to wed you after your little adventure. He is honor bound to ask you, and it will be his ruin. The title is his by right of law, but nothing is entailed on Shalford. The estate which forms the Latimer marquisate, all that my son is entitled to as firstborn, is a ruin of a castle in a rocky, barren part of Northumberland. The Abbey, the townhouse, and the fortune are his father's to leave where he may. And let me assure you, if he weds without his father's approval, he will be virtually a pauper. You may have his title but there will be little else, if you should be so foolish as to accept the offer he is duty bound to make."

Ella's knees began to shake, and she sat down on the nearby chair. In all her misadventure with the earl, never once had it occurred to her that she was being compromised. They had been far more concerned with merely staying alive, and not the aftereffects. Then she remembered that Shalford had said he needed to speak with her about their future. She was foolish to think it meant more than it was. He was an honorable man and would do his duty by her even if it risked his own future. The thought that he would marry her out of duty and not love made her feel sick. She loved him too much to make him give up the life to which he was entitled for her. Suddenly all she wanted was to be gone from the inn, and from Lady Latimer's presence.

It took a moment for Ella to regain her composure. When she looked up, she matched the marchioness's hostile gaze. Ella stood and her chin came up proudly. "Madam, while it is true that I have no fortune, the Sandersons can trace their lineage to Henry the Fifth. If that is not good enough for you and your husband, then so be it. I shall make certain that your son is not forced to make any proposal to me that would ruin his life. Does Mr. Banks come to Kent?"

"I believe it was his intention." The marchioness did a poor job of concealing her delight at Ella's words as a satisfied smile curled her lips.

"Then there is no reason for us to have further communication, madam."

Head held high, Ella strode from the room, down the hallway, and out the inn's front door. Once in the growing darkness her eyes welled with tears, and she nearly stumbled as she made her way to a small garden beside the Crown. It was there that Uncle Addison found her some fifteen minutes later.

He entered by the small gate and she looked up from the bench where she'd settled, the tears glistening on her face in the twilight.

"There, there, my girl. Nothing can be quite as bad as that."

"Oh, Uncle Addison, I want to go home." It seemed strange to Ella that she could consider Newton Park home, but that was where she wanted to be at the moment. Away from the marchioness and all her dislike. Away from the earl and his duty.

The old gentleman rubbed his chin as he looked thoughtfully at the setting sun. "Well, my dear. We can leave the inn at this late hour, but I fear your aunt has thrown you out of Newton Park."

Ella shook her head, unable to comprehend more bad news. "Because of the balloon flight with his lordship? Surely she must realize it was an accident?"

The old gentleman removed his hat. "Not the balloon, dear, Lady Latimer's party."

A dawning expression raced across Ella's face, followed immediately by one of utter desperation as the full meaning of his words sank into her already buffeted senses. "Whatever shall I do? I have no references, no place to live, and no money."

The old gentleman slid onto the bench

with her. "Nonsense, child. You have me and Harper. We want you to come and live with us."

Ella sneezed, then wiped at her nose. "You are too kind, but you cannot take me in. Aunt Leona shall toss you out of the cottage if you defy her in such a manner."

Mr. Banks's voice hardened. "You let me worry about that woman, Ella. I shall manage things very well."

"But I haven't told you the worst, Uncle. We ruined your balloon and I know you haven't the funds to replace it."

He slid an arm round her shoulders. "Never mind about such trifles, Ella. There are things you don't understand about my circumstances. We will discuss our situation after you have had a good night's sleep."

Ella looked at the inn with distaste. "Uncle, must I go back in there?"

His brows rose. "You cannot wish to go back to Surrey tonight, my dear."

"I-I was hoping we might at least move to another inn so that I might not have to encounter any more . . . so that we would have less of a journey in the morning."

"I must guess that you have had an encounter with that dragon, Lady Latimer."

Ella nodded her head and dabbed at the

tears with a handkerchief. "She thinks me some . . . dreadful creature who has trapped her son into a . . . marriage proposal."

"I hope you won't listen to any of her nonsense, my dear. If you do not wish to marry his lordship, you don't have to. We shall leave here and never again speak of Shalford or the lady again."

She loved the dear old man for his sentiment and thumbing his nose at convention. Life wasn't really that simple. Society would be savage to her if this adventure became public. Then the thought of never seeing the earl again made Ella's heart hurt, and nothing else mattered. Still, the loss of his company was preferable to having to see him every day and see the resentment in his face for what he would have sacrificed for her. She sneezed once again. "Can we go at once?"

Mr. Banks rose. "Only as far as Maidstone tonight, child. I fear you are sickening." With that, he strode off to find Mary. He ordered the post boy to hitch a new team and to hire a hack for him for the short journey. He scribbled a note for Daniel to explain that he intended to take Ella home at once. The old gentleman also made arrangements with Mr. Adams to have the remains of the balloon brought down and stored at the inn until such time as he sent for it.

Ten minutes later the post chaise pulled from the inn yard with Mary and Ella inside, Mr. Banks on horseback behind the vehicle. The moon was full and the journey to Maidstone went uneventfully. They secured rooms at an inn on the outskirts of the town and Addison ordered Mary to put Ella to bed immediately. The old gentleman secured a private parlor for himself and a large tankard of ale, then sat down to contemplate the future for both himself and Ella.

Ten

A clock chiming the hour of eleven penetrated Gabriel's fuzzy thoughts. Had he overslept? He could understand if he had, since he felt dreadful. Every muscle in his body ached, as well as his head. Opening his eyes in a strange room, memory flooded back. He was in Kent, injured after the wild balloon ride with Ella.

A smile came to his lips at the thought of her, despite his discomfort. He was in love. The kind of love that lasted a lifetime. He wanted to possess her, to make her burn with passion, but with a dawning perception of his deep emotions, he understood there was so much more to his feelings. He admired and respected her courage and strength of character, as well. Over the course of the past day and a half, there had been no hysterics and no tears once she conquered her shock and fear. She was truly a remarkable young woman. A woman he intended to make his bride. His brows flattened when he remembered it was no small matter that he would also be taking her from the drudgery of life at Newland Cottage.

As he lay alone in the inn's lumpy bed, the thought occurred to Gabriel that he still needed to ask her. Where had Ella gone? He tried to sit up, but pain assailed his knee and ankle. Resting against the pillows, he gave a soft curse at being so incapacitated. Impatiently, he awaited a visitor and he hoped it would be Ella. The inn was quiet, but he heard occasional footsteps going past his room. Finally, after what seemed hours but was a mere twenty minutes, his door softly opened and his brother peered in.

Gabriel frowned. How long had he slept, and when had Danny arrived?

"Awake at last. I was beginning to think that country sawbones had given you enough laudanum to drug an army." Daniel entered and came to Gabriel's side. "How are you feeling?"

"As if that same army marched all over me. When did you arrive?"

"Mother and I have been here since seven this evening."

"Mother?" Gabriel spoke her name with a mixture of disbelief that she'd come, and doubt that she'd bestirred herself on his behalf. But then why else would she journey across two counties?

"She insisted she must come."

Gabriel sighed. "No doubt to ring a peal over me for wasting precious days in my duly assigned task of finding a bride."

Daniel nodded agreement. "Lucky for you she has retired for the evening, thinking you wouldn't wake until the morning. Freddie sends her best and wanted to come, but I convinced her there was no room in the carriage."

"What about Ella?" Gabriel asked, intensity etched on his face. He sat up, disregarding the pain. "Did you see Ella? How is she? Where is she?"

Surprise flitted across Daniel's countenance at his brother's urgency. "I saw her and she appeared fine. Mr. Banks arrived just after us. For some odd reason he made the decision to depart tonight."

"She's gone." Disappointment raced through Gabriel and he slumped back onto the pillows. He wanted to see her, speak with her, tell her all that was in his heart.

"Well, there's no reason to look as if someone stole your best hunter, Gabe. She lives at Newton Park and is at Newland Cottage every day. You need only ride over and see how she fares once you are recovered." Daniel settled in a nearby chair. Fatigue had taken its toll. His eyes were shot with red, his hair awry, and his cravat askew. "I'll take a note over to the cottage for you once we are back at Weycross."

Gabriel stared at the raw-beamed ceiling. "I cannot ask her to marry me in a note."

"Marry?" Daniel sat up and ran a hand through his dark curls, further disturbing his once-neat Brutus style. "Is this all that nonsense Mother has been babbling about? You must marry her to protect her name?"

"No." Gabriel's voice was low but forceful. "I will marry her because I love her." Then his features darkened. " 'Tis odd they would travel so soon after our misadventure. Did Mother, perchance, speak with Ella?"

Daniel frowned. "Perhaps. I left them together in the private parlor for only a moment, but Ella was gone when I returned to inform Mother you were firmly asleep. She made no mention of the matter, nor did Mr. Banks in his note."

Gabriel could only pray that his interfering mother had held her tongue. She might not like the results of the day's happenings, but even she could not expect him to shirk his responsibility. Still, had she been so foolish as to forget herself, he had little doubt what the marchioness would have said. A smile tipped his mouth — whatever his mother had said or done, he would make amends to Ella somehow. "It doesn't matter. I shall ask Ella to marry me once we are returned home."

Daniel stood up, a smile lighting his face. "By Jove, Gabe, that's capital." But the smile didn't last as all the obstacles in their path returned to the young man. "Neither Mother nor Father will approve of Ella any more than Lord Hallet approves of me."

Gabriel's face became a defiant mask as he looked his younger sibling in the eye. "It seems, dear brother, that we are both destined to disappoint all parties involved save the women we love."

A grim smile settled on Daniel's face. "So be it."

The following morning, two separate parties made their way back to Surrey with their ailing passengers. Mr. Banks and the women departed from Maidstone just after seven and reached Newland in midafternoon. By that time Ella's cold had grown worse, and she was put to bed by Mary while Mr. Banks informed Harper, not only about their trip, but about the contents of the letter from London. The two old men spent much of the remainder of the day deciding how best to handle their circumstances. Things would be different since they would now have a young lady residing with them.

Lady Latimer and her two sons didn't depart from the Crown until almost ten on the same day. A delay had occurred when Gabriel requested an interview with his mother. Pressed about her conversation with Ella the previous evening, she'd vehemently denied having been unkind. Yet the earl had his doubts, especially since the marchioness had refused to look him in the eye.

The June sun made the day unbearably warm by the time the Crowe family was ready to depart. The gentleman's injuries were such as to necessitate two ostlers helping him down the stairs and into the carriage. The roomy traveling coach had been arranged in such a manner so that the earl could sit with his injured limbs propped up.

Her ladyship informed the coachman that his very position depended on them getting her son home with the least pain as possible. They started out at a lumbering gait until Gabriel protested that they wouldn't reach Weycross before the middle of next week at such a speed. The coachman, worried about what to do, resumed the journey at a modest pace.

The marchioness's mood was decidedly cheery. She chattered inanely about the countryside they passed through and people she knew from Kent, and then mentioned she would have to postpone a dinner party which she had planned until after Gabriel recovered.

Gabriel's eyes narrowed as he stared at her. "Mother, why plan any dinner party? You, of all people, must realize the implications of all that has happened? My bride has been decided."

The lady began to rummage around in her reticule, then drew out a lace handkerchief and dabbed at her perspiring face. "So you say, but you shall have to discuss the matter with your father when he arrives. Besides, who's to say the young lady will agree to your proposal?"

"Father is coming to Weycross?" Diverted from the main subject by this news, Gabriel's brows rose. The marquess rarely came into the country.

"Did you not think he would come? After all, he must give his approval of your bride." The lady feigned an uncommon interest in a hayrack they were passing to avoid her son's probing gaze.

"You delude yourself, madam. There is nothing to discuss. Even Father will agree. A man must do his duty." Gabriel turned and looked out the window. It was pointless to speak to his mother about his true feelings for Ella. Duty she might understand.

"Things don't always go as we plan, now do they," her ladyship responded without her usual anger, and a smug smile seemed to have found a permanent home on her face.

The subject was dropped, but a growing uneasiness settled into Gabriel. What did his mother know that he did not? Had she said something to Ella during their brief encounter at the inn? Worse, had Ella said something that indicated she would refuse his offer? That sent a sharp ache through his heart far worse than what he was experiencing physically. He loved her and didn't want to think what his life would be without her. Was he doomed to a loveless marriage for the sake of the Crowe line?

By the time they reached the Abbey, near dusk, Gabriel was determined to send Daniel to the cottage first thing in the morning to see how Ella had fared from their adventure and to send her his love. He had one other important mission for his brother, which would require a trip to Guildford. His brother could request that Gabriel might have an interview with her at the earliest possible moment. His thoughts drifted to their kiss in the balloon. He was certain she shared his feelings, which did much to soothe his agitated emotions.

Daniel rode to Guildford at first light the following morning. He ate breakfast at the Angel while his order was prepared, then with package in hand headed back to visit Ella. He arrived at Newland Cottage by ten. He knocked at the door, which was opened by a pretty young maid he'd never before seen. A strange feeling of impending doom came over him. The girl's presence seemed such a little thing, but something had changed here at the cottage. When and why had the old gentleman replaced Ella as his maid? The more important question would be, how did it affect Gabe's chances of marrying Ella?

The little maid waited, as the young man appeared to be lost in thought. When he didn't speak, she inquired, "May I help ye, sir?"

"Is Mr. Banks in?" His gaze lit on what appeared to be several large trunks sitting in the front hall. Who was going on a journey?

"No, sir. Gone to Guildford, he has." She dimpled up at him.

Disappointment raced through Daniel. He'd hope to enlist the old gentleman's help in making Gabriel's wish of marriage come true. "And Miss Sanderson? Ella? Is she here today?"

"Aye, but she ain't receivin', sir. The young lady is ailing." On seeing the look on the gentleman's face, she hurried to add, " 'Tis only a cold, and I think she'll be herself again by the end of the week."

Frustrated not to have been able to speak with either one, Daniel pulled Gabe's note from his pocket and laid it on the package he'd brought from Guildford. "Can you make certain that the lady receives this?"

The maid bobbed a curtsey and took the present. "Aye, sir."

About to depart, curiosity got the better of him and he pointed at the trunks. "Is Mr. Banks going on a journey?"

Mary bit at her lip. "I don't know if I'm

allowed to say, sir, bein' new at my post, but aye, the gentleman has business in London." With that she closed the door, leaving Daniel disheartened. He'd accomplished little that would put his brother's fears to rest.

So Banks had business in London. Strange, Daniel thought as he went back to his horse, he had the impression that Addison Banks had no business. That was why he lived on his sister's estate. It was all a puzzle. But at least he'd learned that Ella was unwell, which made it unlikely she would leave Surrey before Gabe could come and ask for her hand.

Daniel rode straight back to Weycross to give Gabriel the news. Barraged with questions he couldn't answer about her, Daniel thought it best not to mention the trunks he'd seen for fear his brother would try and get out of bed before he was able. Once Gabe had been reassured about the young lady, Daniel slipped away. He had his own affairs of the heart to worry about and intended to pay Lady Amelia a visit. Their own plans had gone awry with the runaway balloon, and he wanted to kiss the sweetest lips in Surrey, look into her beautiful eyes, and tell her that somehow they, too, would make things work out.

Ella held the sealed note from his lordship up to the morning sunlight. The decorative *S* pressed into the red wax was very elegant. She flipped it over and surveyed the earl's neat script with trepidation. Would it hold the dreaded marriage proposal? If the letter contained a proposal, somehow it seemed appropriate to have come in a cold, impersonal request by messenger. How strange that she should fear something that only days before she might have welcomed. Only then she would have known such an offer would have come from his heart, not this dutiful request to protect her name.

Tears welled in her eyes and she laid the missive aside unopened. Her mind was quite made up to refuse. But what was going to happen to her once she recovered? She couldn't stay with Uncle Addison for long or he would risk Aunt Leona's wrath. Clearly the lady had washed her hands of anything to do with her husband's niece. Ella sighed. That meant she must find a position somehow, somewhere. Who did she know that could help?

Her school friends, Sara and Lady Rose, came to mind at once. Strangely, she hadn't heard a word from either of her friends in the month since she had been home. Perhaps they, too, had no one to frank their letters for them. Or had their lives been as completely unpredictable as her own? In truth, it was likely there was little either could do to help her, especially since not one of the three had two coins to rub together. Her friends' situations were little better than her own. One had only a distant stepmother and the other had no mother, only a disinterested father.

Perhaps Uncle Addison knew a lady who could write her a recommendation. He had said they would discuss their future, so she would wait to see what he would suggest. She picked up the letter again and gazed at the cream vellum. She didn't feel well enough at the moment to deal with the contents. She laid it on the night table to read later, when she was more able to stand strong against her heart's desire.

Her hand fell on the unwrapped package and she lifted out one white satin slipper with ribbons attached at the back. She sighed heavily and her throat tightened. She remembered that he had declared she needed shoes that could be tied on her feet. Ella sat up and slid the slipper on. Somehow he had managed to have the cobbler make ones that fit perfectly. She tied the ribbon at her ankle and held out her foot. It was lovely, and she would never be able to wear it, for it would remind her too much of what she had lost. She undid the ribbon and put the slipper back into the package. She shoved the gift in the drawer of the nightstand and tried to put the gentleman from her mind as she lay back down.

A knock sounded at the door and Ella hoarsely called for her visitor to enter. Uncle Addison stepped into the room dressed in his Sunday best, which surprised her.

"How are you feeling, my dear?" He came and sat in a wingback chair beside the bed.

"Not really sick enough to stay in bed, Uncle. It is truly just a cold. I could be up and being useful. Mary is a dear, but she has a great deal to learn."

"Don't worry about the house, Mary can manage for a few days. I want you better as soon as possible."

Ella plucked at the blue counterpane. No doubt he was worried about keeping his place here should his sister find out that her niece was in residence. She couldn't blame him. "I shall be able to begin my search for a new position as —"

"Nonsense, child. I didn't mean I wanted you gone." He reached over and patted her hand. "I have business with my solicitor in London. I want you to come with me. I have just returned from Guildford to engage a carriage for us." He smiled, then winked. "Like it or not, you are part of my family, if not by blood, then by our hearts. I won't go without you."

Tears welled up as his kindness overwhelmed her. She reached out a hand, which he took in his. "I like it a great deal . . . but what about Aunt Leona?"

"She has no heart and we needn't bother about her." The old gentleman's smile widened. He rose. "Truly do not worry, things are not as they once were. I shall explain everything once I get it all sorted out with my solicitor. For now, I shall leave you to rest." He leaned down and kissed her forehead. As he turned to depart, his gaze fell on the unopened letter. "What is this? From his lordship?"

Ella lifted the missive from the table, turning it over to the red seal. "I think he is doing his duty and making me an offer of marriage. What is the point in subjecting myself to the humiliation of such a proposal when I have no intention of accepting?"

Mr. Banks's gaze roved over her sad face. "Are you certain, my dear? There has always been something about the way you looked at him that encouraged me to suspect . . . well, that you harbor tender feelings for him."

"I want no reluctant husband, Uncle. He is doing the honorable thing. Whatever is in my heart, I won't force him into such a marriage." She blinked back her tears. "He will forget me soon enough, once he returns to his life in London. Besides, Lady Latimer made it plain that if he marries me he will be disinherited, or as much as his father possibly can." She put the letter back on the table. "I shall deal with the matter on the morrow when I am feeling better."

"My dear child, don't allow the marchioness to have the final say. Meet with Lord Shalford and let him —"

"I cannot. It is easier this way. Please, do not ask me to do so." Her green eyes glistened with unshed tears and entreaty.

He patted her on the shoulder. "Then I shan't make you, my dear. Write him your refusal if you must."

"Thank you." Relief raced through Ella and she bid the gentleman good day. As the door closed behind him, she realized she was being a coward not to see Gabriel, and to use a letter to inform him she wouldn't allow him to sacrifice himself for her honor. She wasn't sure she could look into those blue eyes and resist his entreaties to marry him. The possibility of being with him forever beckoned her like a siren calling ships to the shoals of ancient Greece, but it would be her life and dreams dashed against the rocks when he realized what she had cost him. She would go to London with Uncle Addison and worry about her future when they returned home.

Over the course of the next two days, Gabriel grew restless awaiting a reply. At last he received a terse response to his letter. Miss Sanderson coolly informed Lord Shalford she was not receiving and there was no need for further communication between them. The note was formal and dismissive. He crushed the paper in his fist and cursed his mother for whatever she'd said to Ella, then endeavored to rise from his sickbed. Luckily, Timbers and Daniel were present and managed to subdue him. They made him see reason. Ella was not well. Even if he went to Newland, he would only agitate her and perhaps even make her condition worse. Still, he tried his weight on one leg and experienced a sharp pain that almost took him down. Gabriel settled back in bed, at last convinced he wasn't ready to be up yet.

Ordered by the family physician later that same day to remain there or risk serious damage to his knee, the earl fretted at not being able to speak with Ella. He must undo whatever harm his mother had done. Before the accident, he'd seen something in Ella's eyes, felt something in her kiss — he couldn't be wrong about her returning his affection.

As two more long days slipped by, Gabriel found he couldn't eat, sleep, or be rational. He pestered Timbers for news of the neighborhood, he pestered Daniel to go back to Newland Cottage and inquire of Ella's health daily, and he pestered Dr. Manton to allow him out of bed.

The physician grew concerned and spoke with Daniel after a visit. They were in conversation outside Shalford's apartments about what could be done for the earl when the young man turned at the sound of footfalls on the carpeted hallway, and his heart plummeted.

"Father!" Daniel grew nervous and wondered when the old gentleman had arrived at Weycross.

The marquess ignored his son and addressed his question to the physician. "Dr. Manton, how is my eldest son?"

The doctor sighed. "I was just explaining to Lord Daniel that his lordship is improving physically, but mentally, my lord, I cannot like his condition. He refuses to eat or sleep and daily risks his health in an effort to use his injured limbs. I fear if something is not done soon, he shall grow seriously ill or be permanently lamed."

The regal gentleman looked to his younger son. "To what do you attribute Shalford's unsettled condition? Did this flying about in a balloon unhinge my heir?"

"He's in love, sir." Son glared defiantly at father.

Lord Latimer did not show the slightest response to his son's announcement, not even the flicker of an eye. "Doctor Manton, it seems that your services are not needed in this particular matter. I shall see that my son does as he is instructed."

The doctor bid them good day and departed. He had scarcely gone halfway down the hall when Lord Latimer demanded, "Tell me all."

The stern look on his father's face made Daniel quake inside, but he gamely laid out the details. "Gabe is in love and our mother has made it clear she does not approve of the young lady."

The marquess's brows drew together. "But your mother just informed me that it is practically settled between Gabriel and Lady Amelia Harris."

"Millie won't have him, Father!" Daniel practically shouted. He regained his composure and said, "Nor does Gabe want Millie. He loves Miss Luella Sanderson, daughter of the late Viscount Sanders, and she is quite penniless. Mother has plots and plans, but they have nothing to do with what we want."

"Gilbert Sanderson is the young lady's father?" The gentleman's expression grew sentimental, an expression which Daniel had never before seen.

"You knew the late viscount?"

"Gilly and I were quite the terror of the dons at Eton." A gentle smile softened the older man's face and his eyes glazed with nostalgic memories. "He hadn't the money for Oxford, and I only rarely saw him after that. I heard he inherited the title and disappeared up north. I never saw him again, only his obituary in the *Post*." A sadness filled the marquess's eyes.

Daniel stood in silent awe. Like most young men, he couldn't imagine his staid father as a youthful prankster. Then a rush of guilt filled him that would at least help his brother's situation. "Father, there is something I must confess."

Suddenly the door to Gabriel's room opened and he stood there leaning heavily on a crutch Timbers had found in the attic. The marquess's eyes widened at the sight of his son. He was much altered from the young man he'd ordered into Surrey only weeks earlier. Beads of sweat speckled his brow from the sheer effort it had taken to walk on his injured limbs to the door.

"Father, Daniel, do come in and stop nattering about my affairs right outside my door as if I were deaf instead of crippled." He turned his back on the pair and slowly limped back to his bed.

The two men entered and the marquess closed the door, but before he could speak a word to his eldest son, who sat slumped on the bed, the earl lashed out, "Father, I love Ella and I *am* going to marry her despite her lack of fortune, despite Mother's plots, and despite your objections."

Latimer drew his hands behind his back,

his face an unreadable mask. "I don't remember saying *I* disapproved."

Gabriel shot a surprised look at his brother. "But Mother has said for weeks that she knew just the type of female you wanted, and Ella certainly doesn't fit that mold."

"If I had chosen a female for you, of course I would choose wealth and position, but Gabriel, I am not a monster. If your heart is engaged, I should have no objection to a gently bred female despite her financial shortcoming."

Both brothers grew speechless at their father's words. At last Gabriel found his tongue. "What about Mother?"

The old gentleman's eyes hardened. "I shall handle the lady."

Daniel took a step toward his parent. "Father, I still must confess. It was I in the brawl at the brothel, it was I who went and issued the apology. Gabriel was only trying to protect me when he took the blame."

To the brothers' surprise, a rare smile transformed the marquess's face. "I am glad you have finally confessed. I learned the truth scarcely a week after you left Town. It makes me proud that you have owned up to the matter, for I fully meant to censure you for allowing your brother to take your punishment. Honor and duty are what make us gentlemen, Daniel."

"Yes, Father." The young man blushed under his father's rebuke.

The marquess frowned at his eldest. "Manton says you still need your rest, Shalford. Back to bed and stay there."

Gabriel reluctantly climbed back under the covers. "Sir, there is one other matter."

"Yes?"

"It regards Daniel's future."

"Well, I have no intention of sending him off —"

Gabriel gestured at Daniel to make him understand what he must do. The younger son straightened. "Sir, I have fallen in love with Lady Amelia and would ask that you intercede on my behalf with Lord Hallet."

The marquess's brows rose. "So that was why you were so vehement about the young lady not wanting your brother. I should have guessed."

Daniel nodded, then his shoulders sagged in defeat. "I approached her father, but Mother has convinced him that Gabe would make Millie an offer. He refused me."

"And does Millie want to be a future marchioness or merely Lady Amelia Crowe?"

The young man beamed. "She wants me, Father."

"There is simply no accounting for taste." Gabriel waggled his brows and the trio laughed.

Latimer clapped his hand on his son's shoulder. "Then I shall do my best, Daniel. Perhaps if I present you with an estate nearby Hallet Hall, that might help change the old gentleman's mind. It will be a wedding gift from me."

Looking more mature, a subdued Daniel shook his father's hand. "Thank you, sir."

The marquess's gaze moved from one son to the other. "Is that all? Is there anything else you would tell me?"

Gabriel stared at his father as if a stranger had replaced the man they had known for years. "May I ask, sir, why? Why this acceptance of our choices?"

The old gentleman's gaze moved to the window. Once again a glaze came over his vision as he journeyed into his past. "I know I haven't been the best of parents, but somehow the choices we make change us and we aren't aware what has happened until it's too late." He grew quiet a moment, then continued, "When I was a young man I fell in love with a mere vicar's daughter. My father refused his permission for us to wed and ordered me to marry your mother instead. I was weak and allowed him to convince me love was too fleeting to give up what your mother would bring to a union. Rebecca is a worthy woman, but I cannot deny that I have often regretted my weakness. I was unhappy in my marriage and I made your mother unhappy. Over time we built this united facade to show the world. But we don't understand one another any more today than we did the day we married. I have often wondered if things would have been different had I married Olivia." His face softened with the memory of his first love.

Both his sons were quiet as he seemed to be in a dream world where life had been what he wanted. At last Gabriel asked, "What happened to her, Father?"

"She was the fortunate one and got a second chance. She married for love some years later." The wistful expression fell from the marquess's face. "I made my choice and must live with it, but I came to understand this week that I was about to force you into the same mistake."

Gabriel's brows rose. "What happened?"

"I encountered Olivia with her daughter and the girl's fiancé. They were in London to arrange Letty's wedding to Sir Edward Spalding." The old gentleman sighed. "That young man looked at Olivia's girl just the way I used to look at Livy." Latimer turned to Gabriel. "Over the course of the next few days it occurred to me that I was denying you the very thing my father had taken from me."

Gabriel was awed by how little he knew of his father's life. At the same time, he was moved to see his father's genuine emotion for his sons for the first time. "Thank you, sir."

A frown touched Latimer's face as he looked to Daniel. "You do understand that I can only do so much with Hallet. The rest will be up to you and Lady Amelia."

"I do, sir." Despite his father's serious tone, Daniel couldn't contain his joy and beamed back at the gentleman.

"Then I must go down and have a few words with your mother. On second thought, I suspect it will be a great many words." The marquess left his sons, but there was no grand celebration. Each still had bridges to cross before they could claim the women they loved.

Eleven

Three days after the conversation with the marquess, Gabriel was seated beside Daniel in the young man's curricle, bowling up the drive of Newland Cottage, the crutch wedged in between them. That morning the doctor had determined the ankle fully healed and given his permission for the earl to move about as long as he relied on the crutch to protect his injured knee. Doubtless, Dr. Manton hadn't meant a journey, but once freed from the confines of his room, Gabriel was determined to see Ella. He also needed to inform Mr. Banks that he fully intended to replace the destroyed balloon.

To the men's amazement, a young lad of about seven was swinging from one of the cottage trees while a little girl of five plucked yellow roses from the trellis around the doorway. On seeing the carriage approach, the girl dashed through the front door of the cottage. Daniel reined the team to a halt precisely at the flagstone path to the door.

"Do you want me to help?"

"I can do it, thanks." Gabriel pulled out the crutch and struggled to climb down.

A plain young woman with light brown hair and unfashionable clothes appeared at the front door, the young girl peering around her mother's skirts. As Gabriel drew near, she politely called, "Good morning, sir. May I help you?"

Gabriel pulled his hat from his head. "Good morning, madam. I am looking for Miss Sanderson." Noting the perplexed expression on the woman's face, he added, "Or Mr. Banks."

"That would be the former tenants, sir?"

"Former?" He frowned, thinking she had misunderstood him.

"Aye, sir, they moved out three days ago. We passed their fourgon as we were coming to look at the cottage. We have let the place for the remainder of the summer."

Gabriel's hand gripped the crutch. Had he come too late? "Would you know where they were going, madam?" The air seemed to hang in his lungs as he awaited her answer.

"Sorry, sir, I don't. Perhaps Mrs. Newton would know. I believe the solicitor who leased us Newland mentioned that the

317

gentleman was some relation of hers."

"Thank you." Hope rushed back along with his breath. Ella lived with her aunt, not Mr. Banks. That was where she would be, Newton Park. After a bow, he replaced his hat and limped back to the carriage where Daniel waited. "To Newton Park. It seems Mr. Banks has departed."

"Gone? Wait, the new maid said he had business in London."

"New maid?" Gabriel climbed awkwardly back into his seat.

Daniel explained about the trunks he'd seen.

"You should have told me, but it doesn't matter. Ella lives at the Park — she wouldn't have accompanied the gentleman to Town."

Daniel put the carriage in motion as Gabriel slumped back against the seat. He didn't like that the old gentleman had gone without a word to them. What had happened? Perhaps Ella would know. Mr. Banks's destroyed balloon weighed heavily on his mind — when his thoughts weren't locked on the woman he loved.

The ride to Newton Park went quickly. Gabriel surveyed the neat and well-maintained structure. Strange that Mrs. Newton lived so well, yet she forced her niece to do menial work for her brother. But then that was the way of the world for poor relations.

No sooner had the curricle drawn to a stop than Gabriel limped to the front door and knocked. Minutes later the portal was opened by the butler. Gabriel handed the man his card. "I should like to speak with Miss Sanderson."

A flicker of something strange passed over the old man's face, but Gabriel couldn't tell whether the reaction was from the man's reading his name or hearing Ella's.

"Do come in, my lord. The ladies are in the rear drawing room."

Relieved that Ella was in residence, the earl followed the old servant into an elegant room done in varying shades of blue. The butler announced him as if he were making an entrance into a ballroom. To Gabriel's disappointment, he found himself in the presence of three ladies, one elderly, the others young, but none of which were Ella.

The older of the three rushed forward, hand extended. "Lord Shalford, to what do we owe this honor?"

"I am looking for your niece, Miss Sanderson. I have hopes to make the lady my wife."

After three shocked gasps, the silence in the room was deafening. Mrs. Newton stood like a marble statue, her mouth hanging open. Then she seemed to gather her wits. "You . . . and . . . Luella . . . marry? But, sir, do you not understand that . . . well, the girl is without fortune?"

"I fully understand Ella's situation, Mrs. Newton. Is she here?" He was surprised at the lady's reaction. Did she not want the best for her young relation?

The lady pressed her lips together and her eyes narrowed. It was almost as if she weren't going to tell him what he needed to know. Then a strange, sly smile appeared. "Sir, I regret to inform you that my niece no longer lives with us. She left with my brother several days ago." The lady sighed. "I fear you are too late. Addison intended to marry her as soon as they reached London. No doubt they are on their honeymoon trip."

"Marry? Are you certain, madam?"

"Of course, the man is my brother, after all. She could not live with him without creating a scandal."

Gabriel's hopes for the future suddenly grew dim. Ella married? It couldn't be. He managed to gather his wits enough to thank the lady and refuse her offer of tea before he abruptly bid them all good day. He limped blindly back to where his brother waited in his curricle.

On seeing his brother approach, Daniel cried, "Good God, Gabe, what the devil is wrong?"

"Banks has married Ella." Gabriel threw himself onto the leather seat and stared with unseeing eyes, his life in ruins.

Daniel gasped in shock. "By Jove, he swore to Mother he would do it when she was making all those dreadful accusations, but I thought it only said in anger."

Gabriel turned to his brother. "What accusations?"

"Oh, that Ella had plotted to entrap you by flying off in the balloon with you. Nonsense like that. Mr. Banks set her straight, but I cannot believe he would marry Ella. He treated her like a daughter."

"It would seem that now she is his wife." Gabriel spoke with an anguish Daniel had never before heard. "Take me home."

Daniel tooled the carriage back toward Weycross Abbey in silence to give Gabriel the needed time to grasp this dark turn of events.

When they entered the gates of the estate, the earl stared at the house that would one day be his. On arrival several weeks earlier, he'd thought the worse prospect facing him was a marriage of convenience. Today he knew there were far harsher realities, like having the woman one loved married to another man, forever beyond reach.

After limping back to his room, Gabriel disappeared behind those doors for a solid week. Save his valet, he granted admittance to no one, not even his brother or sister. A great many brandy bottles disappeared into the darkened depths of his bedroom on Timbers's tray, only to return empty. When Lord Latimer inquired of the valet if his son was any improved, the old servant would shake his head sadly. It had been left to Daniel to inform his parents and the others of the devastating blow which Shalford had received. Later, Daniel heard his parents quarreling in the library, but what was said he did not know, only that his mother was a more subdued woman afterwards.

On the eighth day of Gabriel's hibernation, a message to the earl arrived via Timbers. It was a command, not a request, from the marquess that his son appear in the drawing room before dinner that evening. At seven sharp the young man appeared at the door, looking gaunt and pale, but not the least tipsy. The conversation halted at his arrival, then the marquess rose.

"Come, Shalford, you must be here for the news."

The earl came to stand behind Freddie, who looked at him with such sadness that he put a hand upon her shoulders to reassure her he was surviving his disappointment, albeit not very well at present.

Everyone grew quiet as Latimer drew his hands behind him, a serious expression on his face. "This afternoon Lord Hallet and I met."

Daniel leapt to his feet. "He's agreed to our marriage."

The marquess raised his hand. "Not so fast, young man. He has not agreed."

Daniel sat down hard, the smile slipping from his face.

"Hallet feels that Lady Amelia needs to have at least some introduction into Society since her come-out was repeatedly delayed due to her grandparents' deaths. Especially before she makes such an important decision. He intends to take her to London for the remainder of the summer, since so many celebrations and fetes are planned to celebrate the peace. They plan to remain there until the Little Season has ended."

Lady Latimer nodded. "An excellent notion."

The marquess frowned at his wife, who had the decency to blush at the role she had played in trying to force the girl to marry Gabriel. Latimer then continued. "As I was saying, the viscount will let her make her bow to Society. Then, if she is still of a mind to marry Daniel after that, he will agree to an engagement after Twelfth Night."

Gabriel had thought himself emotionally numb after the previous week, but he was pleased for his brother's good fortune. He said all that was proper when his time came to congratulate Daniel. But his ordeal wasn't yet over, for his father expected him to join in the evening's normal routine. Gabriel got through supper and the small talk with his family before he pled fatigue and retired early. It wasn't until he was again in his room and he had picked up the brandy decanter to pour a generous portion into a glass that his hand froze.

Spirits weren't the answer to his problems; they hadn't changed anything. Each morning he woke with a heavy head and Ella was still married. He put the glass stopper back into the brandy decanter. He'd wallowed in self-pity enough for a lifetime. Ella was gone and while his mother had played some role, he knew he was mostly to blame. He should have asked her at the inn the very moment the doctor left. His mother never would have succeeded had Gabriel not been such a fool and realized sooner that Ella was the woman he wanted. He'd wasted precious time trying to find some ideal wife instead of seeing the ideal woman was right before his eyes.

Nothing could change the past. Ella was now Mrs. Addison Banks. There was little doubt the old gentleman would treat her well. Still, Gabriel loved her enough to hope that she would find happiness.

He walked to the window and looked out over the moonlit gardens. It was time he got back to some semblance of a life. Perhaps if he became involved in politics or something of that nature it would help keep his mind off what he'd lost. With the peace there would be legions of soldiers coming back, needing work. Perhaps he could find a way to help.

A knock sounded at his door and he called for his visitor to enter.

Daniel warily peered round the oak-paneled door. "May I speak with you a moment?"

"Don't look as if I have suddenly turned into a delicate piece of china. I am finished with tippling my way to perdition. I have to accept what I cannot change." He gestured for his brother to come in.

"Well, I think anyone would be bowled over by such a nasty surprise. I cannot think how I would be if Millie were to marry another. I came up to see if you wanted to . . . well, talk about things."

Gabriel moved to a wing chair near the fireplace and eyed his brother. "What are you up to? I have known you long enough to know when something is in the wind. You know there is nothing to discuss. Ella is married, end of story."

Daniel came and sat in the opposite chair, trying to look totally innocent. "I could never fool you. I was thinking I might pay a visit to London and thought you might like to come with me."

"No, you were hoping I would talk Father into letting you go back for the summer, and that won't happen unless I choose to return."

"Well, I think he would have no objection if you made the suggestion, now that he has changed his mind about your being married by the end of the month. I don't think it good that you should be alone at the moment."

Gabriel propped his chin on his fisted hand as he stared at his brother's hopeful face. He wasn't certain that Lord Hallet had intended for Daniel to follow his daughter around like a puppy over the course of the next several months. Still, Gabriel could see where his brother wouldn't want to end up in the same boat as he had, with Lady Amelia swept off her feet and married within a month to some London swell.

He gave the matter some thought, then said, "I have another plan in mind. Come with me to London. I must replace Mr. Banks's balloon. That task alone will take several weeks. Once I have found the old gentleman and given him the new balloon, then you may pester Millie to your heart's content."

Daniel stared back at him with a frown. "Are you certain you want to see Mr. Banks again? Most likely you will see Ella, as well, and that would be hard."

"I know, but I think it my responsibility to give him another balloon after I managed to destroy the one he had."

"Well, I don't see how it was your fault

the dog released the ropes" — Daniel saw the expression on his brother's face — "but if you insist on replacing it, *I* could see he gets it."

Gabriel rose and went to the window. He stood in silence a moment, then said, "I want to make certain she is content in her new life. After that I can at least try to put all this behind me."

Daniel wasn't certain his brother seeing Ella was the best thing, but since Gabe was helping him get to Millie, he agreed to the plan.

June passed into July. Gabriel's knee healed fully and he was once again able to go about his business. The brothers returned to London, where the aristocratic populace remained high, despite the heat, due to the planned celebrations of the Prince Regent. The earl and Daniel pursued their own affairs, however. They worked at finding the proper craftsmen to construct a new gondola and a new silk envelope to help lift the creation. Three weeks after they departed Weycross, the pair sat in the dining room at Latimer House. Gabriel read the message that the butler had just brought to him. He sighed as he tossed it on the table beside his half-eaten breakfast. "The solicitor has had no luck finding Mr. Banks. He said it's as if he and Ella have disappeared into the woodwork."

When they hadn't been overseeing Mr. Banks's new balloon, Gabriel had been visiting with the other members of the Royal Aeronautical Society in the hopes that one of the gentlemen could give him information about Mr. Banks's whereabouts. Most hadn't seen or spoken with the gentleman in years. Others had seen him recently in Town, but were unaware of his current direction.

"He has to be in London still. There is to be an ascension in Hyde Park during the Regent's peace celebration. I cannot imagine him missing such an event."

Daniel, his head bent while he read a delicately scented missive, was only partially paying attention. "The balloon has been finished this past week and more. What do you intend to do?"

"I suppose I shall go to the illumination at the Park the first night of August to see if they —"

Suddenly Daniel looked up. "What day is it?"

" 'Tis July nineteenth, why?" Gabriel's brows rose at the excitement on his brother's face. There could be little doubt that the young man had been less than thrilled to stay away from his Lady Amelia all this time, for he'd not been his usual jovial self.

Without a word, Daniel dropped his letter to the lacquered tabletop and dashed out of the dining room into the hall. After several moments, Gabriel heard a shouted, "Here it is!" Moments later his brother appeared in the dining room doorway brandishing a large vellum invitation with the Regent's crest. "We have been invited to Carlton House for a fete to honor Wellington."

Gabriel stared at his brother as if he'd lost his mind. "You want to dress to the nines, stand about in sweltering hot rooms, and be toadied to and fawned over by most of the matchmaking mamas in Town? Have you been into the brandy now? If you want to meet the general I can have —"

"I don't give a rat's arse about meeting war heroes. Millie will be there. I shall be the one fawning and toadying to her. Besides, I shall have you in all your titled splendor to keep the matchmaking mamas at bay." Daniel grinned.

A half smile tipped Gabriel's mouth. "So I am to be the sacrificial lamb."

"You will go with me, won't you?" Daniel's face became a study of concern.

"Would it not be easier to merely pay her a visit?" Gabriel asked, hoping to avoid the kind of entertainment the Prince Regent was noted for — extravagant and long.

"Father encouraged me to give her and her family a wide berth. In his opinion it is all right if I encounter her at parties, but I am not to seek her out or I might get Hallet's back up."

Gabriel's gaze shifted to the missive lying beside Daniel's empty plate. "So she is informing you of her agenda, and you will 'accidently' encounter her there; is that how it works?"

A sheepish smile appeared on Daniel's face. "Something like that."

"I fear Hallet is wasting his blunt bringing that determined chit to London. Very well, we are for Carlton House."

"I know it's a great deal to ask . . . well, considering . . ." Daniel's voice petered out at the look on his brother's face.

"I must get on with my life." Gabriel rose and strode toward the hall, calling over his shoulder, "Shall we go to Tattersall's and see if the next possible derby winner is for sale?"

Daniel knew his brother had no interest

in purchasing a racer, but it would keep the gentleman's mind off a certain newly married lady.

Two days later, on the night of the fete, the two brothers arrived to find a long line of carriages in a queue as guests climbed down and entered Carlton House. Without ladies in their party, Gabriel and Daniel had made the decision to exit the carriage and walk the distance to the entry gates. The crowds pressed against the fence, hoping to catch a glimpse of Wellington at his arrival. A murmur of disappointment rose when each new carriage didn't hold the war hero.

The Crowe brothers passed through the Regent's extravagantly decorated house into the rear garden. Prinny had commissioned John Nash to construct a special hall just for this occasion. The building was over one hundred feet in diameter, with an umbrella-shaped roof. No expense had been spared; even the ceiling was fully draped with white muslin. As they moved through the press of the crowd, Gabriel could see a large temple had been constructed in the middle of the hall, which housed musicians behind a facade of flowers. Beyond the domed hall in the garden, he could see covered walks which led to supper tents. Had the prince spent all this money for one party? No wonder the man was perpetually in debt.

Before Gabriel could ponder the prince's expenses, Lady Amelia appeared before them, a vision in a white silk gown trimmed with yellow. Her eyes were twinkling unusually bright in the candlelight. "You came," she cried with delight, sliding her arm through Daniel's. They stared into one another's eyes with such intensity, Gabriel once again thought the viscount was wasting his time and money delaying the inevitable.

After giving the pair a moment, he asked, "Are your parents here?"

She nodded without drawing her gaze from Daniel. "They are speaking with Lord Melbourne just beyond the temple."

The pair once again fell silent, gazing raptly into one another's eyes.

Gabriel made one final attempt at conversation. "Have you been enjoying your visit to London?"

The lady tore her gaze from Daniel and seemed surprised to see the earl there, as well. "Oh, I do apologize. What did you say?"

The earl repeated the question, certain he at last had her attention.

"I have, sir. We are meeting a great many people." Her eyes widened, then she leaned near and whispered something to Daniel.

His brother opened his mouth to speak, but Lady Amelia held up a finger, then addressed herself to Gabriel. "Shalford, I have someone I should like to present to you. Lord Brantley's daughter is a friend of mine."

Gabriel sighed with frustration. Was he now to be pushed at every eligible female by his family and friends in the hopes of helping him to forget Ella? She was one of a kind, and it would be some time before he would be able to think of another female. "Thank you, but I see some friends of mine there by the fountain with whom I must speak." Before they could insist, he hurried to where he saw an old friend from school and greeted the gentleman more heartily than normal.

When he looked back, he could see Daniel and Lady Amelia with their heads together. He wished them well, but he would have to speak with his brother about trying to matchmake for him. His old friend, Sir John Aubrey, arrived, and Gabriel began to catch up on the news in Town.

Some minutes later he felt a tap on his shoulder, and turned to find himself looking at the very man he had searched for since coming to London.

His brother was grinning like a besotted monkey behind the gentleman. "Gabe, allow me to present you to Lord Brantley."

Gabriel's gaze swept over Mr. Banks. The old gentleman was elegantly dressed in a well-cut black coat of the finest material. It was nothing like the rather ragtag attire he'd worn in Surrey. "You are Lord Brantley, sir?"

"That I am. Inherited my uncle's barony scarcely a month ago."

Gabriel's gaze began to search the crowd for Ella. In a tight voice he asked, "And is Lady Brantley with you?"

The old gentleman chuckled. "There is no Lady Brantley, sir. Lord Daniel told me you thought I'd fallen into the parson's mousetrap, but I'm too old a dog to learn new tricks. You must be referring to my ward, Miss Sanderson. I believe she is speaking with Mr. Sadler's sons about the ascension to be held next week." The old gentleman turned and pointed beyond the temple to the edge of the hall.

"You didn't marry her?" Elation washed over Gabriel as he grabbed the gentleman.

The new Lord Brantley frowned. "She is like my daughter, sir."

Gabriel spotted her in an instant. His heart jumped in his chest at the sight of her, for she was beautiful and she was unmarried. Her lovely auburn hair had been dressed high upon her head, and she wore a fashionable pale green silk gown which molded to her figure. The sight sent his pulse racing.

Without another word to the others, he moved toward her, but a hand gripped his arm. He looked down into the narrowed eyes of Addison Banks. "You know your mother has made it plain she does not wish Ella to be her daughter-in-law?"

"Never fear, sir. My father has taken care of that lady's objections. I want to marry Ella if she will have me. I intend to marry her no matter who objects." Pure defiance shimmered in the air around him as he made clear to Lord Brantley that even his objections would not deter him.

The old gentleman's chin came up. "She is my ward, but for the present she is still penniless."

"*I don't care.*" Gabriel gave each word emphasis.

The old gentleman's hand dropped away and a smile brightened his face. "You have my blessing, Shalford, but you must go see what Ella has to say. She is no longer a mere barefoot beauty in Surrey. She is my ward, and as such has been much courted since I brought her to London."

With a nod of his head, Gabriel pushed through the crowd.

Daniel, still beside Mr. Banks, watched his brother make for Ella. Then his thoughts turned to the conversation he'd just overheard. "Sir," he said to the former Mr. Banks, "I say, did old Brantley leave you without a feather to fly with? That was bad luck."

The old gentleman grinned. "Not a bit of it. Once all is settled I shall have a tidy sum. Just wanted to see if your brother still wanted Ella if he thought her penniless, since money seemed to be Lady Latimer's concern. After they are wed, I shall make a proper settlement on the dear girl."

Daniel's eyes widened and then he laughed. "I can assure you, sir, he will marry her no matter if she has been tying her garter in public for the last week."

The two men grinned at one another in complete understanding.

Across the hall, Gabriel wound his way to Ella, never taking his eyes from her face. Fear stirred deep within him. What if he was wrong about her feelings? What if her heart had not been touched by him? A determined knot settled deep inside. If he must, he would court her anew, but he intended to make her his bride.

Standing near the temple, strains of Mozart filling the air behind her, Ella looked up at that moment and her gaze locked with Gabriel's. Her knees shook and her heart misbehaved in a strange manner. He was here. What would she say to him if he started to speak of his duty to marry her? She had spent too many agonizing nights wondering if she could resist him, even knowing the real reason he was compelled to ask for her hand. How could she refuse when every fiber of her being wanted her to say yes? But what kind of marriage would she have with a man who'd been forced into marriage?

Suddenly afraid to meet him, Ella turned and excused herself from the gentlemen who were discussing matters of flight beside her. She hurried out of the domed building, then halted, looking for someplace where she could gather her wits. Lanterns hung in the trees, and she moved away from the busy path that teemed with people on their way to the supper tents, toward the shadowy depths of the garden.

Ella had gone scarcely ten feet into the shrubbery when a hand closed over her arm and turned her round. She stared up into the blue eyes that had haunted her dreams since they'd left Surrey. "Lord Shalford, I wrote you there is no need for you —"

"There is every need for me to tell you how much I love you, Ella. When your aunt told me you had married Mr. Banks, my world went dark."

"Married! Aunt Leona told you that? But I'm not married." Anger burned deeply within Ella. She had never truly understood just how petty and cruel the lady was.

"What you may not know was that Mr. Banks had threatened to marry you to keep you from my family. I had no reason to doubt Mrs. Newton." He lifted Ella's hand and pressed a kiss on the gloved surface. "My life has been an utter misery without you, dearest Ella. You must rescue me from the darkness. Tell me that I am not too late. That you have not fallen for some other gentleman."

Her voice grew soft and she looked into his eyes. "There could be no other gentleman for me, my one and only."

Gabriel stepped forward to kiss her, but

inadvertently stepped upon her foot. Laughter bubbled up in the pair as they looked down to see the white satin slippers he'd sent her.

"At first I thought not to wear them, but putting them on made me feel close to you. I couldn't resist them and they fit perfectly." She held out her foot to display the lovely slipper.

He drew her into the curve of his arm and smiled. In a husky voice he said, "Just as you do in my arms." With that he crushed her to him, and kissed her with the pent-up passion of a man who'd found his true love again. For Ella, the moment was sheer discovery that she responded physically as well as emotionally to the embrace. Her heart raced, and a tingle grew from deep inside and seemed to race to every inch of her body. When at last they drew apart, a breathless Ella blinked in astonishment that she felt so weak with passion.

"Marry me, Ella, and make me the happiest of men."

All her doubts rushed back and she said, "How can we marry when your mother told me —"

"Forget about my mother and your aunt and everyone else who has a plan for what is best. I care not what they think, only what you think. Do you love me, Ella?"

"I do." She said it with such emotion he could have no doubt.

"Then say those words to me in front of a vicar as soon as possible." His arm tightened round her.

Ella laughed. "Whenever and wherever you want, my beloved."

The couple spent another ten minutes in the Regent's darkened garden showing the other just how much they cared. At last, realizing their passion might get the better of them, Gabriel suggested they go and find the others.

They found Lord Brantley, Daniel, and Lady Amelia in a supper tent. The gentlemen rose as the pair approached, and Daniel smiled as he noted the look on the couple's face. "I say, am I to be a brother-in-law?"

"You are, sir." Ella looked up at Gabe, who beamed at the gathered party.

Daniel moved round the table to kiss Ella's cheek, as did Lord Brantley and Lady Amelia.

Ever impatient, Daniel asked, "Gabe, when is the ceremony?"

Gabriel looked to the old gentleman. "If

you have no objections, sir, I should like to get a special license and marry within the week."

Ella's eyes widened. "So soon? I had hopes of inviting my school friends, Sara and Lady Rose."

Lord Brantley waved his hand. "Leave your friends to me. I shall make arrangements for them to attend the wedding. Why, I might fly them to London if I must, for I understand from Lord Daniel that I once again possess a balloon, thanks to you, Shalford."

"That is true, sir. 'Tis in a warehouse near the River Thames."

"Fly them to London?" Ella asked warily and looked at Gabriel.

The earl smiled and shrugged. "Or, as we well know, they could end up in Brussels or Paris or some other exotic locale, depending on where the winds are blowing on that fine day. Perhaps, sir, it is best if we plan the wedding for two weeks hence and allow the young ladies to travel by carriage."

Brantley sighed. "Well, if you insist."

"Never fear." Daniel leaned toward the gentleman. "I shall go adventuring with you in your new balloon."

That brightened the old man's countenance and they all sat down to enjoy the Prince Regent's largess.

The better part of the next week was spent with Ella trying to discover the whereabouts of Sara Whiting and Lady Rosamund Dennison. Messengers had been sent to each of their homes, but each missive had been returned with the information that the respective young lady no longer resided there. Ella could only hope that the announcement of her wedding in the *Morning Post* would catch her friends' notice and they would write. It seemed that their new lives had been quite as full of adventure and change as Ella's.

On the day before the wedding, the butler at Brantley House entered the drawing room, where Ella and Gabriel sat making plans.

"Sir Evan and Lady Beaumont are at the door, along with Mr. and Mrs. Fenton."

Gabriel rose. "Garth Fenton? That's Buckleigh's heir. I scarcely know the man. As to Sir Evan, I cannot recall having met him."

"Then let us see what they want." Ella directed Jansen to show the couples in.

When the door opened, Ella leapt from her chair and dashed forward. "Sara, Lady

Rose, you have come."

"Of course we came; we saw the announcement." The blond beauty called Lady Rose embraced Ella, as did the lovely raven-haired woman who Gabriel realized must be Sara. There were introductions all around, and Ella ordered tea. Sensing that the three old friends wanted to talk, Gabriel suggested that the gentlemen go to White's for drinks and allow their wives and his fiancée a reunion. The afternoon was full of tales of love, misunderstanding, and adventures as each lady told her story. Sara was married to Sir Evan, and the guardian of seven young lads who'd brought the couple together. The boys were presently at Beaumont Hall under the watchful eye of a trusted old servant. Lady Rose and Mr. Fenton had met at her family's estate in Yorkshire, and were happily married and running Viscount Buckleigh's estate. The day proved a prefect reunion for the Three Fates. They laughed about the silly pact they'd made, knowing that each had blissfully found her place to be happy.

For Ella, the next morning was everything she'd dreamed about. In a simple ceremony attended by friends and family, even the once disapproving Lady Latimer,

Miss Ella Sanderson was united in holy wedlock with Lord Shalford at St. Paul's. After a sumptuous wedding breakfast at Lord Brantley's town house, the bride and groom departed on their honeymoon trip, going only to Brantley Manor, the baron's newly inherited country house near Bristol in County Gloucestershire. They arrived at the estate early the following morning, after breaking their journey at a beautiful inn near Nettleton.

Ushered to the elegant rear drawing room of the lovely old Elizabethan manor, Ella moved to the long doors to admire the view and await Gabriel, who had stopped to speak with Townley, the butler. She gasped at the sight that met her eyes.

When her husband strode into the room, she called, "Look," and gestured at the fully inflated balloon Gabriel had purchased to replace the one lost in Kent. The towering vessel was tied to a newly erected set of stairs in the large rose garden. Several large lads were sitting on the grass nearby, eying Gabriel's gift with fascination. "Is Uncle Addison coming to join us? He has been most anxious to test out his new balloon and declares Gloucestershire has favorable winds."

Gabriel came up beside her and slid his

arm through hers as he opened the door. "He is not coming until September, but he suggested we take care of a certain matter while we were here." He tugged her into the garden and Ella didn't resist, curious what matter must be dealt with.

They approached the young lads, who scrambled to their feet, tugging their hats from their heads. The earl greeted them before he asked, "Is everything ready?"

One particularly burly lad with blond hair and a neatly trimmed beard spoke. "Just as Lord Brantley ordered, my lord."

"Excellent." Gabriel led Ella up the stairs, then stepped down into the gondola. It had been designed much along the same lines as the first, using the same colors, but this one owned a gondola that was twice the length. The earl turned and smiled at her, extending a helping hand.

Ella gasped and took a step back. "You cannot mean to go up." Her gaze roved over the towering red and blue envelope, which was more ornate than the one that had been destroyed.

"That I do, my love." He extended his hand. "Won't you join me?"

She wrung her hands while the last few minutes of that fateful ride raced through her mind. When she continued to hesitate,

Gabriel added, " 'Tis much like being thrown from a horse. You must get back on and ride again or fear will rule you. It would be the disappointment of Lord Brantley's life if you did not want to fly with him."

Not wanting to disappoint the old gentleman who'd become like a father, Ella reached out and put her hand on her husband's shoulder. She allowed him to sweep her into the balloon, where he kissed her nose then set her upon her feet. After the gondola ceased to dip and sway, Gabriel called to the lads below, "Release the lines."

Her fingers tightened on Gabriel's arms, but Ella showed no other fear. Somehow, in her husband's arms she reasoned she would be safe.

This flight proved different. The balloon drifted upward in a gentle, steady motion. There were almost no winds, so they rose steadily upward with only the slightest drift to the east.

In the distance she could see the Bristol Channel, the River Severn, and beyond that, Wales. When they drifted through one puffy white cloud, she said, "In all the excitement of the crash, I had forgotten how beautiful it was in the clouds."

"You are beautiful *and* brave, my love."

She looked up at him. "I love you." He kissed her. Then her gaze drifted to the envelope above them. "I must suppose that Uncle told you which of these lines is to be pulled to descend."

An intense look came in his blue eyes as his fingers grasped the blue ribbon that laced her blue and white muslin bodice closed. "Oh, I know what line needs to be pulled . . ." He tugged the ribbon, then leaned in and kissed the curve of her neck when the fabric fell open. After several moments he whispered, "I thought that I would never have such moments after the lie your aunt told me. That you were lost to me forever."

Ella's arms slid round his neck. "I am yours forever. How could I not be when these slippers you ordered fit perfectly? It's just like in that old fairy tale."

Gabriel kissed a path to her ear, where he whispered, "I shall certainly live happily ever after as long as I have you by my side."

Ella fully agreed as she surrendered to her husband's kisses.

Several farm lads reported seeing an unmanned balloon drifting over County Gloucestershire that lovely morning. Yet the rumor proved untrue when the brightly hued balloon descended in the village of Siston, and Lord and Lady Shalford climbed out looking a bit disheveled, but supremely happy.

ABOUT THE AUTHOR

Lynn Collum lives with her family in Alabama. She is currently working on her next Zebra Regency romance. Readers can write to Lynn at P.O. Box 814, Valley, AL 36854 or visit her website at www.lynncollum.com.